BEYOND REDEMPTION

L. A. BURCH

BOOK TWO OF THE MASTERMINDS SERIES

L.A. BURCH

Beyond Redemption: 1) Beyond making something or someone better or more acceptable.

2) Beyond the reach of being saved from sin and evil.

L.A. BURCH

KDP Publishing

Cover Design: Michelle D. Josey

Typist/Content Editor: L. A. Burch

ISBN: 9798990247222

Dedication

This book is dedicated to my Big Brother, Walter Keith Rogers. Sadly, he was taken from us too soon. In defense of his country until the day he died, we all lost more than a soldier when God called him home. Love you Big Bro, and know that this is not a goodbye, but an "I'll see you again soon."

Acknowledgements

I want to thank God for giving me the talent, the drive, and the time to sit down and focus on achieving the goal of writing another book.

I thank my family once again for supporting me and making sure I was comfortable after making some tough decisions. Sometimes we have to sacrifice to do the things we want. But, when you have people to ease the burden, the sacrifice doesn't hit too hard.

I want to send a special thanks to all my author friends who are not shy about giving feedback. We all like to get constructive criticism, but sometimes we need people to be brutally honest with us. I had some guys who were willing to give me exactly what I needed to improve my style. I thank them for having the courage and the kindness to help me out.

BEYOND REDEMPTION

L.A. BURCH

Beyond Redemption

BOOK TWO OF
THE MASTERMINDS SERIES

L.A. BURCH

PROLOGUE

"Listen detective," said the killer. "Why are you procrastinating? You know what you have to do. Get it done and free your women."

The detective and the killer were sitting in a cheap motel room in the city of Cary, right outside of Raleigh, North Carolina. The killer had called the detective and asked for this meeting. It took everything in the detective to not draw his gun and murder the man who he most hated in the world.

"I wouldn't have to free anyone if you hadn't kidnapped them," said the detective. "This second task is going to take time. I'm trying to get it done without having every cop in the state on my ass."

Sergeant Detective Walter Rogers worked for the North Carolina State Bureau of Investigations. The handsome, 49-year-old detective had light caramel skin and wore his hair cut low. He stands 5-feet 10-inches and is 230 pounds of solid muscles. With over 27 years of law enforcement, 12 of those as an MP in the Army, he could intimidate even the strongest of men. But not the man sitting across from him.

The killer was a 6-foot, bald, black man who appeared to be somewhere in his mid-30's. He has light brown skin and had recently stopped wearing a mask around Walt. He seemed to know everything and somehow knew that Walt had seen a picture of him so the mask was no longer needed. Anyway, with the evidence he had on the detective, Walt couldn't afford to turn the man in.

The killer laughed at Walt's intimidating stare. "Walt, I hate to tell you this, but you cops are really not that smart. I've been killing in your state for years now and no one even knows who I am. You're supposed to be the best and you're sitting right in front of me and still don't know who I am. I think you're safe from the dumbass N.C. cops."

Walt could hardly disagree with him. He and his partner Ann, who the killer was holding captive, worked for the SBI but were somewhat wildcards. They only worked on the cases that stretched over multiple counties and no one else seemed able to solve. The two of them together have never come across a case they couldn't handle until they were put on the PGK case. The Prison Guard Killer had been murdering inmates and guards for years without leaving any solid evidence behind. The killer was also right when he said, even though he was sitting right here, very little was known about him.

Walt had had a conversation with one of the killer's trainers from the CIA and he now knew some of the guy's background but didn't know his name or origin. The CIA operative, Agent Steve, wouldn't give up that information because he feared for his and his family's lives. With all Walt had learned, he really couldn't blame the man for his fear.

"So, what do you think I should do?" asked Walt. "Just waltz in the prison and grab him and try to make a run for it, killing anybody who gets in my way?"

"I really don't care what you have to do to accomplish the goal. Just get it done. I'm a civilian and it would only take me three hours max to get him out. The problem is you're trying not to get your hands dirty." The killer looked at Walt with a sad expression and a shaking head. "I'm sorry Walt but lives are at stake no matter what. It's up to you to decide who lives and who dies."

The killer looked at his watch and stood up. "I have an appointment to keep." He turned back to Walt and said, "You have 12 hours to complete task two." When Walt started to object, the killer held his hand up for silence. "I gave you everything you need. Get it done. It's 4:00 am, by 4:00 pm I better be looking him in his eyes or I'll be face to face with Ann and Denise."

Without another word, the killer left Walt standing alone in the motel room. Through experience Walt knew the killer kept his word and would hurt the women if he didn't comply. The women were already locked in one of the killer's prisons somewhere underground. Walt would do whatever he had to do to get them back. Even if it meant killing some guards.

With a small sigh, Walt pulled a folded sheet of paper from his pocket. After unfolding it, he read what it said under the heading of second task.

It was short and to the point: Break Bruce Battle out of Central Prison. When he is free, call me from a safe location and I'll tell you where we will meet.

The killer had included a detailed blueprint of the entire prison as well as a rotation assignment schedule. He had also given him a silenced handgun that was truly silenced. No sound at all. And a small black box that was a criminal's dream come true.

Sad that he was already thinking of himself as a criminal, he put everything on the desk and continued to work on his plan for freeing Mr. Battle.

CHAPTER 1

The killer left Walt while sporting a small smile on his handsome face. He knew the detective would do what needed to be done, he just needed to feel like he was backed into a corner. The killer would break him of that or Walt himself would break. Either way was fine with him.

He walked about a quarter of a mile to where he had left his car parked in the driveway of a family gone on vacation. Stupid idiots were posting every ten minutes on what they were doing. If he wasn't in such a rush, he would steal all of their stuff just to teach them a lesson.

The sun was a couple hours from coming up, but even in the dark The Beast was still menacing. The 1969 Dodge Charger R/T couldn't go by a more well-earned nickname. The satin black finish and the black chrome made the 1308 HP, V-10 monster invisible at night. Almost a million dollars in modifications made The Beast the fastest moving tank in the world. It also had an electric mode that made it silent but no less fierce.

He had a long drive ahead of him as he was on his way to his next target. Taking down cops was easy compared to what he was about to attempt. Taking down a gang stronghold was something local cops sometimes asked the military to help with. Manuel Adams, one of the names the killer was using, was going to do it by himself. He had a few tricks up his sleeve but this was by no means a sure thing. He did have a wildcard in play though.

As he turned onto 85 South and opened up The Beast, he let his mind drift to the main reason why this target was so important to him.

When Manuel was incarcerated at Lanesboro Correctional Institution in Polkton North Carolina, gangs determined your standard of life. Manny had been so far deep undercover working for the governor, he was just another inmate in the bunch trying to make it.

One of the most powerful gangs in the prison was the Big Rollin Crips. Anyone who didn't get with their program was either beaten severely or outright killed. So many of the officers were gang bangers, they were actually helping the inmates get away with their dirty deeds instead of stopping them.

But that's not what made this gang stand out as the front runners. Mickey Brown, the gang's local leader, was who made this group super dangerous. If you happened to fall into his sights, he would not kill you, or even beat you. He specialized in emotional and psychological torture. He would find out what you loved most and he would do his best to take it from you. In some cases, he'd been known to wipe out entire families.

A young man who Manny had befriended named Rodney, had run afoul of the gang lord. Something had told Manny to kill the guy right then, but Rodney convinced him it wasn't a big deal. About two weeks later, Rodney came back from the Chaplain's office with the news that his house had burned to the ground with his wife and children inside.

Rodney had sat in his room for three days, with Manny bringing him his food, before he decided he didn't want to live without his family and killed himself. Rodney had been such a good guy, the inmates organized a service in his honor. Mickey had stood at the back of the service laughing and being rude with his goons.

The killer let a month pass before he made his move. Two of the goons worked in the clothes house with the killer. He set himself up to get robbed by the goons for some poisoned spice, which was the most profitable drug in the prison. The gang members took the poison back to the unit and distributed it to the other members. All of them smoked it except for Mickey.

One of the robbers had to have told their leader who they stole the drugs from because, when all his boys died over the next three days, Mickey came to his room with a knife but was no match for the trained killer. He let Mickey live, but with all of his power structure gone, the gang leader was soon forced to transfer to another prison to keep his life.

Now, the gang leader was free and had amassed another legion of followers to terrorize his community. Now that Manny was free to kill at will, there was no way he could let the guy continue to operate.

He reached his destination about 6:00 am. The sun was just coming up and he still had a ton of prep work to do if he wanted to make this work.

First, he drove passed the four houses in a grouping that he knew the gang owned. The city of Kannapolis as a whole was not that bad. The neighborhood where the gang called home was called the Rut, named after one of the guys who built the mill the city was built around. But the city, full of single-family dwellings, was not equipped to handle the problems that gangs brought to a community.

Because of the small-town atmosphere, Mickey Brown ran his empire with impunity. Hopefully, thought the killer, all that would end today. Not that he cared overly much about the town or its people. He just hated the fact that Mickey was living his life to the fullest while his friend and his family were dead.

As expected, there were sentries posted at the four corners of the property. With no regard for the police station less than a half mile away, they all had automatic assault rifles ready to defend their territory.

Manny had blueprints of all the houses, but he needed to get a look at the layout up close to see any and all modifications. All of the houses had enclosed garages added to them that were not on the prints, so the killer needed to see inside each house for anymore added surprises.

He drove all the way around instead of backtracking because he didn't want them to see his car cruise by a second time.

People were ignorant to believe that all gang members are stupid. Most of these gangs are international corporations with structures and managements just like any Fortune 500 company. So, in order to be the best, you have to recruit the best.

The killer knew for a fact that at least ten former military personnel were in the power structure of this local Crip set. He also knew that thousands of other members would converge on this location with one call from its leader. If he wanted to achieve his goal and get out alive, he would have to be very careful with his movements.

He pulled over in a McDonald's parking lot about a half mile from the stronghold. He had to be careful here also as this was one of the businesses owned by the gang. Mickey definitely knew how to run a successful organization so only a small part of his empire was illegal.

Right after Det. Rogers had splattered the brains of the corrupt Captain Dennis all over the Pitt County courthouse steps for his first task, Manny had gone back to one of the CIA supply depots only he knew about and restocked on a few essential items he would need.

Among those items were several different types of drones. Looking around first to make sure the coast was clear, he opened his door and sat down a drone about the size of a hand-held radio. This particular drone was used to scan for heat signatures inside structures. Before he started his assault, he needed to know exactly how many people he had to contend with, and exactly where they were.

It took the drone about a minute to cover the distance back to the four houses. The houses were not very big but were two- and three-bedroom homes. The two houses closest to the street were both three bedrooms and each contained ten people.

The other two houses were both two bedrooms, and only contained two people. The two heat signatures inside both of the back houses were sharing a bed, but he already knew that one of the two in each house were women.

The women would both be affiliated in some kind of way or they wouldn't be trusted to be in the house alone with the leadership. But he did have some firsthand knowledge on the subject.

Four days ago, the killer had tortured one of the members and received a bevy of information about how the gang operated. The man had bared the soul of the organization to stop Manny from sliding the drill into his body again. He was told that Mickey Brown and his general of the month always stayed in the back two houses. The guards on the four corners were rotated at random times and, before they switched, they all do a perimeter walk together with eyes on each other at all times. Some of this he had already known but it was good to confirm information with another source.

They had about fifty more soldiers around the neighborhood in various houses, on standby, just in case of an attack. They also have a contract with every other Crip set in the state to come whenever they called. And they had about 20 women in the area that rotated on a nightly basis to satisfy the leadership.

All this added up to the killer having to use his entire skill set in order to come out on top of this one.

The only thing working in his favor is that there was no security system in any of the houses. Knowing the drug use and alcohol consumption all around him, Mickey made that decision so as not to bring the cops down on them for a false alarm.

If the killer hadn't wanted to face Mickey man to man, he could have just blown the shit up and been done with it. That wasn't an option now anyway. Plus, the killer wanted to look him in his eyes and explain to him why he was dying.

The last line of defense was a panic button that Mickey went nowhere without. If he got the chance to press that button, then it would be next to impossible to escape.

The killer smiled, thinking of all the assassinations he had done for the United States government, and he could end up dying in a backwoods town trying to kill a gang member.

Recalling the drone, the smile faded as Manny went to work on evening up the odds.

CHAPTER 2

Mickey Brown stretched, opened his eyes, and smiled all at the same time. He stared at the ceiling as he froze and just listened to the room. After 15 years in prison, he knew the importance of being still and just feeling your surroundings before making a move.

After about five minutes of silence, he turned to the right and looked at the sleeping beauty beside him. The bed was a California King with enough room for six people, but Alisha was only about three inches from him.

Never really seeing himself with a dark skin woman, he was surprised he had fallen in love with this dark chocolate princess. She was laying on her left side, facing him, still asleep, but with a partial smile on her lovely face.

Alisha was 5-feet 8-inches tall and had a body built like Megan Good's. With her huge brown eyes, and natural long, jet-black hair, she could have been a movie star. But when she smiled, her real radiance shined bright and filled his heart with joy.

He stared at her for another minute and then swung his legs off the side of the bed. He stood up and stretched again. Mickey would never be considered a big guy, but his 5-foot 10-inch frame looked like it was chiseled from pure granite. He only weighed 170 pounds, but you couldn't miss the hidden power lurking behind his long, lean muscles.

He went into the bathroom and relieved himself before standing in front of the mirror. Most people who saw him said he looked like a light skin Snoop Dogg. With his wolven features and long tipped cornrows, he didn't take it as an insult at all. In fact, he enhanced the comparison by dressing just like the OG Crip legend.

He glanced back at Alisha one more time, noting that even her painted toes were beautiful to him, before he closed the door to handle his morning business.

The room he was living in was a special built room with qualities of a bank vault. There were no windows in the bedroom or the attached bathroom, and all the walls were lined with a steel mesh that could stop anything short of a nuclear blast. It also acted as a faraday cage with its heavily grounded copper infusions so no one could pick up any of the nationwide transmissions he had to make on a daily basis.

He opened a modified drawer that would only open with his fingerprints on the lever, and pulled out one of the iPhones hidden inside.

First thing first, he had to check on the stronghold's security so he could report the findings to his OG. This particular phone was used only to call the watch commander's station at the house in the front of the compound.

He dialed the number and sat the phone on the sink after turning the speaker on. When the phone was answered, he said one word, "Report."

Recognizing the voice of one of his military specialists, Mickey listened as he took care of his oral hygiene. "All of the outpost checked in with an all clear. All is quiet on the home front. Shift rotations reported no disturbances during the night or early morning. Both of the VIP suites are still locked up tight. No problems reported from any of our allies. Businesses opened at seven with no trouble. From what I can see, everything is good. You are clear to come out and mingle. Do you have any request or concerns?"

Beezo, having spent ten years in the Marines knew how to give reports to a superior officer. He knew to leave out all the mundane everyday problems and just get to the point.

"None for right now," answered Mickey. "If I need anything, I'll let you know."

He hung up the phone and put it back in the drawer. He pulled out the Samsung Galaxy and laid it in the exact same place as the last phone. He looked at his watch and saw that he still had two minutes to burn, as it was only 8:58 am.

He looked up and locked eyes with himself through the mirror. His eyes were cold and black and revealed the fact that his soul was really and truly gone.

Having become a Crip at the age of eleven, the gangbanging life was all he knew. His parents hadn't cared one little bit what he did so he dropped out of school in the 8th grade. Money had never been a problem as his Dad had been a Judge and his Mom a lawyer. When they died, he dedicated his whole being to the gangbanging lifestyle.

Most nights he dreamed of that fateful night that turned him into an orphan. One of the rival Blood sets from Concord had come calling for his head. It was a rare night that his parents had actually came to one of his AAU Basketball games. His team had crushed the visiting team from Charlotte, and Mickey had been the star of the night.

They had been leaving the gym with his parents raining praises down on him, when out of the corner of his eye, he saw a red flag and heard a saying that caused his hair to stand on end. When the automatic gunfire started, his Dad, in a final show of love, pushed him out of the way and the bullets found homes inside of his parents and four other innocent civilians instead of him.

The anger and hatred for everyone who wasn't on his side of the war started to boil up when the phone on the counter started to ring. He drew all the anger back in so as not to offend the person on the other end of the phone.

When the phone was answered he heard, "What's poppin little homie?" Mickey responded with the customary Crip greeting as love and gratitude filled his heart for his big homie.

Face G was the same age as Mickey, 38, and had been in and out of prison for most of his life. Face G was a Crip legend on par with Snoop, but he kept to the code of "Real G's move in silence." Rarely going out in public flagged up, but if you stepped out of line, he would kill you in the middle of a church service.

After the greeting rituals were done, Face G asked Mickey, "You have anything going on that I need to know about?"

"Nah Cuz. Everything is operating smoothly over here. Had to discipline a few of the little homies out pulling jobs not authorized but nothing for you to worry about," replied Mickey."

"Did you kill one of the little niggas?" asked Face G. When Mickey replied in the negative, Face G said, "You too easy on these G's Cuz. They have to understand that we have a program for a reason. A beat down is nothing to a G. You have to put the fear of death in them."

Mickey knew Face was right, but he had a soft spot for all the little homies. He saw so much of himself and Face G in them.

"Babe? You mind if I come in and use the bathroom?" asked Alisha.

Face G, hearing her, laughed and said, "Damn Cuz, let me let you go before I get you in trouble. Tell Alisha I said what's up." After their ritualistic goodbyes, they both hung up.

He put the second phone back in the drawer and pulled out the last iPhone and put it on the counter. He closed the drawer then called out, "Come on in Sweetie."

Alisha opened the door and started to come in. "Girl, get your ass out there and put some clothes on. You know I have to go." She sucked her teeth and rolled her eyes as she turned her naked body around to grab her panties, bra, and a long T-Shirt that covered her from neck to knees.

"I swear," Mickey said loud enough for her to hear. "Tell a girl you love her and she thinks she can get away with anything."

"Shut up boy! I just have to pee really badly. Go ahead and get your shower so I can take one after you." Smiling, Mickey turned around and cut the water on in the shower.

"Hurry up so I can get my kiss before I get in," he demanded of his Queen. It was crazy but he didn't even mind her morning breath he loved her so much.

She came strutting back into the bathroom as the lights flickered for a few seconds and then went out.

"I know I'm lights out gorgeous, but this is a first for me," joked Alisha. "Did somebody forget to pay the light bill?"

Mickey was silent as he waited the ten seconds it normally took for the generator to kick on. After twenty seconds, he started feeling a chill creep into his bones.

He reached out and grabbed Alisha's hand and said, "Baby, go get dressed and bring my clothes."

Knowing that this was the OG speaking and not her lover, she hastened to do what she was told. Mickey saw her cell phone flashlight come on as she did his bidden as fast as possible.

He also turned the flashlight of his own phone on, cut the shower back off, and reached to open the drawer containing the other two phones. The drawer wouldn't open. "What the fuck!" he murmured as he tried to force the drawer open.

Essentially it was a small safe and he cursed himself and his security because he just now realized that they never tried to open it without the power being on. The 15,000-gallon diesel fuel tank buried under the compound that fed the generator could work for up to three months with no problems. So, this was an issue that never arose.

Alisha came hustling back with his clothes in her hands and he quickly got dressed. He snatched up his phone and went to call the security when he realized that he couldn't because of the faraday cage. The other two phones had been specially configured to only connect to the two numbers that could call them. Any other transmissions were blocked.

17

He raced passed Alisha and grabbed his gun off the side table. He made sure it was loaded and then pulled out the panic button that he lived with in arms reach at all times. The light was still blinking to let him know it was on line, so at least whatever was going on didn't have an effect on that.

He looked up at Alisha's frightened face and asked, "Should I press this button?" She knew what he was asking. If he pressed that button, 1000 Crip and Crip allies would flood the area killing anyone that wasn't recognized. It was a last resort thing that would bring the heat and anger of all the upper management if it was a false alarm.

Alisha shook her head and said, "Baby no. It could be a storm or an accident or hundreds of other things. Let me go out and see what's going on. Give me two minutes and, if I don't come back, then press the button and bring the Calvary."

Mickey thought about it and knew he didn't have any other options. Alisha was still one of his soldiers and he had no doubt that she could handle herself. He turned around and pulled up a section of the floor. "Take this and you better come back to me." He gave her a small modified High Point 9mm handgun, gave her a fast kiss on the lips, and then led her over to the vault like door.

He entered the combination to line up all the tumblers, kissed her one more time and asked, "You know the knock to let me know it's you, and the one to tell me you're in distress?" At her affirmation, he opened the door and she stepped out quickly as he slammed the door shut again.

The two minutes seemed to take forever as he waited for her return. He clutched the panic button so hard, he had to put it back in his pocket for fear of breaking it.

His cell phone showed two minutes and ten seconds had passed when the secret code knock came through the door. He rotated the knob and unlocked the door for his Queens return.

Pushing the door open, Alisha, standing with a smile on her face, started to say something but Mickey snatched her back in and slammed the door shut again.

"Boy! What the hell is wrong with you? Why you slam the door closed like that?" asked Alisha.

"Shut the hell up Alisha," demanded Mickey. He hugged her to him and said, "I was scared to death for you. What the fuck is going on out there?"

Smiling and leaning in for a quick kiss, she said, "Some stupid bastard crashed his car into a light pole up the street and knocked all the power out in the whole neighborhood. Beezo got everyone on the perimeter while Sammy is trying to figure out what's up with the generator."

His heart finally slowing down, Mickey looked at Alisha and walked back to the bed. "Good. Well, we'll stay here until everything is squared away."

Frowning, Alisha said, "No way OG. Beezo said everything was good and you need to get going to that meeting."

"Shit!" said Mickey. "You know I can't leave you in here alone. Sorry but you have to go home until I come back."

"I know that Pookie," said Alisha, causing Mickey to wince at the endearment. "I'll brush my teeth and pee and then we can go." She rushed off to the bathroom after grabbing some more clothes and throwing the gun on the bed.

Mickey put the gun back under the floor and tucked his own behind his back. He stood at the door waiting for her for a couple minutes and then she emerged looking better than any video vixen in her regular jeans and T-Shirt.

He opened the door and they stepped out. He grabbed her hand to stop her when she went to keep walking. As she turned, he kissed her with all the feelings that his unthawing heart could muster. When they pulled apart, he said, "I really do love you. I can't wait to put a couple babies up in you."

She smiled and said, "I love you too Shnookums."

He winced again and said, "You have to chill with all the nicknames. I am still an OG Crip." He shut the door and walked into the living room side by side with his Queen.

When he crossed the threshold, he felt the cold barrel of a gun press into the side of his head. "Don't move a muscle or I'll confirm if you really bleed blue."

A chill went up his spine as he heard the voice of the only man who had ever beaten him at his own game.

CHAPTER 3

Det. Walter Rogers never wore suits. After leaving the military, he vowed to never wear another uniform again in his life. And to Walt, suits were just another kind of uniform. But ever since he'd met the Prison Guard Killer, he'd been doing a lot of things he vowed never to do.

Dressed in his all-black suit, he was sitting in a church parking lot about a quarter of a mile from Central Prison, making the last preparations for what he had to do.

After the killer left him in the motel, a plan had started to form in his head. He had rushed back to his office at SBI headquarters in Raleigh and started going through his files for the perfect offender to make the plan work.

When he found him, he rushed over to the church parking lot to organize everything in his mind. He looked at his phone and saw that he still had 90 minutes until shift change. He had to hurry if the plan would work.

He dialed a number and as soon as it was answered, he said, "I'm on my way," and hung up.

He started his black BMW M5 and took off for the Maximum-Security Prison that housed the Death Row for the North Carolina Department of Public Safety.

Walt had figured that the best way to gain access to the inside of the prison was to go in as legal as possible. Thankfully Officer Woods, who had helped him before when he was trying to identify the killer, was working this shift. The detective had called the officer and set up an urgent meeting with offender Dewayne York. If everything went as planned, no one would have to die.

Walt had studied the prison blueprints and knew how to get to Restrictive Housing, where Bruce Battle was being held, from the interview rooms in the basement.

Det. Rogers flashed his I.D. to gain access to the grounds and made his way to the officer's entrance. Walking towards the door, he saw Officer Woods already waiting for him at the next checkpoint.

He greeted the officer and waited as he turned and whispered something to the guard staffing the checkpoint. The other officer shrugged and Officer Woods motioned for Walt to follow him.

Officer Woods said, "We already have Mr. York waiting in the interview room." He glanced over at Walt with trepidation in his eyes. "You're not going to try and kill this one, are you?"

Walt glanced over at him as they made their way to the interview room. Officer Woods was a 6-foot 3-inch, bald, white guy who looked tough enough to chew nails. Seeing the nervousness in his eyes, Walt said, "Not at all. I just need to ask him a few questions about our killer. You can even stay in the room with us to make sure I behave."

The relief on the officer's face was clear. "This guy carries a lot of weight here. If something happens to him, some of us won't be going home. Hell, we might not even be safe out in the streets."

Having already read the man's file, Walt already knew that Dewayne York was a very dangerous man. Serving 22 years for double murder, his money and powerful friends were the only things that kept him off of Death Row. Walt was going to have to make a deal with him in order to get Bruce Battle out in time.

They reached the door to the interview room and Officer Woods yanked it open and let Walt go in first. A mountain of a man was sitting at the table with a slight smile on his face.

Dewayne York was a dark-skinned man with a head full of lightly curled hair and a full beard with grey shooting through in irregular places. He was only 6-foot 1-inch tall but he had to be 300 pounds of well-defined muscle. He couldn't be an award-winning bodybuilder, but he could definitely hurt someone on the football field.

The offender sat in silence, watching them as Walt and Officer Woods stood watching him. Walt, understanding that Mr. York wasn't going to talk first said, "How would you like to get paroled and walk out of prison in the next 30 days?"

Walt could clearly see the interest in his calculating eyes. Mr. York sat back and said, "I wouldn't be here if you didn't know who I was. I will not snitch or talk to you about anything or anyone."

Walt smiled and said, "That's exactly what I wanted to hear from you. All I need from you is your word that you can keep your mouth shut." He paused and searched the offender's face. "Do I have your word?"

Dewayne York was fully invested in the conversation now. He searched Walt's face for any kind of deception and Walt fixed his face to look as trustworthy as possible. After a full minute Dewayne said, "You have my word as long as you do what you just said you could do."

Walt nodded and looked at the confused face of Officer Woods. He said, "Officer, take the handcuffs off of Mr. York."

Dewayne held his hands out for the officer and as he inserted the key, Walt moved with lightning speed and stuck a needle in Officer Woods' neck. Less than a second later, he was stretched out on the concrete floor dead to the world.

Mr. York jumped up and said, "What the fuck man? I thought you were a cop."

Walt pulled out his credentials and showed them to the man. "I am and I don't have time to go into details. What I need you to do is sit here for the next 30 minutes with the door closed until I come back. Officer Woods won't remember what happened. We'll just say he passed out during the interview. And if anyone ask, I was in here with you the whole time. If you can do that, I'll have you free in 30 days. Okay?"

Dewayne sat back down and laughed. "Deal man. What do I do if this guy wakes up?"

"He won't. I have to stick him with another needle to wake him. I'll be back," Walt said as he dashed to the door.

Walt opened the door and peeked out. No one in sight in either direction. He closed the door behind him and made his way deeper into the basement of the prison.

Navigating this part of the prison unseen was child's play. Since no offenders were ever allowed to be in this section without being cuffed and escorted, there were no cameras and no patrols. Using a seldom used staircase, Walt transitioned from the basement to the attic of the prison without being seen by a camera or a person. This route had been clearly marked on the blueprints by the killer.

Using the overhead catwalk system, it only took him ten minutes to reach the stairway that led to the block where Bruce Battle was being held.

This was the most dangerous part of the mission. An officer was sitting in a booth about 30 yards away, and the control panel would light up if he opened the door. After gaining access to the staircase, he still had to open the door to the block, and every corner of the block was in sight of a camera.

He removed the black box and sat it on the floor. He took his phone out, as well as another container about the same size as a jewelry box. He opened the small container and removed the bee sized drone. He activated it with his phone and set it on course to infiltrate the officer's booth.

After directing it under several doors, the drone entered the booth. The booth was dark but had enough light spilling over from the dorms for Walt to easily make out the officer taking a nap at the front of the booth.

Walt got the drone as close to her face as he could and released a dose of the gas. Through the high-definition lens, he could see the officer fall into a deeper sleep. Walt brought the drone back home and then activated the black box.

He pulled a mask from his waistband to hide his face from the other offenders and picked the lock on the first door. Ten seconds later, he was at the door to the block. The black box knocked out all of the cameras in the whole facility so anyone else who just happened to be looking at the cameras would see nothing but a black screen.

Walt picked the lock to the Restrictive Housing Unit door and scrambled in. Bruce Battle's cell was only three doors down so he began working on his lock seconds after gaining access to the block.

Eighteen minutes of total elapsed time had passed before he opened the cell door and Bruce Battle jumped up out of his bed.

Bruce was a Blood gang member who had run afoul with the killer and had gotten his arm blown off for his troubles. Bruce and the killer seemed to have a grudging respect for each other because Bruce had known his identity and refused to give him up even to go home early. Well, until Walt had beaten him half to death to get the one-armed man to give up the information.

Bruce had once been a big man physically, but the surgeries and segregation time had whittled him down to skin and bones.

"Who the fuck is you man?" Bruce asked the masked detective.

"Your friend Manny sent me to break you out. We don't have much time so get dressed and come the hell on," responded Walt.

Showing some renewed vigor, Bruce dressed in about 30 seconds and Walt led the way back to the stairway. Walt, slapping his own head, went back and closed the cell door and continued closing the doors behind them until they were back in the basement making their way towards the checkpoint.

They bypassed all the interview rooms before Walt held his hand up to stop their progress. He took out his phone and activated the drone again and navigated it to the checkpoint. The same officer was sitting there in a chair behind the desk, looking bored out of his mind. Walt flew the drone directly over his head and released a dose of the sleeping gas. Almost instantly, the officer's head slumped forward in sleep.

Walt called the drone back, put it up, and then directed the offender to follow him. They made it to the door and Walt said, "Stay right here."

He rushed out and got his car moved directly in front of the door. He popped the truck and, even without being told, Bruce ran out and jumped in, closing the lid behind him.

Walt parked the car right where it had been before, removed his mask, got out and walked to the back of the car. "I have to cover our tracks. Stay in the trunk and don't make a fucking sound. You got me?"

"Yeah, I got you," replied Bruce. "Just hurry up, I can barely breathe in this fucking trunk."

Walt rushed back inside, passed the checkpoint and entered the room where Dewayne still sat at the table and Officer Woods was still on the floor. He straightened himself up a little bit and turned to Dewayne. "We good?" he asked the offender. At his nod, Walt produced the other needle and stuck the officer in the neck again.

After a second, Officer Woods started to groan. Walt was on the floor helping the officer to his feet, asking him, "Are you alright? What happened? You just passed out."

The officer looked around confused and asked, "Where am I? What's going on?" Walt explained about setting up the interview and, in the middle of it, the officer just passed out. Something Walt had just noticed and hadn't even thought about; the officer's keys were back on his belt loop and the cuffs were firmly on Mr. York's wrist. When Walt looked at him, the offender still had the same small smile stretched across his face.

Officer Woods looked at his watch and said, "Oh Shit! It's almost shift change. Sorry but I have to get Mr. York back to his cell." Walt nodded his understanding and told the officer that he would see himself out.

Walking back down the hall, Walt deactivated the black box so the camera could pick him up leaving on his own seconds after the officer had checked his watch. That way Officer Woods would actually be his alibi when the inevitable questions came his way.

He walked pass the sleeping officer, strolled outside and got into his car. He drove to the exit checkpoint, flashed his badge and the officer, busy letting in guards for the shift change, waved him on through.

Walt continued out of the city until he entered Durham. He drove to a house that he'd rented a few weeks ago and entered the enclosed garage. He popped the trunk and then got out himself.

Bruce crawled out of the trunk and stretched before he turned around and caught sight of Walt.

His elation at being free evaporated off of his face the second he recognized the detective. "Fuck you motherfucker," he said advancing on Walt. The detective pulled the silenced weapon out and pointed it at the convict who immediately stopped in his tracks.

"I swear I'm not here to hurt you. Manny did send me to get you. Just calm down and let me set up the meeting to hand you over to him." Walt pulled out his phone and dialed the killer. The phone rang and rang. No other time had Walt called him did the phone rang more than once before it was answered.

He looked at the clock on the phone and saw it was almost 9:00 a.m. He glanced back at Bruce and said, "Shit, I think we have a problem," as the phone continued to rang and rang.

CHAPTER 4

"How did you get pass all my security?" asked Mickey.

"What security?" asked Manny. "As far as I know the three of us are the only people left alive." Manny still had his gun pressed against Mickey's head with Alisha standing beside him.

Mickey laughed. "I don't know how you snuck pass all the homies, but if you pull that trigger, you will die right along with me."

"You think so?" asked Manny. "Well, I have an idea. How about I put my gun away and we fight man to man to the death? Would you like that?"

"You don't have the balls to face me man to man. You're nothing without that gun." Mickey had turned to face him by now with a look of pure hatred on his face.

"Take five steps back or I kill you now and take my chances with your homies." Mickey stepped back five steps and Manny put his gun back in his hip holster. Alisha stayed glued to the wall with an utterly passive look on her face. Manny asked him, "Now do you call for your boys, or do we handle this like G's?"

Mickey smirked and said, "G's? Are you serious? You not a real G. You don't deserve me facing you like a real G." Mickey reached and pulled his gun from behind his back and pointed it at Manny's chest. "Fuck you nigga. You got to be one stupid motherfucker to come to my hood, pull a gun on me, and then don't shoot." Motioning down with the gun,

Mickey said, "Get on your knees coward. Talking some gangsta shit with me."

Alisha said, "Baby, stop playing with this fake ass gangsta and kill him so we can go."

Mickey said, "Ok baby." At the same time Manny said, "Not yet baby."

Mickey looked at Manny in confusion, then quickly turned to Alisha as she finally peeled herself from the wall.

She was looking at Mickey with disgust as she walked toward Manny. When she reached him, she grabbed his hand and kissed him on his lips while staring lovingly at his face.

The gun slipped a little in Mickey's hand. "Alisha? What the fuck are you doing?"

"What does it look like I'm doing?" she replied. Kissing Manny again, she said, "I'm supporting my man and my OG."

A look of pure, cold fury blazed in Mickey's eyes as he murmured, "Well fuck you both," and started firing shot after shot at Manny and Alisha.

When the smoke cleared, Manny and Alisha stood hand in hand, smiling at Mickey. Manny looked over at Alisha and said, "You did really good sweetie. I love you."

"I love you too daddy," replied Alisha.

Manny looked at Mickey again as he reflected on the past year that led to this point in time.

· ·

Manny drove passed the Crip stronghold a year before he planned to make his move. He had a lot of research and recon to do before he could even think about making a move. He needed to know numbers and positions and profiles and motivations so he could make informed decisions about the best way to rid the world of this scum.

He started by taking pictures of each member he came across and running facial recognition on each of them. He found that many of them had been in the military and others had been to prison. A lot of them had been to both.

Hanging around the neighborhood would be next to impossible as almost everyone in the area was affiliated in some way. So, he started planting listening devices and cameras in certain members houses until he started to get a general idea of what he was really dealing with.

What he learned as time went on was, no one talked about the leadership compound. He obtained blueprints, but it was plain to see that modifications to the property had been made without worry over legal permits. A lot of reinforcement and shielding and added security and protections. One thing was clear, he needed an inside person who was willing to help him. He knew he could just blow the compound up with a military drone, but he wanted to reduce Mickey to the nothing he was before he killed him face to face.

Then the answer came one night as two women were talking on the couch in one of the houses that he had bugged. He only had sound until he dispatched one of his spy drones to give him a visual of the two suspected female gang members.

"That boy is in love with you Alisha and you know it." This was said by a young woman who bore a striking resemblance to a young Rhianna. That is until she belched like a 300-pound biker and didn't even excuse herself.

"I think he just loves fucking me, Tyiesha. He's old enough to be my dad and I don't want to earn rank by spreading my legs. I want to be the first female OG Crip that the guys under me can respect."

Alisha was nothing short of a dime. She was about 5-foot 8-inches with perfect slim thick curves. Huge doe-like brown eyes and long black hair emphasized her glowing dark chocolate skin.

Tyiesha said, "Well, let's get going to the club. Motions is supposed to be off the chain tonight. Maybe you can find some civilian chump to spend some money on you."

"With us looking this good," Alisha said while doing a slow model spin. "If we can't make some cash tonight, I might just have to rob somebody." It was hard to tell if she was joking or not but Manny was going to be there to find out.

The club Motions was right on the outskirts of the Crip's territory. In fact, it was so close, nobody but Crips and brave civilians showed up. It was packed with young bangers on the come up, but because it was owned by a very connected white guy named Bambam, it was relatively violence free.

Manny was out to be impactful tonight. Normally his life depended on blending in when heading into situations like this. Tonight, he wanted to separate himself from all the fake ballers, so he made a trip back to his house to gear up.

He pulled up to the club wearing a royal blue, three-piece suit. His all white Lexus LFA Nürburgring Edition was one of only 50 in the world. He revved the 562 HP, V-10 engine and let 42 Dugg announce his arrival with his song *4 Da Gang* blasting through his $100,000 stereo system.

By the time he stepped out, he was sure word had already spread that a true baller was on the scene. He anticipated being questioned as to who he was so he put his most confident and privileged persona on display as he strutted to the front of the line, ignoring all the young beautiful ladies.

To his surprise, the bouncers stepped out of his way and he walked unaccosted into the club. He had secretly looked for the young woman Alisha in the line, but guessed she and her friend had already made it inside.

Wayne Wonder's *No Letting Go* was playing over the club's sound system and the dance floor was full of young sexy people rubbing all over each other. He scanned the club and spotted the extremely sexy Alisha dancing with some young guy wearing a blue flag around his head.

Manny stopped a passing waitress and asked if they had a VIP section. She told him yes, but it would cost him $500. He gave her a thousand, told her to keep the change and lead the way.

She led him to a slightly elevated platform that overlooked the dance floor. He didn't know if it was fate or just good luck, but his new position gave him a direct line of sight to Alisha.

It was only one other group in the VIP and it was an older white guy that had three beautiful white women with him.

Manny couldn't be sure, but he looked like one of Bambam's partners.

Some new young black women came in the club and ran up to Tyiesha and Alisha, greeting them with hugs and kisses. They began talking and looking around until one of the new ladies spotted him sitting in the VIP section. She turned and began gesturing for Alisha and Tyiesha to look up at him.

Knowing that a rich, influential man wouldn't play games, he locked eyes with Alisha and let her see the desire in his eyes. What he didn't expect was the true desires being stirred up for this young beauty. At that moment, Drake's *Knife Talk* came on and, still locking eyes, she began to dirty wine.

While all the women in the group were good looking, none of them could hold a candle to Alisha. She was wearing a gold slip-on dress with a royal blue belt and royal blue three-inch heels. Manny inclined his head to her as she spun around and continued her motion while looking at him over her shoulder.

Manny had seen thousands of beautiful, sexy women, but for some reason, Alisha was wreaking havoc on his body. When French Montana's *Unforgettable* started playing, all the sexy women in the club started doing their best ass shaking routines.

Manny was lost in watching this young goddess, but knew it was time to put his game in motion. He waved for her and her friends to come up to the VIP section and join him. She got everyone's attention and the five women made their way to the small staircase. Manny nodded when the

35

waitress looked over with uncertainty in her eyes. She then smiled at the group and allowed them access.

He stood up and greeted each one of them with a handshake and a smile. He memorized all their names and then introduced himself as Manuel Adams. Everyone settled down in the booth and Manny motioned for the waitress to come over.

The VIP waitress was a slim very attractive white women with a slight overbite that some people thought needed correcting and others found adorable. "What can I get for yawl this evening," she asked with her adorable smile.

"I don't need anything but a Coke, but bring the ladies whatever they want," Manny responded. The drink orders ranged from Moet to Cîroc. Alisha ordered a Coke and glanced over at Manny, feeling his constant stare burning into her face. She responded with a small smile and Manny's heart did a little flip flop in his chest.

For the next 30 minutes they all made small talk with him saying little and them trying to milk him for information. Lil Wayne saved the day with his song *Lollipop* because all the women wanted to go back and dance for a while.

When Tyiesha noticed Alisha still sitting down, she gave her a knowing look and hurried the other women along. Manny asked her, "Did you not want to dance?"

Alisha said, "I'm good. I'd rather sit up here and get to know you a little better."

"That's too bad," replied Manny. "All games aside, you are a very beautiful woman and I can't think of anything I'd rather do than sit here and watch you dance." For once

Manny wasn't playing a role or giving a line. He was simply telling her the truth.

At that moment *Streets* by Doja Cat came on and Alisha said, "If you want me to, I can dance for you?" Manny could only nod as Alisha got up and started gently rocking her hips and rolling her mid-section from side to side.

She danced about three feet in front of him and he was able to admire her impeccably proportioned body from her gold painted toe nails, to her raven-black hair. Alisha spun around and her dress was the perfect length to tease him with glimpses of her long, toned legs and the cuff of her stunning ass.

Manny was starting to feel out of his depths because he wasn't sure who was seducing who. When she dropped down and slowly rose her hips back up with her hair still sweeping the floor, all the liquid in his mouth dried up. She continued to draw him in as she moved closer and closer to him.

Up until that point, it was just her looks and her sensual movements that had him enthralled. Then her smell filled his nose and he was helpless to draw a deep breath and release a small, "Oh my God."

She was facing him now and he moaned as she reached up and started rubbing all over his freshly shaved, bald head while biting on her plump, pink lips. She remained locked eye to eye with him as his hands began to migrate and explore up and down the back of her chocolate legs. All Manny could think about was how much trouble he was in and thinking that he would kill the DJ if he allowed the song to end. Might even hunt down Doja Cat and teach her a lesson about making her songs so short.

They continued like this for another 30 seconds before the song started to fade away. Manny actually cut his eyes over to the DJ and made a move to get up when Alisha pushed him back down and said, "Relax Sweetie, we're not done yet."

On cue, Ty Dolla $ign's *Or Nah* came on and Alisha pushed him all the way back in the cushion. After making sure he was comfortable, she turned around and sat in his lap and proceeded to give him the sexiest lap dance he'd ever had the joy of experiencing. Right at the start of The Weekends verse, she spun around to face him and started grinding down really hard.

Manny knew that she could feel him responding, so he held onto her hips as she continued to grind back and forth while staring into his eyes. He was feeling the heat radiating from her core as her lips parted on a small moan. Out of the corner of his eye, he saw the other women coming up the steps and he released her and pointedly looked in that direction. She acknowledged that she saw them but turned his head back and gave him a fast peck on the lips before she moved off of his lap.

They all stayed about another hour before Manny said it was time for him to go. He asked if he could drop them off somewhere, but said it would be a tight squeeze for him to take everyone. They all glanced at Alisha and said they were going to stay for a little while longer. Alisha said that she was ready and would appreciate a ride home.

Manny called the waitress over and gave her $5,000 in hundreds. He said, "Anything they want, they get. The rest you can keep as a tip." He grabbed Alisha's hand and maneuvered her outside to his car.

He hit the remote start and opened her door before he made his way around to the driver's side. He got in and she gave him directions to her house, though she had no idea that he already knew where she lived. They were stopped at a red light when *My All* by Mariah Carey came on and Alisha said, "Oh my God, this is my song," and proceeded to match Mariah note for note with her eyes closed.

Manny sat at the light, listening and watching, as he slowly fell in love with this old soul inside of a young woman's body. It was after two in the morning and there was no traffic, so he just sat, in awe of her talent and passion. When the song ended, she had tears on her face and she looked at him shyly and said, "Sorry." He reached over and pulled her into his lap for a deep kiss and hug.

All at once, he came back into himself and realized that he was in a dangerous situation. He was in enemy territory making out with the King's Queen. He sat her back on her seat and proceeded to her house.

"I'm sorry but I live with my Mom. You can't come in but I had a very good time, Manuel."

He pulled out his phone and asked her to put her number in his contacts. She put the number in, but had a worried look on her face. When she handed him the phone back, he took her hand in both of his and said, "I want to be honest with you, but I can't tell you everything. What I can tell you is that you are wreaking havoc on the reason I am here. I am

39

going to make a promise to you that I have never made to anyone else on this Earth."

When he was sure he had her undivided attention, he said, "I feel a very special bond between the two of us and because of that, no matter what happens, I will not hurt you. Do you believe me?"

She looked a little confused but nodded that she did. He kissed her deeply but quickly and said, "I will call you tomorrow. Now, it would be my pleasure to watch you walk to your house, turn and give me a little wave, and then go inside." She did just that, sporting a sexy grin the whole time, and he drove off with a smile on his face.

Over the next couple of months, they built their relationship into something real. She admitted to what she was and said that she didn't have a choice in being intimate with Mickey Brown. He told her he didn't like it but he understood. He also told her that they wouldn't go all the way because, once he had her, no other man would ever touch her again.

Three months in, she was staying at his compound in Charlotte whenever Mickey wasn't calling on her to perform her duties. Every time she had to leave him, she would cry and Manny felt like just sending that air strike and being done with Mickey.

She broke down one night as they lay in bed and told him that Mickey was in love with her and he was pushing for her to move into the gang stronghold with him. Manny decided it was time to put his faith in someone and tell her some things that would be difficult for her to hear.

"Alisha, I have to tell you something." She looked at him questioningly but didn't say anything. "This will be hard to hear and you might hate me after I tell you, but the promise I told you from the beginning still stands. OK?" She nodded so he went on. "I'm the Prison Guard Killer."

There was dead silence for about ten seconds and then Alisha started to laugh. She slapped his chest and said, "Thanks for lightening up the mood, but be serious."

He got out of the bed and paced over to the window overlooking the pond in the backyard. "Alisha, I'm being totally honest with you. I can tell you the whole story, but I need you to understand that I am dead serious." He turned and looked at her and he could tell when it hit her that he wasn't joking around.

"Have you heard the description on the news?" he asked her. She nodded her head and he motioned for her to take a good look at him.

"You mean to tell me you killed all those people?"

"Yes," he answered her. "And I will kill a lot more."

She laid on the bed staring at the ceiling for a full five minutes without saying a word. Finally, she turned to him and said, "80% of my gang has been to prison at some time over the last 15 years. Are you here for them?"

"Yes."

"Which ones?" she asked him.

"All of them."

She looked around in alarm. "I must be missing something. You're the PGK so I know you're not the police. Are you part of a rival gang?" He responded in the negative.

"Well, you and who else are going to take on the biggest gang in the city?"

He didn't respond. Just turned and looked out over his land. "Oh! I get it. You have a death wish." She threw the covers to the side and started to get dressed. Even though they had not made love, they still enjoyed the pleasure of just holding each other skin to skin.

When Manny heard the rustling, he turned. "So, you care if I die?"

She finished dressing before she spun on him. "That brings me to the next point. What about me? Was all this just a game to turn me against my own people? Answer me dammit!" She was screaming because he was just standing there looking at her.

"I told you from the start that I wouldn't hurt you ...."

"Too late for that," Alisha interrupted.

"And I always keep my word," he finished, ignoring her interruption. "When it started, yes, I needed someone to be my inside person. But Alisha, after the first night with you at the club, all that changed. I love you. I want to spend my life with you. Do I need your help? Yes. But that's just one plan. Baby, I could kill all of them tonight without involving you. I can and will change my plan because I have more than myself to think about now."

He walked over and sat on the bed in front of her. "No lines and no lies. I use people. Okay? I trick people. I lie to people. I kill people for the things that they have done to me or to others. I have a personal mission and I have to carry it out to its conclusion. I know you, and I know you are loyal to the people you love. Listen to me about who I am. Let me explain the reasons why I do what I do. After that, if you don't want to be with me, I'll leave you alone. It won't be easy, but I'll give you whatever you need and whatever you want and I'll make sure you are safe before I make my move."

"What if I decide to help my gang and tell them you're coming?" she asked.

"It won't matter. I'll kill them one by one until it's just you left."

"You do understand that the organization is worldwide and you're just one man?" she asked him.

"I don't have a problem with the whole organization. I have a problem with this particular part of it," he responded. "But anyone who gets in my way, except for you, will die with them."

Shaking her head, she sat down on the floor and said, "Maybe I need to hear this story to understand why you are so confident."

Manny took a fortifying breath and then told her the story of his life. He told her about how it was to grow up a genius. He talked about attending high school and college at such a young age. He explained about his work with the CIA and Military Intelligence. About his time in the Marines. His knack for killing that made him a legend worldwide. Then the story took a negative tilt.

He couldn't keep the disdain out of his voice as he talked about the deal made with the governor to send him into the North Carolina prison system. He revealed some of the things that went on inside and the plot the governor came up with to get rich that cost him ten years of his life. Manny even went into detail about all of the money and assets he stole from the government.

She asked, "And they let you get away with just taking all their stuff? I mean, you're not actually hiding out here." By now they were both laying on the bed with him looking up at the ceiling and her staring at him.

"There is some stuff going on behind the scenes that make my apprehension, let's just say, difficult. I'll say, I work alone, but I'm just a small part of a whole. And I'll leave it at that."

He glanced over at Alisha and grabbed her hand. He could see the love and sympathy shining in her eyes. He didn't know if it would be there five minutes from now, but he had to push on with his story. "There is one last part that I have to tell you."

"It's okay sweetie. You can tell me anything."

Manny was nervous and unsure because he knew things would change after his next revelation, but he had to tell her everything. "This isn't my first run in with your gang." A confused look formed on her face.

"I don't understand," she stated. "I've never seen you before and I've definitely never heard about you, except on the news."

He said the one word that would explain everything. "Lanesboro."

She still looked confused. "Lanesboro? I don't under...." Then it registered and tears filled her eyes. "No." She flung herself up from the bed. "No, Manny!" Tears were now flowing freely down her lovely face.

"I didn't know you then and I really didn't have a choice," he attempted to explain.

She doubled over, clutching her midsection like a powerful blow had been struck. She straightened up and said, "My brother? You're the one who killed my brother?" Then she lunged and attacked while screaming and calling him every foul name she could think of.

He dodged and blocked all the blows, trying his hardest not to hurt her, until she lay spent on the bed, crying her heart out. After a while, she went quiet. "I'm sorry Alisha but…."

"Don't," she interrupted him. "I don't want to hear another word from you. Take me home and I better not ever see you again." A look of hatred spread across her still beautiful face. "And I will be standing with my gang against any and all enemies." She stormed out of the room leaving Manny standing there with a sick feeling in the pit of his stomach.

Months passed as Manny took out his pain and anger on prison guard after prison guard. Inmate after inmate. Each one more brutal than the last. He left Alisha alone but always checked on her covertly to make sure she was okay.

After six months, he was ready to cut his loses with her and make his move on her gang. On surveillance one night, he heard a familiar song coming from Alisha's house. It was Mariah Carey's *My All*, and he could hear Alisha's soft cries over the listening device as she let the song play on repeat. He felt bad for her, but he respected her wishes not to be contacted.

Then a miracle. Two days before he was about to carry out a different plan, his phone lit up with her face on the screen. He accepted the call but stayed silent, giving her the right to speak first. Then, with just three small words, she restored his heart and soul: "What's the plan."

CHAPTER 5

Looking over at Alisha and, for the moment, ignoring the idiot still standing there holding his useless gun, Manny asked her, "What do you want to do? Go wait for me out front, or stay here and watch me take this clown apart?"

"I've only seen you when you were practicing at home," she replied. "I'd love to see you in action."

"You disloyal bitch!" shouted Mickey. "You callin this nigga daddy? You do know that this is the man who killed your brother, right?"

Manny tensed up at the reminder. Alisha had asked for an explanation before she would totally commit to him. He had finally gotten to tell her about Mickey and all the families he had destroyed while he was locked up. Her brother had been one of the guys who had robbed him out of the poisoned K2. He admitted that he wanted all of them to die, but told her that he still felt he had done the right thing.

She had cried for a while but then told him that she forgave him. They had been sitting in Manny's mountain retreat in Burnsville, NC, which was where he had moved to because Alisha knew where the Charlotte compound was.

Now, she looked over at Mickey and said, "Me and my man have no secrets. I'm going to enjoy watching him kill you." She then walked over and sat on the sofa to enjoy the show.

Manny, keeping his eyes on Mickey, unclipped his holster and sat it next to Alisha on the cushion closest to her.

He could see the fear clearly on Mickey's face as he remembered the last beatdown Manny gave him. This time, he didn't even have a knife to help him defend himself.

They squared off in the wide-open space of the living room, and Manny made the fight last a lot longer than it needed to. At the beginning, Manny threw a lot of painful blocks that had Mickey hesitant to even throw another punch. Then the methodical assault commenced.

Manny started with Mickey's body. Landing kick after kick and blow after blow until Mickey was on his knees throwing up blood, barely able to breathe.

All of a sudden, Mickey smiled and started patting his pockets and looking around on the floor. "Looking for this?" asked Alisha.

Mickey looked over at her and the smile vanished as he saw that she was clutching his panic button in her hand. He collected enough breath to say, "You're going to die bitch," before he coughed up more blood.

"Eventually, but not before you from the looks of it," she replied.

Then Manny started breaking things. Fingers. Toes. Wrists. Ankles. Until the Crip OG was on his back begging for mercy. After one gruesome arm break, Manny glanced over at Alisha and saw the shock and horror on her face. It was that look that forced Manny to end things. He quickly rolled Mickey onto his lap and whispered, "That was for Rodney. This is for me," and broke his neck. Manny rolled the dead man off of him and then went to the bathroom down the hall for a quick clean up.

Charges had already been set to burn the compound to the ground, so, as Manny escorted his Queen to the car parked around the corner, he pulled out his phone and dialed the command to start the fire.

The drive down to Charlotte was mostly filled with silence. About five minutes from the house, Alisha turned to him and said, "That was horrifying, but also amazing. I've seen him fight and win against five guys at one time, and you just destroyed him without breaking a sweat."

With wide eyes, she said, "You are a very dangerous man, and now I see why you are always so confident."

Manny didn't say anything until they were sitting in front of the gate to his compound. "I have to go handle some things with Det. Rogers." He looked at her questioningly. "Are you good to stay here or do you want to go to your mother's house?"

When Manny had been sure that they were truly back together, he'd moved her mother out of their old house and brought one down the street from his Charlotte compound. If anything had went wrong with the plan, he didn't want her to become the target of the gang's wrath, so he'd moved her out of harm's way.

"I'm good," she said with a smile. "Especially since, now that Mickey is dead, we can consummate our relationship as soon as you get back." She was already on his lap by the time she said the last word. They ended up making out like a couple of horny teenagers until Manny opened his door and practically threw her off of him.

Manny was breathing hard and wouldn't even look at her as he said, "See you later," slammed his door, and sped off.

Thirty seconds later a text came in from her: Coward. Run while you can. "Jesus. She's trying to kill me." It took all of his discipline to keep the car pointed north towards Raleigh instead of going back and making love to his woman right in the middle of the street.

It was only 11:00 am, but Walt had been calling him every five minutes since about 9:00 am. He had checked the news feeds while he'd held a gun to Beezo's head in order to force him to give the "everything is okay" report to Mickey. He knew that Walt had already freed Bruce Battle, but using some other contacts, Manny knew that the police had no clue at all about who or how.

Shaking his head, Manny couldn't do anything except give Walt his props for that. He did hear some speculation that the PGK had finally showed up to free Bruce for his loyalty. Well, if the news people said it, then it must be the truth, right?

Manny sent Walt a text on where to take Bruce. Almost immediately Walt responded saying it was impossible to move him from where he was stashed. Furthermore, Walt had been called in to help find the motherfucker. Walt gave Manny the address where Bruce was and confidently declared himself done with task 2. Manny laughed at Walt's audacity and then entered the new address in the navigation system.

He was still careful when dealing with Walt because he didn't know when he would say, screw it, and set him up to get captured, sacrificing himself in the process. So, a couple hours later, he was canvasing the area around the house where Bruce was hold up. He parked about two miles away and sent out a drone to check the area.

It was a well populated area but the houses were set up to provide the most privacy possible. It would have been perfect for what he had planned, but Walt needed to understand that he wasn't the one in charge.

Manny recalled the drone and then sent a text to Walt. Within a minute, his phone was ringing. He answered with a smile. "What's going on detective?"

"What the hell man? I gave you the address where he is. Just go over there and get him," demanded Walt.

"Remember who you're talking to. You don't tell me to do shit. Now, I sent you the address where I want the exchange to happen. It's now 1:35 pm. You have two hours and 25 minutes to get him there or you fail the task. I don't think Ann and Denise would appreciate that."

"You're a real live piece of shit man. I'm outside of the prison trying to figure out how the inmate, that I broke out, got away. Cut me some slack here." Walt was sounding desperate, but also resolved because he knew no mercy would be offered.

"Walt, you're wasting time. I want you to win Walt, but I really don't give a fuck if you fail. If you're giving me all this trouble on task two, maybe we should just skip to the part where the ladies die and you go to prison. Is that what you want?"

After a moment of silence, Walt said, "Fuck you," and hung up.

Manny laughed and proceeded to the address that he'd just given Walt. It was only 20 minutes from where Bruce was at this moment, but rules were rules. If he let Walt get away with it this time, then it would bite him in the end.

The address took him to a building in the warehouse district and Manny had cameras covering every square inch of the whole neighborhood. Manny entered one of the warehouses and set up a laptop so he could watch for anything out of the usual for the area. He sat down and made a few calls to pass the time until Walt arrived with his cargo.

At 3:40 he saw Walt's car enter the district. He propped open the warehouse door and then returned to his seat. It took Walt a couple minutes until he found the entrance, and Manny heard his car pull up at the door. He watched on the laptop as Walt popped the trunk and Bruce Battle climbed out and slammed the lid.

They both trotted in with Bruce smiling and Walt frowning at the sight of the killer sitting in front of them. Walt, sensing something wasn't right, held back at the door. Bruce, on the other hand, strolled forward confidently saying, "Thanks man. I knew you wouldn't take my arm and then leave me in that hellhole."

"You're very welcome," was all Manny said before pulling out a gun and shooting Bruce right between the eyes. He crumpled instantly to the floor and silence overtook the warehouse.

Manny and Walt stared at each other for a couple minutes before Walt asked, "Can I go now?" He was visibly angry but was controlling it very well.

"Hold on for a minute. I have a surprise for you." Manny motioned him over to the laptop setup on the table. After he finished what he was doing, he looked up to find Walt still standing at the door. "Something wrong?" he asked him.

"Why would you have me go through all of that if you were just going to shoot him?" asked Walt.

"If you can't figure it out then you wouldn't understand my explanation anyway," replied Manny.

After a minute Walt said, "A test."

"Bingo," said Manny. "See, you're not as stupid as you look. I want you to learn that there are many ways to do something. You didn't want to kill. I wanted to see if you could figure out a way to do what needed to be done while staying in your comfort zone. Sometimes that won't be possible. Other times, you just won't be smart enough to figure it out."

"Can you at least tell me why you killed him?" asked Walt.

"He was a dangerous loose end for both of us," replied Manny. "He would have eventually come up with some scheme to blackmail one or both of us, and it might have been harder to kill him after he linked up with his people. You remember what they taught us in the military? A potential threat is already a threat."

Manny stood up and walked deeper into the warehouse. He said, "Press enter on the laptop when you're ready," as he turned a corner and walked out of sight.

Walt, not knowing what to expect, walked over to the laptop sitting open on the table. The screen was blank but a low hum told him that it was indeed on. He glanced in the direction the killer had gone and then sat down and pressed enter.

The machine whirled and for a few seconds the screen remained dark. Then the picture blinked on and Walt almost jumped out of the chair from shock. Two of the most important people in the world to him were sitting in front of a camera smiling and waving at him.

They were both sitting on a bed in what appeared to be an upscale hotel room, but Walt knew to be a suite in one of the killer's underground prisons. They appeared to be making a lot of noise, but no sound was coming through. Walt pressed a few buttons and then the soft voices of the women floated from the internal speakers.

"Oh my God Walt, you look terrible!" This from Walt's beautiful, younger partner, Detective Ann Grace. She was 5-foot 8-inches tall, 130 pounds, and her mixed white and Cherokee heritage contributed to her light skin and long black hair. She was in her mid-30's and had been in law enforcement for almost 15 years. Ann was the closest thing to a little sister Walt had ever had, even though he knew that she used to have a crush on him. Walt started to tear up as he studied his partner in her usual khaki skirt and elegant teal blouse. She looked happy and well cared for.

"Don't listen to her. You look amazing as always." Denise McCarthy was as beautiful as she was smart. She was a journalist at Channel 5 based in Raleigh. Standing at 5-foot 5-inches, she carried her 120 pounds just as well as her 40 years of age. With her short dark hair and glowing brown complexion, Walt thought she was the most stunning woman in the world. The killer had actually pushed them together, but he was also the cause for them being apart.

Feeling fuzzy headed from happiness, he said, "Hi my two beautiful ladies. I am so happy to see you doing so well."

Denise said, "We'll be doing a whole lot better when that bastard lets us out of here."

"It could be a lot worse," countered Ann. "We have pretty much everything we could ever need, except for sunlight and a cool breeze. He's making sure we're as comfortable as possible. Well, as long as we don't piss him off."

Denise rolled her eyes and said, "I'm really getting worried about your partner Walt. She keeps forgetting that this sweet, caring man is our fucking kidnapper." By the last few words, she was looking at Ann like she was crazy and she was screaming. "Really Ann, stop defending him."

Walt piped in before an argument exploded between the two strong willed women. "Well, I finished task two and will be starting on three soon. In no time at all I'll have both of you out of there. Is there anything going on that I need to know about?" Walt looked around, making sure he was still alone. "Is there anything either of you can tell me about where you are?"

"Well, I was in the trunk during the ride here and was passed out for most of it. I also had a blindfold on when I was transferred from the car to the building." Denise had gone home after what everyone thought was a successful trap for the killer. She had taken a bath and went to sleep at her house, but woke up in the trunk of her own car, a prisoner to the man everyone thought was dead.

"Mine was similar Walt. I was blindfolded and he kept giving me a drug that made me paralyzed and sleepy at the same time. I did see the inside of the structure that conceals the elevator down into the prison. It looks like the inside of a rundown cabin. Sorry Walt," she said on a shrug. "Me and Denise have talked about this and we can't help you with finding us."

Ann had been abducted when they thought they had the killer on the run and he had turned the tables on them. He had just killed a guard that had been out of contact too long and, while Walt was running in the woods looking for him, the killer had been kidnapping Ann and stealing Walt's car. They found the car down the road but Ann had been missing ever since.

Ann continued. "What we both want to know is how you are doing? I can only imagine what he has you doing in order to free us. I don't think it's worth it to sacrifice your life or your freedom for us. Just stay safe and we'll all be together again in no time."

Walt thought about what she said and then asked Denise how she felt. "I guess I want to say do whatever he tells you so that I can get out of here. I know that is selfish and not what I should say, but Walt, I really want to go home." Out of everyone involved, Denise was the only civilian. So, Walt did feel where she was coming from.

Walt glanced to his left and the killer was standing about ten feet away from him. He hadn't even heard him walk up. Manny said, "Denise is a very smart woman. If I could get Ann to stop being so hard headed, things could go a lot smoother."

Walt knew that Ann was super independent and vey hard headed, but he'd be damned if he would agree with the killer out loud.

Manny said, "Walt, get up for a second."

Walt turned back to the screen and said, "Ladies, I love you both and I am doing everything in my power to get you back. Stay strong and I'll see you soon." After some heart felt goodbyes, Walt stood up.

The killer walked over and stood just outside of camera range, and said, "Ladies, I am about to put my trust in you. I think you are picturing me as a monster because you have no idea what I look like." With that, he walked in sight of the camera and took a seat.

Denise seemed to not care at all that he'd just exposed himself to them. "So, what, you're cute. You think we all haven't seen cute monsters before? Put on any Disney movie and I'll show you at least one."

But Ann's response was totally different. She drew in a shaky breath and said, "Oh my God!" She was looking at him with her expressive brown eyes like he was a movie star. She actually got up and walked out of the camera's view.

"Okay," said Manny. "I guess you can relay this message to her later. Call me Manny. I don't want either of you to be afraid of me. We all have things we have to do that we might not like. I can honestly say that holding you ladies in that prison is one of them for me. If I didn't think it was necessary then I wouldn't have done it.

"On another note, and I've said this to all of you before, none of you know what's going on. I have a broader view than you, but I don't even have the whole picture yet. Just bear with me and I think everything will work out fine."

Denise sat there looking at him like he was a piece of shit sitting on her kitchen table. "Is that all?" she asked.

Manny laughed and said, "Sure Denise, that's all."

"Well, in that case, bye Walt. I'm going to go check on Ann."

As she got up, the killer shut the laptop and turned to look at Walt. "I will have to show you a couple things before you can tackle task three. It should only take a few days."

"Are you really going to sit here and not explain what you just said?" asked Walt. "You just revealed that you are working for someone else. Are you serious?"

The killer stood up and that dangerous look came across his face. "I'll let you know what I want you to know when I want you to know it. Stop fucking trying me, Walt. My patience is running out on all of you."

Manny abruptly turned and headed for the door. "I'll text you where to meet me tomorrow. 2:00 pm and not a second late." At the door, he stopped but didn't turn around. "I'm trying Walt. This playing nice with others is a new thing for me. I'm trying to show you guys the real me. The person who agreed to spend two years of his life in prison just to help people. But every time one of you looks at me like I'm a monster, I get that itch to just kill you all and damn the consequences." With that, he walked out and closed the door softly behind him.

Manny knew that he couldn't go home to Alisha like this. Sometimes he could ignore other people's feelings toward him, but he felt like he was taking a huge leap of faith by showing the women his face. The response told him that he might have made a huge miscalculation and that just pissed him off more.

He drove out of the warehouse district but pulled over at the first gas station he came to. He glanced at his phone and saw that it was fairly early, only 5:20 pm.

Manny knew what would boost his mood. He needed to burn off some steam and he had a job he'd been putting off for too long anyway. Now seemed the perfect time to go visit a friend, and in the process, take care of a few enemies.

CHAPTER 6

The killer had a major debt that he had to repay. So, two hours after leaving Walt in the warehouse, he was sitting down the road from a familiar house in Dunn. He had already sent his drone in and found that a man and two young girls were in the house.

The man was Officer Nicolas Black, a guard at a minimum custody prison in Raleigh. The two girls were his adopted daughters, Emily and Gabby Black. Tonight, the killer needed to right a wrong that had been eating at him for a while.

Not too long ago, he'd heard some rumors about Nicolas Black's husband, Greg Black, and had put in some work to either prove or disprove the whispers. What the killer had uncovered was that Greg had raped a lot of inmates and gotten away with it because of a corrupt system that protected guards no matter what they did. The killer made him pay for his transgressions with his life. But during the murder, he had learned that Greg also molested the girl living under his roof.

Emily had been lucky because she had eventually gone off to college and escaped the abuse. Gabby had not been so lucky. In an act of compassion for the child, who was present at the time of the murder, the killer had showed her his face to form a bond with her. The police had interviewed her extensively, but at no time did she reveal that she had seen his face.

The killer felt he owed her for that, and also the fact that he had waited months after he knew Greg was dirty to come kill him. During that time, she had been living a terror filled life, and he had left her to that fate.

That was only the half of it though. The killer had left a few cameras in the house after he'd killed Greg and, even though it was no longer sexual abuse, Gabby was still abused on a regular basis. Well, not after tonight.

The killer was in his element and he was ready to serve up a little well-earned justice. He had his bag strapped to his back. He was dressed all in black. And he was on the hunt for one of the worst kinds of people; a child abuser.

He had also gotten lucky tonight because Emily was in the house with her family. She was 20 years old and a sophomore at N.C. State University. The fact that she had abandoned Gabby, leaving her to be abused, didn't sit well with the killer. If she didn't have some damn good answers for him, then she would follow her two fathers in death.

The area around the house was very country. Wide open fields and woods were the only things in sight. A long driveway led up to the front of the house, but that wasn't the route the killer was going to take. Right now, he was posted up just inside of the tree line at the rear of the residence.

He didn't want to hurt anyone prematurely, so he dispatched another drone that contained a sleeper agent to render the occupants of the home unconscious. When he was satisfied with the drone's results, he boldly walked to the back door and enter the house.

Thinking about Alisha and how she would react to the decision he had come to, he got to work setting everything up. He smirked to himself. He was more worried about coming home too late than murdering one, possibly two, people. Oh, how the mighty had fallen, but he wouldn't have it any other way.

He rounded up all the occupants and secured them in the living room. Gabby was not restrained in any way but her sister and dad were chained from neck to feet with their backs pressed together. They also had blindfolds on because the killer didn't have a mask on. He wanted Gabby to be able to see his face as soon as she woke up so she wouldn't be afraid even for a second.

Since they all received the same dose, Nick and Emily started to stir first. The bigger you are, the faster the drug would wear off. Nick, being a smaller man, was about the same size as Emily. It would be about another five minutes before the ten-year-old Gabby started to wake up.

When Manny had been doing his research on the family the first time, he had learned that Emily and Gabby were real sisters. Eight years ago, their parents had died in a home invasion while Emily hid in a closet with baby Gabby.

Greg and Nick had seemed like heroes as they stepped up to adopt the young girls who didn't have any other family to take them in. Emily had gone into fits whenever she was separated from her baby sister, so everyone applauded the two men for stepping up and adopting both girls.

Manny knew that Emily had suffered too, but he didn't think that was a good enough excuse to leave your sibling behind to suffer in your place. She could have alerted the authorities at any time. So, in the absence of a good reason, she was just as guilty as the two men.

"What's going on?" asked Nick, being the first one to gain his senses. "Who's there? Listen, take whatever you want, just don't hurt my family."

Manny walked over and kicked the man as hard as he could in the stomach. He watched as he retched and attempted to double over but the chains made that impossible. "Shut the fuck up unless I tell you to speak. The next kick will be to your head."

There was going to be no second chance for Nick Black, so Manny yanked the blindfold away from his face and let Nick see that death had come calling.

"No, no, no, no, no! Please not my family. Please man. Haven't you hurt us enough?" wailed Officer Black. All of the officers in the state had been given a vague description of him, so under the circumstances, it wasn't surprising that it only took a second for Nick to recognize him.

Manny was about to deliver the promised kick to his head for talking, when Emily came to. "Dad? Daddy? What's going on? Why am I tied up?"

"Be quiet Emily. We are going to be fine. I'm handling this," replied Nick.

"Handling what? And why were you screaming?" asked Emily.

Manny decided to step in. "He's screaming because I'm back to take care of daddy number two. He's screaming because he knows that he's been a bad daddy and that his life is going to end tonight. Now, if I were you Emily, I would shut the fuck up so that maybe my body count stops at one tonight." Emily, being a smart girl, instantly stopped talking.

"I never touched these girls. I swear it. You can ask them. That was Greg and you've already killed him. I begged him to stop, even threatened to leave him. But he said he would take me down with him with his lies. Don't kill me man. I'm sorry." Nick continued to beg for his life until Manny did deliver the kick just to shut him up.

"So, you want me to believe that you are daddy of the year material? Let me show you something." Manny walked over and pointed to a black dot high up on the wall. "This is one of the cameras I left in the house to watch over your family. But the things I heard and saw regarding that little girl over there, you're just as bad as Greg."

Nick was silent as he recovered from the blow to his head. When he could speak again, he said, "She is a child. The Bible says that if you love a child, then you have to discipline them. You're going to kill me for loving that little girl?"

"So, calling her a little slut and a little whore is discipline? Telling her she is lucky that you don't like little girls like Greg did is showing her love? You didn't have to hit her or touch her to terrorize her." Manny had his full focus on Nick until he saw movement on the chair where he had placed Gabby.

She wiped her eyes like she was waking from a full night's sleep. When she saw him, she smiled for the first time that he had ever seen, and Manny smiled back with a lump in his throat. "Hi little angel," said Manny.

"Hi," she replied back with a little wave. "Are you here to kill Nick and Emily?" She didn't sound upset or happy, she just sounded curious.

"Nick is definitely going to die for how he's been treating you." He paused for a few seconds. "Me and you will talk about Emily, but ultimately her death will be up to you and her."

Manny reached in his bag and pulled out a small plastic bag with a rubber innertube attached to the opening. "Mr. Black. I've done some research on you." Manny got up and walked into the kitchen. He opened the fridge and took out a gallon jug of cold water.

He continued. "When you were a child, you almost drowned at a water park. I think it was in a wave pool that the incident occurred. From that experience, you've developed an illogical fear or drowning, right? Well, tonight that fear will become logical," he stated coming back into the living room.

Nick had already eyed the bag, but seeing the gallon of water made him start up his begging once again. "Please no! Pleeassseee! Gabby, I love you. I've never hurt you. Please tell him to stop. Hey man, I get it. I learned my lesson. I will never talk down to her again. I swear you don't have to kill me."

"I know you'll never talk down to her again," said Manny. "Kind of hard to curse a little girl when your head is surrounded by water." He pulled out a small automatic pump and began hooking it up to a port on the bag. As soon as he produced an attachment that dipped into the water, Nick started screaming.

"Heellllpppp! Heeellllpppppp! Please help me!"

Up until this second, Emily had been quietly crying. Now, she was wailing loudly while trying to put as much distance as possible between herself and her doomed adopted father.

Manny glanced at Gabby to gauge her reaction to what was going on. She was watching her family the way a middle-aged woman might watch a boring movie: With no emotion at all.

Manny sucked in a breath as he realized something for the first time. With her dark skin and long dark hair, she looked just like a miniature version of Alisha. He wondered how anyone could bear to hurt this little princess without feeling guilty. After tonight, if anyone hurt her, they would pay with their life.

With that thought in his mind, he slipped the bag over Nick's head and pulled the cord to inflate the tube. It created an airtight seal using the innertube without choking the person wearing it.

Nick was shaking his head and trying to drag the bag off by rutting on the floor like a pig. Manny didn't want him to just suffocate, so he flipped the switch to turn on the pump. As soon as the water touched Nick's face, he went apeshit trying to remove the bag.

It took about 30 seconds for the bag to fill up and about 30 seconds after that, Mr. Black started to drown. His body was bucking so hard that he was jerking Emily around like a rag doll. It was a horrible, painful, ugly way to die and Manny felt the man had earned every second of it.

Manny walked over to Gabby and sat beside her on the chair. His heart broke a little more as she gave him a way too mature smile and leaned into his side.

Nick's ending came with a series of whole-body jerks and then a stillness that only the dead could achieve.

Manny patted Gabby on her leg and then got up and reversed the pump to suck all the water back into the jug. He then removed the bag and packed everything back into his backpack. He carried the water jug back to the kitchen and poured the water in the sink.

During all this, Emily continued to cry and beg for her life. "Please don't kill me. I'm sorry for whatever I did. Gabby, please don't let him kill me. I am all the family you have left. Don't you love me? I saved you before. When you were a baby. Please Gabby, save me." On and on until Manny told her to shut the fuck up.

He walked over and snatched the blindfold off of the now silent young lady. Then he went and sat back down next to Gabby. "Emily, I can only promise you this. If you have to die here tonight, I will not torture you. I will make it fast and painless."

He paused and looked over at Gabby. "I really hate to put you in this position Gabby, but her life is in your hands. I will ask Emily some questions and if you are satisfied with her answers, then she will live. If you don't feel like she is being truthful, or you just don't like her answers, then she will die. Do you understand?" Gabby nodded and they both turned to look at Emily, still strapped to the dead man on the floor.

"Did you know what was happening to Gabby?" Manny asked Emily.

"Yes, but I couldn't do anything about it. It was happening to me too."

"Why didn't you go to the police or contact someone to help the both of you?"

Emily took a deep breath and said, "Because they threatened to separate us. They said no one would believe me, and they would send me somewhere else and keep Gabby. I made myself available so that Greg would focus on me as long as possible."

Manny said, "But you ended up leaving her here by herself anyway. Can you explain to me why you would do that? And this is the part where you want to be truthful and precise in your explanation."

Manny heard a sniffle from beside him and he looked over to find Gabby crying softly. She had been so strong during his other encounter with her that he sometimes forgot she was still a little girl. He put his arm around her and pulled her closer to him.

Emily watched them for a minute before answering. "I didn't have a choice in the matter. Right before I left for college, both of my fathers sat me down and told me that they would kill Gabby if I told anybody anything. They convinced me that they would label me as a liar and in the confusion, Gabby would go missing and no one would ever find her. They both said that they knew guys that used to be locked up that would love to have a pretty little girl like her. We were both in fucked up spots, but I was just trying to make it so she survived. And I told her that, as soon as I could afford my own place, I would come for her. That's why I've been working even though I have a scholarship."

"But he hurt me Em! He hurt me over and over again. And you never came to help me," cried Gabby. "Even when

I screamed for you to come and you were right here, you would ignore me. I thought you loved me." She dissolved into a soul tearing cry and Manny had had enough. He was not going to let anymore tears of pain and anguish come out of this child.

"It's okay Sweetie, I got you," said Manny, holding the child and pulling out his gun. "I know you're hurting Gabby, but you have to tell me what to do with your sister. I can take her with us and both of you can be safe. It's up to you."

"Please Gabby. I'm so sorry...." Emily started but was quickly silenced by a deadly look from the killer.

"You've had your say, now shut up and let her decide." Gabby mumbled something from where Manny had tucked her under his arm. "What did you say Sweetie?"

"I said I don't have a sister. I don't need a sister. And I don't want a sister," declared Gabby while staring up at Manny. There was no need to ask her if she was sure. He could see the determination in her red rimmed brown eyes. Manny squeezed her hand and then stood up.

"No Gabby! How could you say that? I've loved you with all my heart all your life. Please Gabby," begged Emily.

Manny was standing over her with his silenced gun and he looked back at Gabby to see if she was sure. She left little doubt as to how she was feeling as she gave a small nod for him to proceed. In the middle of Emily's constant pleas, Manny shot her once in the right temple and quickly put the gun away.

He decided to leave Nick and Emily exactly as they were and he walked back over and sat next to Gabby with a sigh.

"So, Gabby," Manny started as he looked at the little girl. "What do you want to do now?"

She looked at him with a calm expression on her small, pretty face. "Are you going to kill me now too?" she asked as if she was just curious.

"Hell no, Gabby. I will never hurt you. In fact, little Princess, you can think of me as your new guardian angel. I will protect you against the devil himself if he tries to hurt you." He didn't have any problems with his declarations because he meant every word.

"I don't have anything to give you, like money or anything," the child stated. "You can just leave me here and I'll tell the cops that I never saw your face like I did last time."

"Is that what you want me to do?" asked Manny. "You want me to leave you here?" The little girl thought on it and shook her head no. "Tell me what you want to do Princess."

She lowered her head and said softly, "I want to go with you." She hurried on like she was afraid to hear his response. "I promise I'll be good. I always brush my teeth before bed. I keep my room clean. I promise to do whatever you tell me to do." She looked so earnest, if he hadn't made up his mind before he had even entered the house, the look on her face now would have sealed the deal.

"Is there anything that you want to take with us?" he asked her.

She rose up and jumped into his lap saying, "Thank you, thank you, thank you," over and over again, while crying her eyes out.

He held her, thinking about going after the adoption agency that placed her in this toxic home in the first place. What a hell her life had to have been for her to be so happy to be placed in the care of a mass murderer. Yeah, he definitely would be paying a visit to that agency.

Eventually she stopped crying and she fell asleep in his arms like she had been waiting to feel safe enough to sleep for years. He stood up and walked over to the couch to lay her down. He then walked over to her bedroom and began going through her meager belongings.

He was going to buy her new everything, but he wanted to see if she had any personal things that she might want to keep. They could track her phone so he would have to leave that behind also. He did insert a little device that copied all of her files so he could upload them onto the new phone. He had just about finished going through her things when he came across a well-worn photo.

It was of a couple in their 30's holding a newborn baby with another girl about 10 years old, cheesing, sitting on a couch. These had to be Gabby's parents because the 10-year-old girl was a young Emily and both of the young girls were the spitting image of their mother. Manny put the picture in his pocket and exited the room.

Watching Gabby in her peaceful sleep, he pulled out his phone and sent a text for Alisha to meet him at a fast-food place about a mile from their home. He knew that she had probably been busy setting the scene for tonight's celebration, so he also apologized but promised her that it was very important. He added that it might take him a few hours to get there, so she could take her time. She responded with an okay and an I love you. He returned the sentiment and put the phone away.

After leaving Walt, Manny had switched cars because he knew then what he was going to do. He was now driving an Audi A8 four door sedan that he had taken from a CIA warehouse outside of Raleigh. He made sure Gabby was resting peacefully, then took off from the house at a run to get the car. He had hidden the car in the same turn off he had used to kidnap Det. Ann Grace.

He drove the car back to the house and rushed inside to grab the sleeping child. He carried her out and deposited her along the backseat and then turned to take a last look at the house.

Emily had taken a semester off from school, so it would be a while before anyone missed her. Nick, on the other hand, was supposed to be at work in a couple days. If he burned the place down, it would obliterate any evidence of what went down, but the police would come in minutes. Weighing his options for a bit, he decided to leave them to rot. In two days, he would have a new identity for Gabby anyway. The fact that she looks so much like Alisha would help her blend in while they were out and about. Decision made, he jumped into the driver's seat and started the trek back to his home area.

When he arrived at the restaurant, he circled the lot twice but he didn't see any familiar cars. Thinking they would eat before Alisha arrived, he parked and turned to wake up the sleeping Gabby. He tapped her and called her name softly. She became instantly awake, sat up, and just looked at him with wide eyes.

She didn't complain about being tired. Didn't ask any questions. Just sat there looking at him like she was awaiting orders. He knew some people who would kill to get him to behave in the same manner.

"Are you hungry Princess?" When she nodded, he said, "Well, come on and you can order whatever you want." They both climbed out and entered the restaurant with her hand planted firmly in his.

After they got their food, Manny led her to a booth in the middle of the eating area. He wanted as many bodies between them and the windows as possible.

As they ate, Manny watched the little girl. She ate with the manners of a nun. Chewed with her mouth closed. Didn't make a mess. She even said a quick prayer before she started. He wondered how she could still believe in a God to pray to after all she had been through. Then again, maybe that was what kept her moving forward. He did notice that she was squirming around in her seat as she ate.

"Shit," said Manny. "Gabby, do you need to use the bathroom?" It had been hours since he had used the sleeper agent on her while she listened to music in her room.

"Yes," was her soft answer.

"Sweetie, look at me," demanded Manny. When she looked up, he said, "You are safe now, okay? No one will hurt you again. I don't know much about kids so you have to work with me. When you are hungry, let me know or just eat something if we are home. If you have to use the bathroom, and we're out somewhere, let me know and then go. Okay Sweetheart?" She nodded yes and then jumped up and raced to the bathroom.

As he watched her run off, his eyes tracked to Alisha standing just inside the door watching the child run by. She was in a pair of black spandex leggings and a blue sports bra and had her hair pulled back in a ponytail. Manny laughed to himself because she was wearing her fight clothes. Leave it to her to think that, if he called her and said it was important, she might have to whip a bitch ass. All the laughter faded when she turned to face him.

His heart did that flip flop thing and he couldn't stop staring at her beautiful face as she walked towards him. She sat in the chair across from him that Gabby had not been using, and used one of his methods as she just sat looking at him in silence.

"Alisha, I can't explain everything right now because there isn't enough time. Her name is Gabby Black. She is ten years old. She witnessed me killing her dad a while back, and then her other dad and sister tonight. She is under my protection now and I have to look after her. Is that going to be a problem?" Manny asked her.

Alisha sat for a while longer and said, "Our. We."

"What?" said Manny in confusion.

"You said. 'she is under my protection now and I have to look after her.' No Manny. She is under our protection now and we have to look after her." She didn't even know the child and she was looking like a mama bear ready to protect her cub.

Manny stood up and pulled her out of her chair, hugging her. "I love you Alisha and whatever you need or want in order to help this girl, let me know."

"I love you too babe," she said holding him tightly.

He released her and, out of the corner of his eye, he saw Gabby standing off to the side. "Gabby, please come here. I have someone I'd like you to meet."

She walked over and stood in front of Alisha, looking up at her face. Alisha said, "Hi Gabby. My name is Alisha. I'm Manny's girlfriend." She extended her hand to the girl and Gabby shook it.

"Shit," said Manny. "Forgot to tell you Gabby. I'm Manny." He noticed the look on Alisha's face and said, "Had a lot of other stuff on my mind. Let's sit down and finish our food. Alisha, you want something?" She said no and they sat down and made small talk until Gabby was done with her meal.

They discarded their trash when they were done and made their way to the parking lot. Manny looked around in puzzlement and then glanced at Alisha. She said, "I wanted to ride with you so I took an Uber." Many nodded and led the way over to his car.

They loaded in and Manny drove them home to his Charlotte compound. When they got there, Alisha took over duties to get Gabby settled into one of the rooms. She made sure Gabby was good and then met Manny in their bedroom.

Alisha sat down and said, "Tell me." Manny filled her in on the life Gabby had lived over the past ten years. After he finished, she said, "That poor baby. Well, she doesn't have to worry about anything else happening to her."

"I'm going after the agency tomorrow. Her social worker will also die." He paused and laid down next to her on the bed. "I want you to take her shopping in the morning. Get her anything she wants. Take her where ever she wants to go. We'll get a decorator in here to fix up whichever room she wants, however she wants it. I never want her to be unhappy, but don't spoil her too much."

"You better tell yourself that!" exclaimed Alisha. "You love her already and you feel guilty. Just remember, kids need discipline too."

"Is she asleep?" Manny asked while getting up, stripping his clothes off, and heading for the bathroom. She nodded and looked him up and down when he stood before her totally naked. "Well, all that shit you was talking about me being scared, it's time for you to back that up. And I mean that in every way possible." He walked into the bathroom and turned the shower on with a voice command.

He had seen her naked hundreds of times, but never when he was about to make love to her. She walked ahead of him, slowly stripping out of her fight clothes, until she was naked with the water cascading down on her beautiful body. The shower is where they ended up spending the next two hours.

When they were finally satisfied, they dried each other off and made slow love one more time in the King-sized bed. Manny would have loved to fall asleep with a satisfied smile on his face. Instead, the killer was plotting the worst possible revenge for the people who hurt Gabby. He grabbed his phone so he could do some research before he planned the upcoming day.

CHAPTER 7

Walt woke up with the mother of all headaches. Yesterday had been a day of extremes. Completing task two by breaking Bruce Battle out of prison, then watching him die at the hands of the killer. Talking to and seeing Denise and Ann whole and healthy, then being left with the dead body of Bruce to deal with.

The last thing being the easiest of them to handle. Walt had simply wiped the computer down that the killer had left behind, walked around the warehouse to make sure he didn't leave anything behind himself, and then left.

He'd driven back to Central Prison and rejoined the efforts to find how Bruce had gotten out, and where he was hiding at now. Since it was technically a local matter until the escapee was spotted outside of Raleigh, Walt just stayed back and listened, taking notes to see if they would discover anything that would point to him.

From what Walt had been told, every prison in the state was on lockdown and all available officers were out searching for Bruce. The local P.D.'s and Sheriff offices had road blocks set up all over the state. Since the last confirmed check of Mr. Battle had been hours before his room was discovered empty, law enforcement had no idea how far he had gone.

Walt knew that his early morning visit would come out, so when he saw the Warden and the lead detective talking, he went over and volunteered the information.

77

Walt had expected some form of suspicion or interrogation. All he got was a mildly interested question by the detective if he had seen anything out of the ordinary. When Walt said no and explained where he was while inside the prison and why, the detective shrugged and walked off, looking for better information elsewhere.

Warden Thomas, who Walt had met before in his efforts to catch the killer said, "I knew something like this was going to happen. That fucking killer just cost me my job!"

"Why would you say that?" asked Walt.

"The Commissioner of Prisons tells every Warden the day they're hired that if you lose an inmate, and it makes the news, go ahead and start looking for another job." With that statement, Warden Thomas walked off shaking his head and mumbling to himself.

For the rest of the day, they had fielded tip after tip and Walt had felt safe because none of them were close to where Bruce actually lay dead at this moment. A lady did call in a tip from the first neighborhood Walt had taken him to, but of course it didn't pan out.

Now, Walt was sitting in his kitchen after finishing breakfast, when his cell phone rang. He glanced at the display and saw it was a call from his boss at the SBI, Captain William Graham.

Will was an ex-jock, ex-frat boy, who had a superiority complex like no other. He was the same age as Walt, had all-American good looks, and always wore the proper clothes for the occasion. They had joined the SBI the same year, but Will possessed a political suave that took him higher, faster. His boss was loyal and honest and a huge pain in Walt's ass.

Walt answered with, "Hello Boss. What can I do for you?"

"Get your ass in gear. We got a solid tip and a witness that puts Bruce Battle in the warehouse district with two other guys," said Will.

And just like that, Walt's stomach fell to his knees. "A witness? How reliable is this witness?" he asked, jumping up and grabbing his gear.

"It's a homeless drunk, but the witness claims a man fitting the killer's description arrived first in a black muscle car. Then, sometime later, another black luxury car pulled up and a middle age black guy got out the driver's seat. Then a man fitting Bruce Battle's description hopped out of the trunk. Shortly after the second group went inside, a gunshot was heard. The witness says the two men left separately, but Bruce never came back out."

Cpt. Graham said something to someone else then came back. "I'm sending you the address. We're meeting at a gas station down the street from the target address. You better hurry because we're hitting it within the hour."

"Hold on Will! Will?" But he was already gone. Walt didn't know if he should go at all. If this witness identified him, it might be too many coincidences for some to ignore. He couldn't believe what he was thinking, but he needed to get to this witness. More than just his freedom was at stake.

First thing first, he couldn't go to the scene in his black BMW. The witness had seen it and it might trigger a memory that Walt didn't need him to have. He went out and pulled the cover off of his 1970 Plymouth Barracuda. It was gray with black trim, so it wouldn't be something the witness would have forgotten.

Walt transferred all his gear from the BMW, jumped into the Barracuda, and raced to meet up with the takedown team.

When he arrived at the gas station, what he saw amazed him. There were enough local and state cops to take on some small countries. Everyone was outfitted in full riot gear and the SBI SWAT team had come out to lead the takedown. The local SWAT team had been killed in the same failed trap for the killer that got Denise kidnapped. A new one was being trained, but was not yet ready for something of this magnitude.

Walt spotted Cpt. Graham by one of the SWAT vehicles, so he drove over close to him and parked.

They shook hands after Walt got out and Will said, "After this, we have to drive down to the Charlotte area to check something out."

Walt wanted to ask about the witness, but with the plan he had for him, he didn't want to be the one to bring it up. "If this guy is in the warehouse, we'll be here all day. What's so important down there that we have to leave?"

"How about 50 or so dead gang bangers?" asked Will. "Unless we have a rogue military unit going around killing people, I think our killer has been busy."

"I don't understand," said Walt. "Charlotte's hours from here. If the killer was up here doing this, how did he kill 50 people way down there?"

"That's the thing," replied Will. "Whoever killed the bangers started a fire to destroy the evidence. The local P.D.

went in and found 12 shell casings in one of the houses, but that house contained only one body. The other houses with bodies in them didn't have any casings found and none of the bodies have bullet holes in them. In fact, except for the lone body, it looks as if all the other ones died of natural causes." Will paused and glanced at Walt with a smile. "Sounds like our guy, doesn't it?"

Walt said, "I don't know man. Sounds like another gang moving in on their territory."

"I would have thought the same thing," said Will. "But it seems most of these guys have been in prison. So, I did a little digging and Manuel Adams had a run in with the gang on the inside. He filed a report on them a few months before most of them died one by one. The local leader, the lone body, was the only one who survived the previous encounter. That leader, Mickey Brown, was beaten to a pulp then had his neck broken. Some of the others were Special Forces and the security on the compound was military based. No rival gang could have done this.

"The problem is," Will continued. "The killer couldn't have broken Bruce Battle out because we narrowed that time down to between 6:00 am to 8:00 am. Our killer didn't start the fire until about 9:30 am. Taking into account the time needed to have killed the soldiers, it's not possible for him to have done both, unless he had a time machine. So, if this witness is right, then that third man has to be the one helping the killer."

Walt jumped on the opportunity despite his mouth going dry from the recent revelations. "Where is this witness anyway?"

"Right over there sleeping in the back of the unmarked," answered Will, pointing to a car on the side of the gas station.

The SWAT commander came up and started talking to Cpt. Graham so, as nonchalant as possible, Walt made his way to the cop car to take a look inside. Once again, he got the shock of his life.

Will had said it was a homeless drunk, so Walt's mind immediately drew a picture of an old dirty man, stumbling while chugging booze. In reality, it was a fairly clean old woman about 70 years old. It was a black woman who really just looked down on her luck, not someone who has been on the streets long. Walt admitted to himself, he could have killed the old, dirty man. He wasn't so sure he could do the same to the kindly looking woman. He quickly turned away and rejoined his boss before the woman could spot him.

Walt was about to ask Will for a word when someone yelled, "Mount up. Let's roll," and everyone took off for their vehicles.

It was a fast moving, well-coordinated operation and, in less than two minutes, the identified warehouse was surrounded. It had already been determined that, because of all the windows, as soon as the warehouse was boxed on all sides, the SWAT team would breach.

Walt, Will, and some of the local brasses were actually in a parking lot across from the target when Walt's cell phone rang. It was an unknown number, but he had a feeling he knew exactly who it would be.

He stepped off a bit and answered the call as he watched the teams converging on the warehouse. "Hello," said Walt.

"I'm so glad your dumbass didn't decide to participate. Oh, and you won't be going to Kannapolis, you'll be kind of busy with the clean-up," the killer proclaimed before hanging up on him.

It took Walt a second, but then it hit him what was about to happen. He started screaming, waving his hands, and running, hoping to stop the advance. "Don't go in! Stop! Stop!" Then the whole warehouse disintegrated and knocked Walt flat on his ass.

He lost consciousness for a few seconds and then came to with debris falling all around him. He rolled around in pain, trying to orient himself before he was able to stand up. He checked his body and discovered only minor cuts and bruises, although he was pretty sure he had a concussion.

When he had his bearings, he focused his eyes on the warehouse. It was Ashley Kirt's house all over again. Manny seemed to have no scruples about killing cops and he didn't value human life at all. For someone who didn't want others to see him as a monster, he had a funny way of reaching that goal.

There were a lot of bodies lying around on the ground, but not as many as Walt would have guessed. He could only see two sides of the rubble that used to be the warehouse, but only five cops looked to be dead. There were a ton of injured, but most of them were still moving around, if only slightly.

Walt glanced back to where Will was still standing with the brass and noticed that they were untouched by the blast. He guessed that they had avoided damage by ducking down behind the cars.

It took Walt a couple minute to get his hearing back, but when it returned, he could hear his phone ringing again. Now, the killer's number came up on the display.

"What the fuck was that man? You're going to bring the whole world down on your ass you keep doing dumb shit like this!" Walt had to force himself not to yell or everyone would know he was conversing with the killer.

"First off, fuck the world. There are only a few people in it that I give a damn about. So, let the world come and you'll see the world set on fire. Anyway, I did this for both of us. Soon as the brass head in for their shine time, the witness who can ID you will be left alone. I don't care, but I know you do. You can thank me later." Then Manny disconnected.

Walt didn't think all of this was needed for a diversion, but now that it had been pointed out, it was the perfect solution. Not to mention the explosion killed any lingering evidence in the warehouse. He did hope it was enough of Bruce left to identify. That way he wouldn't have to keep faking like he was looking for him.

On cue, all the brass took off running to help the injured officers. When the media showed up, every inch of the place would be under a microscope. With that in mind, Det. Rogers eased his way back to where the witness had been left alone in the back of the cop car.

Walt knew the woman couldn't still be sleep after the explosion, so he prepared himself to have to look her in the face as he killed her. He went to his trunk and got the silent pistol and made his way to the unmarked.

He had been harboring a small hope that killing her might not even be necessary, but the look on her face as he came level with the car erased all doubt. Her eyes got big in fear and she scrambled around trying to lock the doors that couldn't be locked from the inside.

No one else was around, but Walt knew that could change at any time. He fished out the pistol and aimed it at the old lady through the glass. She had stopped trying to get away and was staring at Walt with tears streaming down her wrinkled face. Walt mouthed the word sorry and then shot the woman in the head.

He looked around and saw that he was still alone. So, he opened the door and shot her once more in the head and twice in the chest. Walt felt bad, but knew he would do it again if in the same situation. Truth was, he knew he would have to kill some more before this was all over. This had been a hard one, but Walt admitted the killer was getting exactly what he wanted. He was becoming more jaded with each dead body.

Walt closed everything up, wiped the gun down, and dropped it right outside the door. He walked back to his car and sprayed his hands down with bleach to get rid of the gunshot residue. When he was confident he was safe, he eased his way into the fray of helping officers mend their wounds.

Within five minutes, media was having to be held back and a perimeter set up because they kept getting into the crime scene. After another 20 minutes, one of the reporters found the dead body of the witness in the back seat of the cop car.

They didn't know who the woman was at first. Once the media found out that she was the witness who had pointed them to the warehouse, they begin questioning why she had been left unattended. One reporter said that the old woman had been served up to her killer on a dish with the way she had been trapped in the car.

The cops were catching it from all directions today and when Will finally caught up with Walt, it got worse.

"Can I speak to you for a minute?" Will asked him.

"Sure," said Walt as Will led him away from everyone else.

When they were alone, Will said, "Two things. First, you got a call before the explosion. Tell me about it."

"The killer called my phone from a blocked number and said he had a surprise for all the dumbass cops who go in the warehouse. Knowing what he did at Ashley Kirt's neighbor's house, I guessed that it was some kind of bomb or something. They were already breaching, so there was really no time to stop them." Normally Walt would talk shit to his boss, but now was a time for him to be serious.

"Why would he call you, and how did he know to call right then?" asked Will.

"The bastard has had a hard on for me since I started going after him. He was amused as he told me about the surprise, so I can guess that he thought it would be funny. You and I both know that he loves to watch with his drones and cameras. He probably has cameras all around here and he called right then because he knew it would be too late." Walt didn't know for a fact that Manny had cameras, but if he did, he now had another video of him killing someone.

The killer could send Walt to Death Row whenever he felt like it.

Will glanced about and then lowered his voice. "Is there anyone in the government that we can ask for help? This is their guy and, just being honest here, we're not equipped to handle him. No offense, but you're supposed to be the best and he seems amused by that fact. Can you talk to that Agent Steve?"

The Agent Steve that Will was referring to was the guy who recruited the killer into the CIA when he was only 16. The agent was a 30-year CIA veteran who had come to Walt's house to give him the low down on Manny. He basically told Walt that the government wouldn't get involved.

Walt said, "Agent Steve wouldn't help even if I could get in contact with him. I hate to say it but we are on our own and we just have to hope and pray that he messes up and we get lucky." Walt paused and then said, "What was the second thing you wanted to talk about?"

"More bad news on the killer's front," said Will shaking his head.

Walt didn't know of anything else so he didn't have to fake his confusion. "If you're talking about the stuff near Charlotte, I think that's going to have to wait."

"No, it's something else. You remember Greg Black? The officer that was raping inmates and became a target of the PGK?" Walt nodded thinking it was at this officer's house that Ann was taken.

87

Will continued. "His husband Nicolas Black and his oldest adopted daughter was found this morning murdered in their home."

Walt was dumbfounded. This guy was killing all over the state like it was legal. "How do they know it was him?" asked Walt.

"Nick and his daughter Emily were chained together in the living room. Nick was drowned with what the M.E. thinks was a water bag, and he'd been beaten too. Emily was shot one time in the head like a mercy killing."

"OK," said Walt. "It was gruesome, but that doesn't mean the killer did it."

"Yeah, well a man fitting his description also went to the adoption agency that handled the placement of the girls and killed some people there in a gruesome way. Too much of a coincidence for it not to have been him at both scenes."

"Maybe," said Walt. "Wait, there was a young girl too. What happened to her?"

"Oh, you mean Gabriella Black, or Gabby for short? Yeah, she's missing. We have amber alerts going out to the whole southeast part of the country. But we both know she could be right here and we wouldn't know it." Will paused and looked up in thought. "Once again the killer was somewhere else when a crime we put on him happened. He couldn't have killed the witness. He's getting help. Maybe I'll reach out and see if I can get some help for our side." With that cryptic comment, Cpt. Will Graham nodded and walked off.

"Why in the fuck did you take that little girl Manny?" Walt asked out loud. Walt could put his morals to the side for a lot of things, but if Manny hurt that poor innocent child, Walt was going to bury his ass.

CHAPTER 8

Manny woke up that morning to a wonderful sensation. Alisha had started without him, but he made sure she finished a few times before he found his own release.

While they went about their daily morning routines, they talked about their plans for the day. Manny said, "Use the Black Card today and make sure both of my ladies come home happy." He was brushing his teeth while Alisha showered.

"Oh shit," said Alisha. "I forgot to tell you, earlier I got up to check on Gabby and the T.V. was on in her room. She was asleep, but there was an Amber Alert issued for her. So, from what they said," she continued to explain while getting out of the shower, "The prison called to ask her dad to come in and help with the search for Bruce Battle. When they couldn't reach him, they asked the police to go do a welfare check. They found Nick and his daughter, Emily, dead in the house with no sign of Gabby. It might be a good idea to lay low for a while," suggested Alisha.

"Fuck that," said Manny. "That girl is going to live a life of luxury from now on. No one but us will dictate what she can and can't do."

"But what happens if someone recognizes her and they take her away and lock me up?" asked Alisha. By now, they were both dressed for the day and were standing in the bedroom.

Manny turned to her and said, "Wherever they take you, I would kill everyone and get you back. Wherever they take Gabby, I would kill everyone and get her back. Then we would live happily ever after here or anywhere else you wanted to go."

Smiling, Alisha said, "Babe, you're not invincible. People do get lucky. With the way you live, you could die any day. Then where would your two ladies be?"

Manny hugged her close because he could sense she needed it. He said, "My influence goes beyond the grave. Trust me on this, if I die today, everyone in my care will be taken care of. You were right. I love that little girl already, and she will be well taken care of until the day she dies. That goes for you too." He kissed her softly but deeply and said, "Let's go check on our little girl."

Alisha wiped away the tears that threatened to escape as they walked hand in hand down the hall to the room Gabby had decided would be hers. Alisha knocked and they heard a soft, "Come in."

Gabby was sitting on the bed watching cartoons like a normal, happy 10-year-old. She smiled when she saw them and said, "I took a shower, but I didn't have any clothes to change into. Sorry I didn't ask to turn the T.V. on."

Manny said, "That is your T.V. Turn it on and off whenever you feel like it."

Alisha jumped in. "Unless it's after bedtime. Then it has to go off," she said eyeing Manny.

"Yeah, Alisha's right. Listen," Manny said a little uneasily. "Obviously we are not your real parents. You can call us Manny and Alisha. But when we are out in public, I'll need you to refer to us as Mom and Dad."

In a soft, shy voice, Gabby asked, "Is it okay if I call you Mom and Dad all the time?"

Alisha said, "Of course it is sweetheart." In response, Gabby beamed that beautiful smile at both of them.

"Right now," Manny continued while trying to hide his emotions. "There are a lot of people looking for you." When a worried look crossed her face, Manny hurried to say, "But as long as you want to stay with us, I will do everything in my power to keep you."

Gabby jumped off the bed and launched herself into Manny's arms. "Thank you so much. I know you will keep me safe, Dad." She had silent tears running down her face as she clung to his neck with all of her strength.

Manny, close to crying himself, said, "I'm sorry sweetheart for not coming sooner. But from now on, you can count on both of us to be there for you."

Laughing, he pried her arms from around his neck and set her on her feet. "Alisha is going to take you shopping today. I need you to listen to her at all times so both of you can be safe. Can you do that for me?" When she smiled and nodded, he said, "Good girl."

He turned and kissed Alisha on her soft, pink lips, and said, "I have a few things I need to take care of. You girls have fun. Call me when you're on your way home."

Manny walked down to the garage and jumped into the Audi RS7, leaving the Audi A8 for Alisha to drive. It was inconspicuous and it offered a lot more room for their purchases. Manny loved fast, sleek, cars, but he would have to pick up a few family-friendly cars now that he had Gabby and Alisha to think about.

He drove about 80 miles north of Charlotte to Greensboro, North Carolina. There were a couple of stops he needed to make before officially starting his day. He pulled into a parking lot and shut the engine off before looking up at the sign.

The Happy Family Adoption Agency. The only thing about it that made Manny happy was that it housed both Gabby's adoption agent and her social worker. So, he could kill two birds with one stop.

He activated the black box to kill any cameras or alarm systems, and walked to the front door of the office. He had his bag strapped to his back under a light coat, and he had his silent gun in a shoulder holster.

Manny would need some alone time with the two people he had come to see, so he was going to shut down the agency for the day. The receptionist was an understated, attractive, white woman who smiled as soon as she saw him. "And how can The Happy Family Adoption Agency help you today, Sir?" she asked him.

He didn't even waste his time with an answer. Just pulled his gun and shot her right between the eyes. She looked confused for a second, then slumped over on her desk, dead.

He walked around and fished the keys from her pocket and came back around to lock the door. In a folder next to the door was an assortment of cards to hang up from a hook on the door. He found one that said, 'Closed for the day' and hung it up before turning back to the interior. He then pulled out a few small, unmarked aerosol cans from his bag.

There would be a lot of noise and he didn't see the need to kill everyone. He went from door to door placing the opened cans at the bottom crack to release the spray into the rooms. Within minutes, he heard the sound of bodies hitting the floor.

He gave it enough time to put everyone to sleep and then he went room to room restraining the people that he would allow to live. The two that would die, he dragged into a conference room in the back. He stripped them both down to nothing and tied them both spread eagle on the huge table.

Mr. Chad Edelman, the adoption agent, was a slightly overweight, middle aged, black man. He was a proud homosexual, as all his social media proclaimed, and he was responsible for Gabby and Emily being placed with the Blacks. He would learn the error of his ways, but wouldn't be around to prove he'd learned his lesson.

Ms. Allison McDonald was what some would call a MILF. She was in her late 40's, but with her slim, compact, curvaceous body, she would give most college girls a run for their money. She was of mixed heritage, and she had been blessed with the best of both worlds. She had the long, flowing, blond hair and blue eyes of her European ancestors, and the curves and thickness of her African ancestors. She bore a passing resemblance to Megan Markle, but her eyes, an airy sky blue, made he prettier. This was the social worker who had the job of checking on Emily and Gabby, but hardly ever got around to doing her job.

Both of them were gagged, but not blindfolded. He would work on Allison first so he could build up the terror in the ex-football player turned adoption agent. He hit both of them with shots of adrenaline to wake them up. The others would be out for a couple more hours.

Once they were both squirming and mumbling, he stepped into view. As expected, Allison was more worried about her nudity and was panicking because she thought of rape first.

"Hey guys," said the killer. "To put your minds at ease, I am not a rapist. I have a beautiful woman out shopping with our new little girl and I wouldn't cheat on her to save my life. Not to mention, she's an ex-gang Queen and would most likely try to kill me. The other thing is, I just don't like the two of you. Matter of fact, I hate the two of you. Over the next hour or two, I'll be explaining why."

As he'd been talking, he unpacked a few devices from his bag. Those tools were now sitting in the middle of the table where both of their heads could turn and see them. "Now, I want you both to listen carefully. I'm going to hurt you bad. But you might escape with your lives if you do what I tell you to. I'm going to remove the gags. If you try to holler for help, that person will die at the end of this. If you take your pain like a grown up, then you will learn your lesson and I'll leave you be. Do you both understand?" They both nodded. "Oh, one more thing. Don't talk unless I ask you a question. If you do, I will hurt you more." With that, he removed the gags and both prisoners remained silent.

"Allison, we will start with you." He picked up the heavy-duty stapler and pulled some of the skin from her torso.

Without another word, he stapled a row of ten down her side, leaving a ten-inch stretch of skin about two inches deep hanging off her side. She screamed from the pain and ended up throwing up all over herself. The killer just stood watching until she calmed down.

When she was quiet again, he walked around the table to her other side and said, "Now, I will ask you some questions. Depending on what you say, it will determine how much more pain you feel. First, do you know who Emily and Gabriella Black are?"

"Yes," she said in a pain filled whisper.

"Tell me who they are," demanded the killer.

"They are the biological sisters from High Point that were placed with the couple Nicolas and Gregory Black."

"And you were aware that these girls were being molested and abused on a daily basis?" asked the killer.

"Absolutely not," she said in outrage. "If I had known such a thing was going on, I would have removed them and called the cops."

Manny stared deeply into her eyes. "I believe you," he said causing some relief to fill Allison's eyes. "Can you explain to me how you didn't know?"

"Well, they never…. I never…. I asked," she stammered a couple of times trying to explain.

"The fact is you falsified reports saying that you went out there to check on them and you never did. In fact, all you did was call one of the Dads and asked them how everything was going. Then you wrote reports on whatever they said." He paused and waited for her to deny it. "Is that what you did?" he finally asked.

"Yes. And I'm so sorry. I just have such a huge work load. Wait! No! Let me explain!" Then nothing but screams as the killer repeated the staple attack on her left side.

She blubbered for a while until he threatened to kill her if she didn't shut up. He then continued his questions. "Are you aware that not too long ago, Greg was murdered?"

"Yes," she whispered again.

"And yet you still didn't go and check on Gabby and Emily. How could you be so indifferent to those young girls?" She remained silent which was probably the best thing she could do. "Well, let me fill you in on something. I'm the one who killed him." He let that soak in for a second.

She said, "But the officers said the Prison Guard Killer…."

"Exactly. That's exactly who killed him," he said picking up a two-pound sledge hammer. "And everyone who contributed to those girls' pain is going to pay for it."

He brought the sledge hammer down on her shin and she yelped and passed out. He shot her with the adrenaline and, as soon as she came to, he smashed her other shin and she passed out again. This time he left her alone.

He glanced over to the wide eyes of Chad and said, "How has your day been so far Sir?" The killer was smiling as he put the hammer down and picked up the heavy-duty taser.

"Please," said Chad. "I vetted those men and they were clean. They were both employed, legally married, and neither had a criminal background. Once I place them, it's all up to the social worker to maintain contact. I'm out of it."

"Okay, so I'll just ask you one question. I already know the answer, but I want to hear what lie you'll come up with to excuse what you did."

The killer was silent for ten seconds, then said, "You met with Greg Black's supervisor at Central Prison four weeks before you placed those girls. You asked him if Greg had been investigated or come under suspicion for anything of note. Now, we both know what that person told you. What made you approve the adoption anyway?"

Chad laid there looking up at the killer for a full minute before the killer shrugged and lit his ass up. He pressed the taser into his armpit on full blast and didn't stop until that bacon smell filled the air around him. When he turned it off, all the hair had burned off the right side of the man's torso. Chad twitched in pain, but couldn't control his movements yet.

"Answer my question or I move on to the torch," demanded the killer.

Chad mumbled for a while until he could form words again. "They had no proof. I asked to talk to some of the inmates, they said no. I asked to see video, they said, due to security policies, I couldn't view them. I asked the Warden what he thought and he said he felt the inmates were making it up because they didn't want a gay man working at the prison. With me being gay and facing some of the same reactions from people, I sympathized with him and I approved the adoption. I'm sorry those girls were hurt, but I did my job and I don't think I should suffer for it."

"You're right Chad. You shouldn't." The killer shot him once in the head because he had to die but he didn't have to suffer for making an honest mistake.

Allison was coming to and he stood where she could see him holding the gun. She focused on him and said, "I took it like a woman. I never called for help. You said I could live if I took it."

"So what," said the killer. "I lied." He shot her in the throat, taking care to miss the major arteries. He wanted her to die a slow death, suffocating and drowning in her own blood at the same time.

He left everything like it was, grabbed his bag, and walked out. He unlocked the front door, tossed the keys back inside on the floor, and was preparing to leave when he got the alert of activity at the warehouse.

He pulled up the video after stepping back inside the agency and saw all the police converging on the building. He armed the charges using his phone and then called up Walt's position on his GPS. He saw that Walt was across the street, so he made his taunting call, then blew up the warehouse.

He watched for a few seconds, then walked outside. He nodded to an old white lady, hopped into his car, and drove off. He looked at his dash and saw that he still had time for one more stop before it was time to go meet Walt. It was in the same direction, so he might as well get it done. Manny placed one more phone call to Walt, then focused on his own mission.

Manny called the Dunn Police Department dispatcher and identified himself using a valid FBI name and rank. After the dispatcher verified his credentials, he asked for the location of a certain officer. Manny was told that the officer was out on patrol. He asked if he could set up a meeting with the officer in one hour. The dispatcher came back with a location and Manny continued on his way.

When Manny arrived, he spotted the patrol car in the back corner of the Wendy's parking lot. He pulled up beside it and got out, holding up his badge and I.D. Officer Green looked it over and laughed. "Anybody ever tell you you fit the description of that killer running around?"

"Actually no," replied Manny. "But I guess to you a lot of people who look like me fit the description of a killer. Right?" That wiped the smile off of the officer's face real fast.

Officer David Green had been with the Dunn P.D. for ten years. He was short and fat, but it was the hard fat that made people think they were tougher than they really were. The racist bastard was going to find out what tough really was today.

Manny, getting back in his car, said, "Follow me."

"Wait!" said the officer. "What is this about?"

"I need to talk to you about a case I'm working and I don't want to do it in a fucking Wendy's parking lot," Manny said aggressively. He didn't say anything else, just jumped in his car and pulled off. Officer Green fell in line behind him.

While Manny had been leaning on the cop car, he'd fixed a small circuit to the top. It would cut off the tracking system that all cop cars had. Anyone looking for him would still see the car sitting in that parking lot.

Manny led him to a field with a dilapidated shed set about 30 yards from the road. He drove and parked about 10 feet from the structure and got out.

The officer pulled up behind him and got out complaining. "Man, you bring me all the way out here? This isn't even my jurisdiction."

Manny stood expressionless until the officer finished. Then said, "Four years ago you responded to a call about a little girl who was claiming she was raped. Correct?"

"I respond to hundreds, maybe even thousands, of calls every year. I can't remember every single one."

"Well, this one was unusual in some ways," said Manny. "It was a six-year-old black girl named Gabriella Black. She had been adopted by two gay, black men and she was claiming that one of the men was molesting her."

"Oh yeah, now I remember," the officer replied laughing. "The call turned out to be a prank by the little girl. I let her off with a warning," he said with a wink.

"How did you come to the conclusion it was a prank call?" asked Manny.

"The two men were gay. If it had been a little boy, maybe it could have been something. Those two fags didn't want no girl." The cop looked around. "What does that have to do with this place anyway?"

Manny ignored the question. "You are aware that the Prison Guard Killer went back and killed the guy who she accused of rape, right?"

"Yeah, sure. Word was he was raping inmates up there at Central Prison. But hey, you get locked up, you get what comes with it. Look man," said the officer. "I could have told you all this at the Wendy's. What was so important that we had to come way out here?"

At this point, Manny was about three feet from the cop. He said, "Way easier to abduct someone when they willingly participate in their own abduction."

The officer was so slow, he still didn't get it. "Ok. I'm still not following you."

Manny punched the officer one time on the chin, knocking him flat on his back, out cold. Before the officer even hit the ground, Manny had turned and pulled out his phone. He placed a quick call, hung up, and then stripped the officer down to his boxers and socks.

All the cop's clothes and gear went into the backseat of his patrol car. Manny then walked over to the cop and pulled his gun out. He didn't have time to waste with this piece of shit right now. So, to wake him up, Manny shot him in the arm.

The cop came instantly awake, clutching his arm, and rolling around screaming in agony. Manny said, "Get the fuck up or the next one is in your head." The cop quickly rolled to his feet and stood up with a little whimper.

"So, that little girl, because of you, went the next four years of her life being raped and abused. All you had to do was your job, and she could have lived the life that she deserved to live." As Manny was talking, a black Town Car rolled to a stop behind them. A man got out of the passenger side, ran over to the cop car, started it up, and drove away with the black sedan following it.

"Now, you will live the next four years of your life being tortured and abused, and then you will die. That's if you can last the next four years." Manny pointed the gun at his head and said, "Now move." He walked closely behind the cop as he directed him over to the shed.

"Lay on the ground with your hands on the back of your head," demanded Manny. When Officer Green complied, Manny pulled out the key and unlocked the shed door. "Get up you soft ass motherfucker and walk on in." The cop got to his feet and walked into the shed. Manny closed and locked the door behind them.

Manny pulled out his phone and, after pressing a few buttons, said, "Sorry ladies, but I need you both to lockdown for a few minutes." He watched them lockdown on the video feed and he secured them in their cells. He then called the elevator to the surface.

Finally, the officer found his tongue. "Who are you man? Why are you doing this to me?"

"You said yourself who I am. Don't I fit the description? I'm the PGK. Today, I'm the cop kidnapper. I will be the cop killer if you open your mouth again," said Manny. Officer Green chose to shut up for the time being.

The elevator arrived and Manny directed the cop on board. They rode down in silence and the door opened to a cop's worst nightmare. An underground, maximum security prison that was controlled by apps on Manny's cell phone.

The prison used to be a government Black Site that hid dangerous criminals. It was designed in a half circle and contained 48 cells that ranged from 2-Star hotel suites, to medieval dungeon. All the cells faced a central control booth made entirely of glass. A hallway that ran to the left and right was all the reception area the prison offered. The suites were to the left. Manny led the cop to the right.

When they entered the cell area, he ordered the cop to stop. He pressed a button on his phone and the first door on the right opened up. The cop looked in and whimpered again.

The cell was about the size of a medium sized closet. It was dark and all it contained was a bucket sitting in the middle. The only way to lay down in the cramped cell was to turn your body diagonally and lay in the fetal position. Officer Green looked at him and Manny pointed the gun and motioned him inside. Like the coward he was, the officer went in with his head hung low, still clutching his injured arm.

Manny closed the door and looked in at him. He said through the intercom, "You will eat when I remember to feed you. I will let you empty your bucket about once a week, again, if I remember. There is a vent about twenty feet up. If you make noise, I will freeze you to death. If you try to talk to the other captives or do anything I don't like, I will fry your pig ass until you look like pork jerky. You have any questions for me?"

"What about my family?" asked the officer.

"You want me to go visit your family?" asked Manny.

"No, no, no, no, no. Never mind."

"I thought not. Remember, you're suffering because you earned it. Whenever it gets to be too much, and you feel like you can't go on, imagine how that little girl felt. If I could find some big guy to come pay you a visit every night, then you might start to understand what she went through." Manny cut off the intercom and walked away.

He followed the circle around to the other end of the prison where the suites were located. He turned on the intercoms to the first two rooms. "Can I open your doors and speak to you ladies for a minute?" Both of them said yes, so he opened their doors and they came out.

Denise looked at him like he was a piece of shit floating in her oatmeal. It was her usual look for him, but it was really starting to piss him off.

Ann was usually pretty upbeat when he was around, but ever since he had shown his face, she was nervous around him. He thought he knew why.

"First off, you guys now have a visitor down in the last punishment cell. One of you can take him a bottle of water every other day, and a pouch of dog food every three days. Don't try to talk to him or sneak him anything because, whoever does will be in the cell next to him. Understand?" he asked them. They both nodded.

"Second, Denise, I know you hate me. I don't particularly like you either. I will promise you something though. If you keep looking at me like that, I'll have you eating dog food, butt naked, right in the cell with the new guy. Am I making myself clear?" Denise nodded and then put a sarcastic smile on her face.

"Keep it up," he said advancing on her.

"Manny!" Ann said forcefully. He stopped and glanced at her.

He turned back to Denise and said, "I've been instructed not to hurt Ann, but I've received no such instructions about you. Don't forget who I am. I'll torture your ass, kill you, film it all, and make sure your little boyfriend watches the whole thing."

"Wait," said Ann. "Who gave you those instructions and why?"

Manny stared at Denise until he saw real fear flicker across her face. Then he turned to Ann. "The who is no concern to you. The why, I can't say because I have no idea." She opened her mouth to speak and he talked over her. "Ann, stop. I can't say anymore. Just know that you have a guardian angel, or devil in this case, looking after you."

He rubbed his head, and said, "I showed you my face because I don't want you to fear me. I don't have to like you," he said looking at Denise, "but we are in this together. You can't turn me in if you are released because I'll take Walt to Death Row with me. He's become quite the badass if you can believe it.

"Anyway, I just stopped by to let you know that I don't plan on hurting either of you. But, guardian angel or not, if you force my hand, I'll kill you. Either of you. And I'll deal with the consequences later. Have a good day and stay out of trouble. I have to go meet Walt now."

He made his way to the elevator and saw the women arguing through the glass booth. He closed the elevator door and hit the intercom button on his phone to listen in.

Ann: "You need to give it a rest Denise."

Denise: "No, you need to tell me why you're all of a sudden untouchable."

Ann: "I can't okay. Stop fucking badgering me. I don't know what will happen if I tell you. It could go bad for both of us."

Denise: "Fuck you Ann. What did you do? You give the handsome killer some ass back in the day?"

Manny had just activated the camera view when Ann smacked the shit out of Denise. For a minute they both froze with their mouths hanging open. Manny had reached the top, but he prepared to go back down because Ann would kill the other women in a fight.

Denise: "You know what? You've been jealous of me from the start. Mad because Walt wanted a real woman and not some little girl playing dress up. So, keep your secrets. And don't say another word to me while we're down here."

She stormed off and left Ann standing in the loop. Manny had been hoping that Denise could get Ann to confess. He also wanted to know what was so important about her. The person who placed her under their protection was definitely not known for their generosity.

He put the phone up and made his way out to his car, locking up behind him. He got in and roared off. He had a date with the lady killer detective. From the new video he had made at the warehouse, Walt was now a lady killer in every sense of the phrase.

CHAPTER 9

The two weeks after the warehouse explosion were hell on Det. Rogers. Even though he was learning a lot, training with a psychotic genius was very taxing. The things he was made to do to the human body were beyond bizarre. Walt had never been squeamish, but he had thrown up at least three times a day and it got worse before it got better.

Everyday Manny and Walt would meet in a suburban house's basement. Manny would have a man or a woman strapped to a table and would have torture devices lined up waiting to demonstrate to Walt how they worked.

Sometimes the person would be drugged. Other times they would beg and plead and scream until they died. This is when Walt found out Manny was actually a medical doctor with degrees in several specialized fields.

Walt didn't ask where Manny kept getting the people from, but somedays they would go through three or four. Manny was so good, he could keep a person living with just a head and torso. That's after he finished cutting the limbs off using various tools. It was amazing and horrifying and Manny was hell bent on teaching Walt the basics.

At first Walt had refused and stormed out of the house. When he got in the car, his cell phone lit up with a live video feed of Ann and Denise being recalled into their cells. Once the doors were closed, a fog of gas started filling up the rooms. They banged on the glass and begged for help until they started coughing and choking.

The killer had kept up a steady commentary on the fact that they were suffering because Walt wasn't complying. He said that the gas would make them slowly suffocate by contracting their lungs until they just couldn't draw a breath. He predicted it would take about ten minutes of painful coughing before they died.

Walt had hustled back into the house and down to the basement where he told the killer he would cooperate. Manny eyed him for a full minute while the women could still be heard choking to death. Then he hit a button on his phone and Walt watched the gas dissipate and the women breathing normal before the video cut off.

Manny had then issued a warning. "They are only alive because I have faith in you. When that faith is no longer there, they will die. I will strap both of them to tables just like this and I'll send you pieces of them until there is nothing left to send. Stop fucking around, do what I tell you to do, and all this will end."

So, Walt had become better and better at torturing people and making them live longer. Every time Manny taught him a new technique, Walt would kill a couple of people getting it right, but then he'd get better. Manny would then add something else that would kill the person anyway. Over those 16 days, Walt lost count of how many people died in that basement. On the 17th day, everything changed.

Walt had gotten use to receiving a text every morning with the time to meet Manny at the torture house. Today, he got a text telling him to be dressed when he came out of his room because Manny was in his house waiting for him.

He jumped out of bed, took care of all his hygiene needs, dressed, and stepped out into the hallway. He could hear the T.V. playing in the living room, but no other sound could be heard. Walt crept down the hall and peered into the living area. Manny was sitting in a chair with his back to the door watching the News.

The reporter was giving an update on the missing 10-year-old Gabriella Black. He was speculating on the fact that everyone thought the Prison Guard Killer had murdered her family and had probably murdered her too. He showed a picture of the Oakland family and explained how the killer had tortured and killed the Mom and two little boys. He also explained that the killer had left the father alive just to send a message to other guards. He ended with a prayer for mercy and a speedy return of the little girl.

"Go ahead and ask so you won't be sulking later on," said Manny. Walt hadn't made a sound but he wasn't surprised Manny knew he was there. Nothing got by the bastard and Walt wasn't going to act like he was confused about the subject.

"Did you kill that little girl?"

Manny turned and asked, "What do you think?"

"I think that you're a murdering, psychotic, twisted, piece of shit who will do anything to anybody to fulfill your need for revenge." Walt always felt it was best to be truthful, even if it got him killed.

Manny looked at him with a calm expression. "I have my reasons but then again, so do you. When you pick a life over a life, the end result is the same. A lost life. The difference is, I know why you kill, and it's selfish and self-serving.

"You, on the other hand, have no idea why I'm doing what I do. The fact that I'm not dead or in jail should tell you it's bigger than me." Manny stood up and said, "Well, you're in it now. Sooner or later, you'll open your eyes and see the truth. And just to let you know, Gabriella Black is not dead. Now, come over here, we have work to do."

Walt walked over and saw an assortment of gear spread across the living room table. Knives, snips, pliers, scissors, saws, bolt cutters, ropes, straps, an injection kit, lock picks, cameras. About one of everything needed to torture someone and record it for later enjoyment.

Manny produced a back pack and said, "Pack all your gear so that you can wear it and it won't make a sound if you have to run. You should have learned how while in the service." He picked up one of the small cameras. "Put this one on your shirt so it will give me a first-person point of view. The other ones, I want you to set up at different angles so I can see what you are doing."

Walt nodded and said, "Ok. Where am I setting this stuff up and what will I be doing?"

Manny smiled and said, "Task three is going down tonight. What the hell do you think I've been training you for?"

Walt's stomach fell to his feet. He knew it was coming, and he knew he had to do it to free the girls. But he still dreaded it none the less. "Are you coming with me?" he asked Manny.

"I wouldn't need you to set cameras up if I was coming with you genius. It's time for you to step out on your own

111

and show me what you've learned." It irked the hell out of Walt that Manny was so amused.

The killer continued, "His wife will be at the house with him, so you'll need to incapacitate her first. Just follow the instructions and you'll be fine. Oh, and try not to throw up. I don't care if I leave DNA behind at crime scenes because it won't lead to anything. If yours come up, then you go to jail. Then I'll have to explain to those two beautiful women that you failed and they have to die."

Walt swallowed the lump in his throat. "When do I do it?"

"He doesn't work today. However you want to do it, whenever you want to do it, I don't care. It will be sometime today, and the end result will be what I stipulated. Do you understand?"

"Yeah," replied Walt. "You're the boss."

Manny turned on his heels and walked out of Walt's house without a backwards glance. He even closed the door softly like they had just finished up with a pleasant conversation.

Walt packed up all the supplies except for the little camera, which went into his pocket. He then deposited the bag in the truck of his BMW. He had switched back to the vehicle the day after he had murdered the witness because there was no risk in driving it anymore.

To get to the target's house would take a couple hours drive. Walt didn't want to go in cold, so he wanted to leave enough time to recon the area before moving in. He looked at his watch and saw it wasn't even 8:00 in the morning yet.

Walt needed to burn about eight hours before it would be time to head east.

Over the past few weeks, Walt had been working on the release of two offenders. One was Mr. York, the offender who had helped him in breaking out Bruce Battle. The other was the wrongfully convicted Timothy Washington.

In reality, Manny was the reason why Mr. Washington was getting out. He was also the reason why it was taking so long for the state to release him. Procedure had to be followed to the letter. No favors or shortcuts. That was because the whole country thought the PGK was killing to free him.

After the evidence gathered on Candace Price, the lieutenant who accused Timothy of rape, came to light, everyone knew he was innocent. But a lot of law makers and law enforcement thought, to free him would be giving into the killer. Walt was confident he would be free in the next week.

Mr. Dewayne York, on the other hand, was guilty as hell, and 100 times more dangerous than Mr. Washington. He had been convicted of double murder and had continued his streak of violence while in prison. He was still in maximum security after ten years because of his numerous assaults on staff and other inmates.

Even with all that, Mr. York was coming out of prison today to serve his last twelve years on house arrest. The North Carolina legal system was laughable in its fairness.

Neither case needed his attention today as the court system was now handling them both, but Walt still needed to show his face in the office. Not only did he need to act as if he was hunting the PGK, but Manny had taught him it was always good to put forth an image of innocence when you were about to commit a crime. Who would think that a cop would go to work for the day, leave, and kill one, possibly two people? So, Walt needed to interact and be seen by a few people to project that image.

Walt went to work and made a point to check in with as many people as possible. He was still overseeing numerous cases, like the disappearance of Denise McCarthy. He didn't want to overdo it because then people would remember he'd been acting weird. By the time 4:00 pm rolled around, he was revving to go ahead and get this task over with.

He made a couple of offhand remarks to his colleagues implying that he was going home to catch up on sleep, and then wished everyone a good night.

Walt made his way to his house, dropped off his main cell phone so if anyone thought to trace it later, it would show he'd been home all night. Then he kept going right out his back door.

He got about a hundred yards away before he remembered the back pack and had to retrace his path to retrieve it from the trunk of his car. Then he took off down the road again.

About five minutes of walking brought him in sight of a dark blue Honda Accord parked on the side of the road. Walt got in and drove off, heading towards the interstate.

An hour before Walt had knocked off from work, he had received a text from Manny about the Accord. Walt knew that both of his cars stood out, but had never even thought about his vehicle being spotted by people or cameras that could trip up his alibi of being home sleep. Walt guessed that's what made Manny such a good criminal. He thought of all the little things.

By 7:00 pm, he was sitting in the car down the road from the target's house. He was using a surveillance drone to make sure there were no surprises around the structure. The houses in this part of Craven county were only about 25 yards from each other, so there was not much room for error on any part of this mission. A neighbor seeing or hearing the wrong thing and Walt, Ann, and Denise could end up dead because of it. So, he took his time and made sure everything was good.

This drone was too big to sneak into the house with. So, he recalled it and sent the one with the sleeping gas on board. It didn't take him long to find the couple.

The drone entered the house through a barely opened window in the master bathroom. The whole room was fogged up and the sound of the running shower was loud through the tiny speakers of the burner phone. But the sounds of passion were even louder.

"Oh God! Yes baby! Yes baby! Right there! Oh God!" yelled a female voice.

"You like that baby? You like when I go deep like that?" asked a male voice.

Walt couldn't see the couple because of all the steam, but the repeated sound of flesh hammering into flesh was getting faster and louder. What he could see was that the glass front of the shower didn't go all the way up to the ceiling. He guided the drone into the shower stall.

He still couldn't see any facial features to confirm identity, but he could make out two white bodies, one male and one female. The man was behind the woman who was slightly bent over with her ass poking out and her hands splayed on the tile wall. Things were roaring towards their natural ending.

"Oh God! Oh God! Ohhhh Jerome!" yelled the woman as her body convulsed with waves of pleasure.

"Oh, shit Olivia! I'm cominggggg!" yelled the man as his body did some convulsing of its own.

Since the yelled names confirmed both identities, not that he thought Manny had given him bad information, Walt didn't wait any longer. He had no idea if the steam would affect the sleeping gas, but both of them were in the same place, breathing deeply, and he might not get another chance this good. He kept hitting the release button on the app until it showed that no more gas was left inside of the drone.

The couple took a few more deep breaths and then the woman stood up straight and they started kissing deeply like they were gearing up for round two. In the middle of the kiss, the man yawned hugely and said, "Babe, I think you wore me out. I can barely keep my eyes open."

The woman slumped over onto the wall and said, "I think we wore each other out. My body feels…." And just like that, they both crashed to the tiled floor of the shower.

Drowning was a major concern at this point, so he recalled the drone, drove the car down an embankment, parked it deeper in the woods, and took off on foot to secure his target.

He boldly walked to the front door and rang the bell to keep up appearances for any neighbors watching. As soon as he had entered the neighborhood, he had activated his little black box because he knew everyone had doorbell cameras now and he couldn't afford to have one pick up his face. It was dark out by now, but he couldn't just walk down the middle of the street with a mask on.

After a few seconds of standing on the front stoop, Walt turned off the black box and tried the door. Just like in small towns all across America, people here had trust in their neighbors. The door was unlocked, so he walked right on in.

He could hear the sound of the shower coming from the back of the house, so he hurried to the bathroom to pull the couple out of harm's way. According to the task, he wasn't supposed to kill the officer, just totally fuck him up.

The couple wasn't drowning. They were both sleeping and now Walt could clearly see them to verify it was indeed Jerome and Olivia Fox. He could see now because the hot water had run out and the shower head was now dumping freezing cold water all over the couple.

Walt turned the water off and began the process of setting everything up for the killer's entertainment.

The first thing that needed to be done was the securing of the captives. He dragged both of their wet, naked bodies out of the bathroom and into the bedroom. He stripped the bed down to the mattress and then secured Jerome Fox to the middle of the bed, face down in the shape of a cross.

He then brought a chair from the kitchen, propped the naked Olivia into it, and used zip ties to secure her four limbs to the chair. He put a tight gag in her mouth and then turned his attention back to Jerome.

Walt had no idea who this man was, or what he had done beyond what Manny had told him. Officer Jerome Fox was a relatively new hire at Craven Correctional Institution. He had only been there for a little over a year. But in that time, he had been very busy and Manny thought it was time to send another message.

Jerome was a member of the officer hit squad that specialized in brutalizing inmates. They didn't care if you were white, black, young, or old. If you were an inmate, then you were fair game.

Officer Fox was a 22 years old white man who had some martial arts training. He was 6-foot 6-inches tall and was 240 pounds of ripped up muscles. He was responsible for the deaths of two inmates over the last six months, but he had been cleared of any wrong doing in both cases.

He had once been a promising college football player until one day in practice, he had beat one of his teammates so bad, the guy was now in a wheelchair for life. Jerome had been kicked out of school but again, no charges were filed.

Jerome had met Olivia, a 20-year-old blond bombshell, in college and when he left, she left with him. They had gotten married, settled down in their new house, and Jerome started his new job. Fast forward 14 months and now the officer's life was about to change for the worse.

Walt clipped the body camera onto the front of his shirt and then went around the room sticking the extra cameras at different angles to the bed. Little motions from his captives showed that the gas was started to wear off. Walt's phone rang.

The killer was the only one with the number to this phone, so Walt answered with a smart, "What do you want? The show is about to start."

"Do you want to add Jerome and Olivia to your growing body count and fail this task?" asked Manny.

"I did everything you said. They are secured. Why would I have to kill them?" asked Walt.

Manny paused for a few beats. "Put your fucking mask on you idiot," then he hung up on Walt.

"Shit," said Walt, pulling the mask out of his back pack. It was over his face just in the nick of time, because five seconds later, he was looking into the drowsy eyes of Olivia Fox.

"Who the fuck are you?" Olivia asked drunkenly through her gag. It didn't come out that way, but Walt understood enough to know what she was asking.

"Olivia? What's going on? I told you last time, I don't like being tied up. Come take this shit off right now!" Because of his position, Jerome couldn't see what was going on behind him.

Olivia started going crazy the second she woke up enough to realize that something was very wrong. She was screaming louder than Walt had thought possible with the gag in place. She was also bucking so hard Walt feared the whole chair would come apart.

Walt's phone beeped with an incoming text. He looked at the screen: Give them a reason to be quiet. Tighten the fuck up. Control the situation.

Walt figured the best tool to achieve that was tucked in the back of his pants. He pulled out another Manny provided silent gun and pointed it at the back of Jerome's head. Olivia immediately became quiet and still.

"Olivia? Olivia? What the hell are you doing? I swear I'm going to beat your ass if you don't stop playing and free me." Jerome wasn't exactly yelling, but he wasn't quiet either.

Walt decided it was time to introduce himself. "Right now, your beautiful, naked wife is strapped to a chair. You are tied down helplessly to that bed. I also have a gun pointed at the back of your head. You make another sound and the first bullet goes into your wife."

"Fuck you, you son of a bitch! You do anything to her, I'll kill you!" exclaimed Jerome.

Walt walked over to Olivia and picked the chair up, moving it so that now Jerome could see her tied up. When Walt was tired of listening to Jerome issue his threats, he put his hand over Olivia's mouth and shot her through the shoulder. Manny had taught him where best to shoot people to make the most mess, but wouldn't be life threatening. Olivia screamed in pain behind Walt's hand as blood sprayed all over Jerome.

Jerome kept up the comments and threats, so Walt, feeling a little sick, switched hands and shot Olivia in the other shoulder. She was crying and shaking with the pain, but it was enough to finally make Jerome be quiet.

"Olivia, I'm going to have to insist that you be quiet," Walt said. "You didn't have to be hurt, but you can see how much your husband cares about you. All he had to do was shut up and you would still be healthy and whole."

Manny had taught him that also. If you can get the captives mad at each other, then they comply with you if only to outlive the other captives.

"Now that I have both of your attention, Jerome, I'm sure you know who I am. This isn't about getting any information from you at all. This is about pure vengeance for how you've been treating the offenders in your care. Do you have anything to say before we get started?" When the officer stayed silent, Walt said, "Good."

He started pulling out his torture tools and spreading them out on the bed for both of them to see. When he pulled out the small torch, Olivia became irate again. When he touched the gun, she calmed down, but continued to emit a low keening sound. The gag just wasn't going to cut it.

"Okay. I didn't want to do this, but I see I can't count on the two of you to be quiet." Walt produced a jar that contained a paste that looked like concrete. He pulled out a latex glove and put it on over the leather one he was already wearing. He reached his fingers into the jar and pulled out a big clump. He said, "Close your mouths all the way. If any of this gets in, it will cause your stomach to harden and you'll die a slow horrible death."

Walt felt bad because both would need several surgeries to fix their faces after the paste hardened, but that would be the least of Jerome's problems. He did Olivia first, then swung around and put a healthy dose on Jerome's mouth. It would only take about five minutes to harden, so neither of them would be making any more noise tonight.

They all sat in silence. Them looking at Walt and Walt looking back and forth between them. Walt had just stood up to start the show when his phone rang. He was getting mad at all the interruptions, and he was going to let Manny know.

"What the fuck do you want? I'm doing it, okay? Just give me some damn time," demanded Walt.

"You're out of time dumbass. A cop car just pulled up in front with two cops inside. One is already on his way around the house looking in windows," said Manny.

"Shit," murmured Walt. He dashed over to the window and made sure the blinds were right and the curtain wouldn't allow anyone to see inside. He turned to Jerome and Olivia and said, "Either of you makes a sound I'll kill both of you." As soon as the words left his mouth, the doorbell rang.

He put his finger up to his lips to remind the couple to be quiet, and made his way over to the bedroom door.

"Hello! Anyone home? Sheriff's Department." It was definitely a cop. The words were spoken with authority and force. Each word said, answer me now, or you're in big trouble. "We got a complaint from a neighbor about some strange noises. If you don't respond, I've been authorized to break in for a wellness check."

Walt, still holding the phone, asked, "What the hell do I do now?"

"Right now, the cops are separated. If you want to finish this task then you know what you have to do. Time is running out Walt. Who lives and who dies is now up to you." Manny paused for a second. "No matter what, for Ann and Denise sake, I hope you make the right choice and finish the task." He then disconnected the call.

"Manny? Manny?" whispered Walt. "Fuck," he said putting the phone away. With resolve in his heart and on his face, he glanced one more time at the couple, then marched to the front of the house.

Without hesitation, Walt snatched the door open and shot the surprised deputy right in the forehead. He walked right over his still twitching body and went down the four steps. He had no idea which direction the other cop went, so he turned right at random, hoping to come up behind the guy.

He hurried his step when he didn't see the cop on the first side. When he turned the corner to head around back, the other deputy was ten feet away, walking right at him. This deputy was also caught off guard and took a bullet right in the face.

Walt didn't have time. When those cops didn't check in, tons of back up would converge on this location. He sprinted back into the house, leaving the two officers where they were.

He rushed into the bedroom to find Olivia, still strapped to the chair, over at the window moving the blinds around with her face. Walt didn't have time to deal with her, so he shot her in her leg and she, along with the chair, crashed to the floor.

The bindings holding Jerome to the bed had been done very tight for a reason. He had long ago lost feeling in his hands and feet. Manny had taught him to do it that way so the prisoner couldn't make a fist when you went after a finger. Or in this case, all the fingers and toes.

Walt was supposed to use a bolt cutter on each digit, but that was no longer an option with the new time constraints. He picked up the razor-sharp hatchet and placed a cutting board under Jerome's right hand.

"Wom wam. Wam wom ugh," Jerome tried to plead. Walt brought the knife down and removed the four fingers in one swipe. Through the loud moaning, blood, and gore, Walt chopped the thumb off before moving over to the other side of the bed and repeating the process.

Olivia was still on the floor crying and wailing as she watched Walt mutilate her husband. Walt placed the board under both feet and got all the toes with only two hacks. Then he picked up the small torch.

Jerome would bleed out in minutes if Walt left him, even with the tight bindings cutting off most of the circulation. So, Walt needed to stop the bleeding. Since he was already at his feet, he clicked the starter on the mini tank and lit it up. He adjusted the flame and applied it to the open wounds. After about three seconds of screaming, Jerome passed out from the pain.

Walt finished his feet and moved on to each hand. After he was done, he packed all the tools into the back pack except for a four-inch, fixed blade, knife. He rubbed along the top of Jerome's spine until he found the spot he was looking for. He slid the knife in slowly but forcefully until it was in to the hilt. He actually felt the tear that he needed, so he was satisfied he had done the job right.

His task had been to remove all ten fingers and toes and then to leave Jerome Fox a quadriplegic. He would still have his mind, but essentially his body would be gone.

Soon as Walt finished the last cut, he left the knife in, grabbed up the back pack, and took off out of the house. This was a country road, so it was pitch black outside. He activated the black box one more time, but didn't remove his mask because people could still record him with their cell phones.

He actually made it back to the car before he heard the first sirens. He was two miles from the house before he turned the box off and passed the first cop car heading towards the crime scene.

Walt was elated and breathed a huge sigh of relief when the sign came up saying the Interstate was only a mile away. He knew that if he made it there without encountering a road block, he was home free.

He had become so focused on making it to the Interstate, that he stopped watching his rearview mirror. The flashing blue lights and the Whoop Whoop of the siren took him completely by surprise.

It's over, was Walt's first thought. It was an all-black unmarked and there was no way the Honda Accord could outrun it. Walt reached and pulled out the phone and the gun. His hand tracked from one to the other, not sure which one to use.

CHAPTER 10

While Walt was at work that day, stressing over what he was gonna have to do later that night, Manny was also working. He had finally tracked down the last person that needed to die for hurting Gabby.

Patrick Young, A.K.A Black Ops, was a career criminal. He was a specialist in midnight burglary. Ten years ago, he use to run with a crew, but after a year of near misses with the law, he decided that they were holding him back. He decided to go solo.

To this day, Patrick had never seen the inside of a prison cell. He had been to a couple of police stations for questioning, but the police could never get him any farther than that. It helped that he was also a lawyer, so he knew his rights and exercised them.

Patrick was a tall black man who was perpetually in a bad mood. Your average person tried to avoid him at all cost because of how scary he looked and his natural in-your-face persona. Violence just radiated off of him and his profane dialog discouraged any form of polite conversation.

Eight years ago, Black Ops had acted on some bad intelligence involving a doctor's house in Greensboro, North Carolina. His colleague had told him that the doctor was taking her husband and two young daughters on a cruise for a week. The house would be vacant while they were gone.

The day was right, the month was right, even the time was right. The only part of the intel that was wrong was the year.

Dr. Savanah Josey and her husband Warreck, who was a software developer, always planned their vacations a year in advance. Because their daughter Gabby was still too young, they decided to push their cruise back another year so both girls could come with them. It was a decision that cost both adults their lives and both children their childhood.

Patrick had showed up the first night they were supposed to be gone and found a dark house. He hadn't known anyone was in the house until Warreck came down the steps clutching a baseball bat. He shot the man in the back of the head and rushed upstairs to try and get Savanah before she could call the police for help.

He could have just run, but Manny thought the man was upset he wasn't going to get the payday he expected. Dr. Josey was already screaming into the phone when he kicked the door in. He shot her four times in the torso while the dumbass 911 operator asked repeatedly if she was in any immediate danger. Black Ops calmly walked over and hung the phone up.

Manny knew all of this because the whole house had been covered by several indoor cameras and microphones. That's also how he knew that Black Ops had searched for the girls until he heard the first siren signaling the cops were getting close. The masked man had then exited the house and was long gone when the cops finally arrived. Only after the cops started clearing the house did Emily come out of the closet holding a sedate Gabby.

The police had investigated, but could developed no leads. The case went cold over time and the Blacks adopted the girls, so the police just put it down as another unsolved double murder in Guilford county.

Black Ops had fell off the radar for about a year and then went on with his criminal ways. He had ended up killing three more people in his burglaries over the years, but he did try to avoid bloodshed if possible. Being a born predator, Patrick Young was not going to stop on his own. He needed someone to come and help him. Manny was a more than willing volunteer.

Patrick was now living in a townhouse in downtown Highpoint, a small city near Greensboro. Manny had used his FBI contacts to learn everything about the man's movements and habits over the last few years. The tidbit that he was going to exploit was Patrick's willingness to cooperate with law enforcement. He was so cocky and confident, anytime the police called for him to come in, he would show up with a willing to help attitude. He never really helped the police, but he did know how to put on a good show.

At 10:00 that morning, Manny called to set up a meeting with the criminal.

Patrick answered on the second ring. "Patrick Young speaking. How can I help you?"

"Hi Mr. Young. This is Clint Roberts with the FBI Office out of Charlotte, North Carolina. I was in the middle of an investigation when your name came up. I'm over her in Greensboro now and I was wondering if I could talk to you for a minute?" Manny asked.

"Sure Agent Roberts. What do you want to talk about?"

"If you don't mind sir, I'd like to talk to you in person," replied Manny. "If there is somewhere I can meet you, that would be great." Manny knew Black Ops didn't operate in the Charlotte area, so he was hoping that would boost his willingness to be helpful.

After a brief hesitation, Patrick said, "How about my house? I wasn't planning on going anywhere today."

"That's good. Do you still live at …...?" Manny recited the address and Patrick confirmed he still lived there. They agreed to meet at 2:00 pm. Manny thanked him and hung up.

There was absolutely no way for Manny to carry out his plan at Patrick's house. It really didn't even have a yard. It was in the middle of 15 townhouses, so privacy was non-existent. Plus, the police department was less than a mile away. Manny wasn't scared of jail; he'd be out in under an hour. But some trigger-happy cop getting a free shot at a black man might get lucky and kill him.

He had hoped to get the man to meet him somewhere and then pull him over in route to the meeting place. But Manny being Manny definitely had a plan B.

At 2:05 pm, Manny parked his "unmarked cop car" in front of Mr. Young's house. Manny was wearing a pair of khakis and an orange button up to present the image of a soft ass, non-threatening cop.

The car was a modified Crown Vic that was a kidnapper's dream come true. It looked just like an official unmarked with antennas and blacked out windows. But anything that goes into the backseat will stay there until Manny said otherwise. It was soundproof, damage proof, escape proof, and every other proof there was. All Manny had to do was fake arrest Mr. Young and get him in the car and that would be all she wrote.

Manny walked up and rang the bell, then took a few steps back. He had already activated his black box and thought Black Ops might be wondering why his cameras weren't working.

After 30 seconds, the door opened. Manny instantly saw why the average person would be scared. Black Ops was the blackest person Manny had ever seen in his life. No wonder he was so good at crimes done in the dark. He looked like midnight on a country road. And his bald head was gleaming so bright, it was like an oil slick had come to life.

He had coal black eyes. He was 6-foot 4-inches and about 230 pounds. Black Ops had spent ten years in the military, that's where the moniker came from. His muscular build still showed his years of training and working out.

"What the fuck do you want?" was the first thing out of Patrick's mouth.

"Oh, sorry Mr. Young. I'm Agent Clint Roberts. I called you earlier and we agreed to meet."

"You have any I.D.? You don't look like no punk ass cop," said Black Ops.

Manny pulled out his credentials and in a meek voice said, "I wouldn't say I'm a punk ass cop, but I am a cop." Manny got his I.D. back and said, "Can we step inside and talk?"

Black Ops looked around for a few seconds and said, "Come on." He turned and walked back inside, leaving the door open for Manny to follow.

Manny knew the rudeness and junk talk was just part of the man's personality. Pretty soon he would be begging and crying like a hungry dog, so Manny ignored the wise cracks.

Black Ops sat down in a recliner and then gestured for Manny to sit on a straight back, hard as hell chair that was perfect to discourage people from long visits.

Mr. Young said, "Now, what can I do to help an agent from the Charlotte FBI?"

"Well Mr. Young, I am investigating a murder that happened two weeks ago in the middle of an apparent burglary," Manny began to explain.

Patrick cut him off. "Hold up, hold up, hold up. Why would the FBI be investigating a burglary\murder? That's a local matter."

"Normally you'd be right. But the person killed was a federal informant in an on-going RICO investigation."

"So, has it crossed your stupid ass mind that the people he was snitching on killed him?" asked Black Ops.

"All of them are behind bars. Anyway, these are the type of people who hire out that kind of work. But during my investigation, I kept hearing your name."

"And what name is that?" he asked.

"Black Ops," said Manny. After a minute of silence, Manny said, "That is the name you go by, right?"

Black Ops laughed. It was hard to imagine but even his laugh was filled with aggression and violence. "You came all the way up here, fucking with me on my day off, to accuse me of being this Black Ops mother fucker? Get the fuck out of my house. This meeting is over." He stood up and looked down on "Agent Roberts" daring him to do anything except get up and leave.

Manny stayed seated. "Mr. Young, I didn't come up here on a hunch. You were seen in the Charlotte area the day of this murder. The FBI has done extensive research into you and we know exactly who you are. For those reasons, I am going to place you under arrest on suspicion of murder."

Manny stood up and pulled out handcuffs. Bringing out a little of his true self, he said, "Now turn around and put your fucking hands behind your back. Or do you want to add resisting and assault of a government agent to the list of charges?"

Black Ops weighed his options for a few seconds and then began to negotiate. "Listen Agent Roberts, this is my home. This is my neighborhood. You and I both know this is a wild goose chase. You march me out of here this time of day with cuffs on and my name is ruined. I'll go quietly if you leave off the cuffs."

"No bullshit?" asked Manny.

"I promise, no bullshit," answered Black Ops.

"Alright then, let's go." Manny performed a quick search of the man to make sure he didn't have any weapons. Mr. Young asked the agent to take his cell phone and wallet with them. So, Manny put both items in his own pocket and marched Mr. Young out of the house.

Manny opened the back door to the car and Black Ops got in, an accomplice to his own murder. Manny had no reason to fake anymore, so he pulled out Mr. Young's phone, slammed it on the ground and stepped on it. He then pulled out his wallet, took out all the cash and dropped the wallet on the curb with the phone.

He was sure Patrick was going crazy in the back seat because he could see everything Manny was doing. Inside the compartment he was now encased in, no one could hear it except Patrick himself.

Manny walked around and got in the driver's seat and took off. He could hear a slight rumble from the back, signifying Mr. Young was now physically trying to break out of the escape proof cage.

Laughing, Manny reached to turn on the intercom to piss Black Ops off more, when his cell phone rang. He saw the beautiful face of Alisha fill the screen, so he answered it immediately.

"What's going on baby? How are my two beautiful girls coming along?" Manny asked.

Alisha said, "Your two girls are doing good, but we're still at the house."

"Why? What happened?" Every morning since Gabby arrived, they had been leaving the house to go shopping together.

"Well Manny, I know this house has three separate areas where you store cars. I searched through all of them because I figured you of all people would understand the need to blend in. Sweetie, I can't find a car that we can take that won't draw attention."

"You have the Audi A8 right out front. Why don't you want to drive that?" asked Manny. This was the car she normally used.

"It's a hundred-thousand-dollar car! And it's white on white. It stands out like a stripper in church!" exclaimed Alisha. She had complained about all the attention the car was getting.

"Okay. What about the Challenger? It's black and there are plenty of them on the road."

"You probably have half a million in upgrades on that thing. Do you have anything that doesn't cost over $100,000? You know, like a normal car?"

Manny thought about it for a few seconds. "I'm sorry babe, but the closest I have is the BMW M5. It's black and it's a four door, so it might blend in a little."

Alisha laughed at him and Manny found himself getting annoyed. What the hell kind of woman wants cheaper cars anyway? He was crazy in love with this woman, but she was just as strange as most women were.

When Alisha calmed down, she said, "I keep forgetting that you've been rich your entire life. You don't understand that to a normal person, a hundred-thousand-dollar car stands out. It's not bad, in fact I think it's kind of sweet. But right now, your family needs a car that will blend in so we can be safe."

Manny didn't have time for this. He said, "Listen, I'm kind of in the middle of something. Call this number and tell them to bring you whatever kind of car you want." He gave her the number and said, "I love you and have fun with our little girl." She returned the sentiment and they both hung up.

During the phone call, Patrick had gone silent. Manny decided to push him a little bit so he would be really mad at the end. He hit the intercom button and said, "How are you doing in there? You still alive?"

Black Ops didn't sound mad at all. "You know I'm going to kill you as soon as you open this door, right? You picked the wrong motherfucker to try this shit on." Everything he said was delivered in a matter-of-fact way.

"Well," said Manny, "You will surely get your chance. When we get where we're going, I'll open your door and we will go head-to-head until one of us is dead. Just to let you know who you're dealing with, I'm the Prison Guard Killer, not some punk ass cop. You hurt someone close to me and now you will pay."

"I don't give a rat's ass who you are," said Black Ops. "If you did your research on me, you know what I am capable of. Oh, and for the record, fuck whoever is close to you."

"Patrick, I did do my research. I was so worried that I let you get in with no cuffs on. Maybe you should ask yourself what I'm capable of if I'm not worried about you at all." Manny cut the intercom off before Black Ops could respond. After a minute of silence, the midnight burglar went back to trying to break out.

Manny smiled. He knew Black Ops was the real deal. If he hadn't been so evil and criminally inclined, they might have been colleagues. Manny was going to have a real fight on his hands when he opened that door. If Black Ops was as smart as Manny thought he was, he'd save all that energy for their upcoming battle. On cue, the cage went silent and Manny continued on to their destination.

About 30 minutes later, Manny pulled into a parking garage and proceeded to go four stories down to the bottom floor. There were no other cars on the two lower levels because there was no elevator and anyone with sense wouldn't want to be caught down there alone. Manny knew for a fact it was a favorite spot for the local police to beat on their captives. Under the circumstances, it would serve Manny well.

He parked all the way in the back and then turned the intercom on. "I'm leaving all my weapons in here and I'm putting the keys in my pocket. You kill me and take the car, no one will come looking for you. You will be free to live out the rest of your life in peace."

Manny knew this was a lie. If the giant did manage to kill him, he would be dead within the hour. Either way it went, Black Ops would be no more after today.

"I'm going to walk to the middle of the garage and then pop your door. You'll have two minutes to ready yourself," said Manny.

"You gonna talk me to death, or open the fucking door? I'm ready now. You better be the one getting ready motherfucker," responded Patrick.

Manny got out of the car and walked off about ten feet. He took off his shirt and did a slow spin to show he didn't have any weapons. Then he walked on another 80 feet, turned around, and popped the back door.

Black Ops came out of the car with the grace of a panther. He looked at Manny with a smile on his face that was part amused and part predatory. He closed the door softly behind him, looked around, and then stalked towards Manny like he was cornered prey.

It took Patrick about two minutes to close the distance, but eventually, he stood ten feet in front of Manny. "I'm just curious. Who is the son of a bitch you're willing to die for?" asked Black Ops.

"About eight years ago, you broke into a house and killed a doctor and her husband. Then you went looking for their kids before you ran to avoid capture. The baby girl is now my adopted daughter. Because of what you did that night, her life has been hell. I'm going to make you pay for all of her pain." Manny switched up his whole demeanor so the man could see the monster he was about to face.

Black Ops did his evil laugh. "Hehehehehe. I want you to know, after I finish with you, I'm going to finish what I started eight years ago."

Nothing more needed to be said. Both men now knew this was truly a fight to the death. Neither was afraid because both were extremely confident in the skills they possessed. Neither would ever underestimate an opponent, so they advanced cautiously towards each other.

The first exchange was a feeling out to see if the other was even worthy of a serious fight. Both threw a series of kicks and punches with nothing serious landing for either of them.

They both took a step back and circled, looking for an opening or a mistake. Manny was holding back, but he was positive the oil slick motherfucker was holding back too. Manny had no doubt he would win, but time wasn't on his side.

Black Ops was about four inches taller and thirty pounds heavier. He also appeared to be in perfect shape for a man his age. Most fights like this went by a schedule. Each "round" the opponents would step it up a little more until one made a mistake that they couldn't recover from. Manny was about to break protocol.

The next exchange began with a series of kicks by Black Ops that Manny blocked or dodged with ease. When Black Ops switched to vicious punches, Manny ducked under one and threw a powerful right hook directly to the inside of his elbow that instantly dislocated the joint. Black Ops retreated, and with a sickening sound, popped the bone back into place. Manny knew the dislocation and the correction were painful, but the other man never made a sound of distress.

The next interaction led to Manny making a mistake. He went hard at the man knowing his right arm would be throbbing from his recent injury. Black Ops surprised him with a violent and precise three piece that had Manny taking a step back to avoid the fourth punch that would have taken him out.

"Hehehehehe," laughed Black Ops. "Didn't expect that did you motherfucker?"

Manny didn't have time to answer as Black Ops decided to push the advantage he had just gained. Knowing any more games could lead to Manny losing, he made the choice to end things now.

This round, Manny took a couple hits in order to get inside of Black Ops' guard. Manny only had a split second but he made the most of it. He delivered a perfect right elbow to the underarm that separated the other man's right shoulder. He then executed a tight spin around the back of the bigger man and sent the same elbow crashing into the left shoulder blade that dislocated that joint also. The fight was over. Black Ops now couldn't lift either of his arms.

Manny pressed the issue with a combination of fist and elbow strikes that left the big man bleeding from several cuts on his head and face. Manny had to give it to him, at no time did he try to retreat or run. Instead, he used his legs to continue to fight until his knees hit the ground. Even then, he still looked defiantly at Manny.

"You better finish me now," said Black Ops. "If I get back to my feet, I promise you are a dead man."

"No, I'm not," said Manny. "But just in case," Manny did a round house kick right to the other man's Adams apple. Black Ops instantly started to choke as his eyes showed fear for the first time.

Manny knew the man was dead, but that didn't stop Black Ops from getting to his feet. He continued to try and draw a breath, but his crushed wind pipe was preventing it. After a few seconds, he fell back down to his knees.

Manny said, "Gabriella Josey, now Gabriella Adams. That's the person you hurt. I'll make sure to describe how you died the next time I see her. On your knees, just like the coward you are."

A look of pure rage entered Black Ops' eyes. He used the last of his essence to get one foot under himself before he fell over sideways, dead.

Manny walked back to the car and popped the trunk. He pulled out a can of gas and walked back over to the dead man.

To delay identification as long as possible, Manny burned the body and then shot the jaw off so dental records would be useless.

Manny hadn't lied to the man. He would tell Gabby exactly what he had done and exactly how the man had died. It wouldn't be anytime soon, but it was a conversation they would have.

Once the body was a charred pile of bones, he jumped in the car and made his way back to the surface. Before he set things up with Walt, Manny was planning on spending some quality time with his two special ladies.

CHAPTER 11

Ultimately, Walt decided the best thing to do was pull over. He was actually in the process of doing just that when the car cut off on its own. It scared the shit out of him and he pulled over to the side of the road and reached for the burner phone. He got another shock when he realized the phone wouldn't even turn on.

The first thing came to his mind was that Manny was nearby and was fucking with him. But the person who emerged from the cop car was not Manny. The cop's headlights were still on, so Walt couldn't see everything clearly. But it looked like a skinny white guy was walking towards his car.

Walt didn't want to kill any more cops, but something wasn't right with this scene. He could see someone else was sitting in the cop car. If they thought they were pulling over a cop killer, both should be out of the car with more back up on their heels. Walt clutched the gun and tried to see who was coming up to his driver's side window.

The cop, wearing a state trooper's uniform, stopped about three feet from the car and said, "I'm going to be mad as hell if you shoot me Walt. Why don't you put the gun down and step out so we can talk?"

Walt's head whipped around because he actually knew that voice. He scrambled out of the car and came face to face with the elusive Agent Steve. "What the hell are you doing here? Are you following me?"

The CIA agent looked back towards the car where a man sat in shadows on the passenger seat. "I'm going to need you to follow me because some people want to have a word with you."

"Is that Manny in the car?" Walt asked and started in that direction.

Agent Steve put his arm out and said, "That isn't Manny and the only reason you're not dead or in cuffs right now is because I promised you would go without a problem. Get back in your car and follow me before we both end up dead." To emphasize his point, three cop cars zoomed pass in the direction of the two dead cops.

"What about Manny?" asked Walt. "He can see everything happening right now. You're not worried about him?"

"Manny can't see shit. And even if he could, he can't help you now. Trust me Walt, get in the fucking car and let's go," demanded Agent Steve.

The man turned back around and walked to the cop car. Walt, not seeing another option, went and got back in the Honda Accord. Just as the car had cut off on its own, it now started up the same way. He picked up the phone, but it was still dead. Something was going on, but Walt didn't know if it would help or hinder him. One thing he was sure of, it was in opposition to Manny and whatever plans he had.

Agent Steve drove passed, and Walt fell in behind him. They ended up taking the same Interstate Walt himself had prepared to take, heading west back towards Raleigh. Walt hit autopilot on his brain as he thought about this latest development and the consequences it could have on Ann, Denise, and himself.

He had no idea if Agent Steve knew about the predicament he was in. The agent might not fear or be worried about Manny, but Walt didn't have that luxury. Walt had no help. No one to back him up or look out for him. So, if he pissed Manny off, or got himself killed, those two women would pay the price for Walt's choices.

There was also another way Walt could look at this situation. If Agent Steve feared these people more than Manny, and the agent seemed to know more about Manny than anyone, maybe it was a benefit to Walt to meet with them.

The problem was, these people wouldn't care about a little collateral damage. And that's exactly what they would see Ann and Denise as. People with power always felt that the greater good was more important than a single life. They even thought you were selfish if you wouldn't sacrifice yourself for their cause. Well, fuck them. If they thought Ann and Denise would become acceptable losses then they would have another enemy on their hands.

Walt worked to draw back his anger. He was getting ahead of himself. For all he knew, these people were pulling him in because of the two women. Well, he would soon find out because Agent Steve was just exiting the Interstate.

He kicked himself mentally because he hadn't even been paying attention to where he was. He knew they had been driving for less than an hour, so nowhere near Raleigh. Walt followed the agent down a couple of very dark back roads before coming to a stop on the side of the road.

Agent Steve exited the car once again and approached the driver's side window. Walt lowered the window and the man said, "Get out and get in the passenger seat. I have to drive from here on." Walt got out and walked around the front of the car, trying to get a glimpse of the mystery man still in the cop car.

The agent was already in the car and Walt got in to find the man holding a mask. "Put this on. For your own protection, you don't want to see where we're going."

Walt didn't even bother to argue or question him. He just put the mask on and sat back in the seat. The agent beeped the horn and five seconds later they drove off into the night.

The agent started talking almost immediately. "So, I'm authorized to tell you some things that will help you understand what's going on. I can't tell you any names, that's up to each person, but I can fill in a lot of blank spaces for you."

"You were scared to tell me anything about Manny before. If these people are worse than him, why are you willing to help me now?" asked Walt.

"First of all, Manny is crazy. He didn't use to be like that, but his need for vengeance has corrupted his mind. Secondly, no one can hear us. No one at all. I have been given free rein to tell you everything I know except for names. We have about another hour to drive. Until we get to our destination, we can talk about anything and everything," said the CIA agent.

Walt had no idea if he could trust the man. He had first met the agent on the night that Ann was to be murdered by Manny. He had showed up at Walt's house and ultimately tried to convince Walt to leave the killer alone. He'd explained some of the killer's history and warned Walt that his life could be forfeit if he kept up his search. Walt had ignored the man and the result was Walt pretty much belonged to Manny now.

"Alright," said Walt. "Explain to me why Manny is so fixated on me."

"I wouldn't expect you to have figured it out, but you must have some idea as to why he's 'training' you."

"I have no idea at all," Walt replied. "Since we only have an hour, how about let's stop playing games and you give me some real information."

"Okay. He's fixated on you because he's trying to save your life." The agent let a minute pass before saying, "And Denise's life. Ann is pretty much untouchable but we'll get to that later. Right now, you need to understand that Manny is doing what he's doing to keep you safe."

"Ha," Walt barked. "How in the hell is he saving our lives? He has kidnapped Denise and he has me going around as his slave assassin."

"That's your view of it without knowing all the facts. The group that Manny really works with ordered both of your deaths over a month ago." He let that sink in before he continued. "He hasn't kidnapped Denise, he is hiding her. And he's not treating you as a slave, he's proving to the organization that you can be useful. He's training you to be an asset instead of a target."

Walt was speechless. The ring of truth in the agent's words was too loud to ignore. "Why wouldn't he just kill us and be done with it?"

"Because, contrary to what you think about him, he is a stand-up guy. He really does like you and he sees a ton of potential in you. He doesn't like Denise at all, but he feels guilty because he was the one to bring her into this madness."

"How do you know so much? I'm pretty sure you and Manny don't chat over coffee," said Walt.

"You're right, but he isn't the only person with spy gear. He's not the only genius in the world. Ever since he went rogue, the WRA has been keeping tabs on him." He took a breath and said, "We both work for the WRA."

"What the hell is the WRA? I thought you were CIA and he was Military Intelligence."

"You're right, we both are, but we also belong to the WRA, which is the World Redemption Agency. It's a deep cover U.S. Agency that does exactly what the title says; It tries to redeem the world."

"If Manny is an example of trying to redeem the world, the people over him must be monsters," said Walt.

"You have no idea. Some of these people are 100 times worse than anything you've seen from Manny. But, like I said, Manny has gone rogue. When you meet some of the WRA agents, you'll understand a lot more. The bottom line is the Agency betrayed Manny for greed. These are the types of people who believe everybody is expendable, and anyone who gets in their way has to die. Even their own agents."

Walt had a feeling time was running out. He had to get the answer to one question before the agent stopped sharing. "Why is Ann untouchable?"

The agent laughed. "It's actually a funny story. A bunch of years ago, Ann had a relationship with one of the WRA agents. A very, very senior agent. Relationships are allowed, but you have to get approval from the Agency before you reveal your real name or job to an outsider. This agent fell head over heels in love with her and he sought approval.

"He wanted to bring her in as an agent. She was working for CMPD at the time. The Agency said no. When she threatened to leave if the guy didn't fess up and tell her what was going on, they thought he broke the rules and told her anyway. The leadership threatened to kill them both if he ever saw her again. They sent someone to give her the same warning. After that, they had no more contact."

Walt was confused. "What's so funny about that story? Sounds serious to me."

The agent laughed again. "That's one that I could tell you, but I'll let you see for yourself."

Walt would have to be patient because he knew the man wouldn't tell him anymore on the subject. "So, how did the Agency betray Manny?"

"We're almost there, so I'll make this quick. All jobs are supposed to come from an agent's handlers. I was one of Manny's at the beginning. Anyway, you are never to take a dangerous job unless it's for the WRA. When Manny took the prison job, it was an unsanctioned job.

"He was new and didn't do all the right research before he committed to the job. If he had, he would have known that the operation he was attempting to shutdown was a WRA operation. The governor was actually an old asset tasked with setting up a system to use the corruption in the prisons to funnel cash to the Agency. Things started getting out of control and people started dying because of the gangs and drugs. The governor knew if he showed any sign of slowing down, the Agency would kill him. So, he reached out to the president and made it seem like the FED's were forcing the issue.

"Manny was sent in before anyone knew what he was doing, and the Agency punished him by making him stay in for ten years instead of two. They also made sure none of his reports made it to anyone who would care.

"When he finally got out and realized the Agency was the one that held him inside, he declared war on everyone involved. But he toes the line on certain things so the Agency doesn't come too hard at him."

The story left Walt dumbfounded. One thing was still nagging him. "Why doesn't the Agency just kill him and us? Seems that would be the easiest thing to do."

"I told you the reason before. They're hoping that he'll burn out on this revenge stuff and come back. He is a very important agent, and he contributes tons to their overall objective." The CIA/WRA agent paused and slowed down the car. He made a right turn onto a gravel road. As he continued to drive slowly, he said, "The main reason will be revealed to you in a few minutes. Just be prepared to get the shock of your life."

All of a sudden, the road turned into a smooth drive and they entered some kind of structure. Walt could tell because he could hear the engines echoing around the enclosed space. The mask was ripped from his face and Walt blinked as bright lights tried their best to blind him.

The building was like a small warehouse, or an airplane hangar. He glanced back and saw what looked like a barn door closing behind them. As far as he could tell looking around, that was the only way in or out of the structure. No windows to even hint at where they were. Just concrete and metal everywhere he looked.

The agent followed the black sedan up a ramp and both cars stopped side by side on the platform. Walt glanced over at the agent who was wearing a fake highway patrolman uniform.

Agent Steve was pale white and looked to be in his mid-fifties. He was tall and slim, weighed no more than 170 pounds, but had not one ounce of extra body fat. He had the movements and carriage of a career military man. The agent smiled and extended his had to Walt.

"My real name is Paul Stevens. I hate that every time we meet it is under life-or-death circumstances." Walt shook the man's hand as the platform began to lower into the ground. Neither said another word as the cars descended about 50 feet into total darkness. When they reached the bottom, both cars turned their headlights on and went down a ramp and proceeded down a short driveway that ended in an underground parking area.

Both cars parked and Paul said, "Listen Walt. Stay calm. Keep your head and don't argue with these people. If they think you're not on board, they will kill you. It's up to you who you ultimately decide to help, but remember, both sides have their pros and cons. And no matter what you decide, you'll have a deadly enemy on your back, but a powerful ally by your side. One last thing. Not trying to influence you, I just want you to know the truth. Promises or guarantees don't mean shit to these people. And they all know how important Ann and Denise are to you. Just know, they have no way of getting them back for you. Manny is the only person who can do that. And if he feels you've betrayed him, those women will die." With that, the agent motioned for Walt to get out and they both exited the vehicle.

A group of about twenty was standing around a collection of computers studying something on the screens. The group was mixed with different genders and races, but a small sub group of six was off in a circle talking amongst themselves. Paul led Walt over to the sub group and in masse, they turned towards the newcomers, except for one who kept his back towards them.

Paul did the introductions. "What's going on everyone? This is Sergeant Detective Walter Rogers of the NC SBI. You guys can introduce yourselves to him."

Before anyone could say anything, the guy who had kept his back to Walt turned around and faced him head on. Walt took a step back and looked at Paul in shock. "Is this a fucking joke? What the hell is going on here?"

It wasn't Paul who answered, it was the guy with the familiar face who said, "No Walt, this isn't a fucking game or a joke. And if you keep your mouth shut, you might learn what the hell is going on here."

Walt looked around at everyone but kept coming back to Paul. The last hour of conversation meant little. All the information he had been given amounted to nothing. He looked back at the speaker's eyes and did exactly what he advised. Walt closed his mouth and prayed someone would explain the chaos he now found himself in.

CHAPTER 12

Manny got a text from his source that a two-year-old Ford Explorer had been delivered to Alisha at 3:00 pm. Since he didn't get the text until he was on his way back to Charlotte, he guessed that his girls were at the mall by now. A quick text and answer from Alisha confirmed his guess.

He was only about twenty minutes from the mall, but he needed to clean up and change his clothes. Because of his proclivity to kill at any moment, he always kept a change of clothes in any car he drove. With that in mind, he exited the Interstate and pulled into a cheap motel parking lot.

Thirty minutes later, he was fresh and clean with some casual, but expensive, clothes on. He was a little bruised, but ready and excited about spending some time with his new family.

He would have to keep the modified police car until he got close to home, but that shouldn't be a problem. There were so many government unmarked cars floating around, one more shouldn't cause a stir. He checked on Walt's progress and saw that he was on the road headed east. He smiled as he climbed into the Crown Vic and took off.

Manny had a good feeling about Walt. He thought the man would eventually come around and become the killer Manny knew he could be. After the torture classes and the deaths that resulted, Walt's body count was now in the double digits. And Manny had video of them all.

Walt thought the videos were to keep him in line, which was only partly true. That wasn't the main reason. The main reason was to show certain people that Walt would be of better use alive than dead. The WRA didn't like to change its mind once a decision was made, but Manny was going to stand firm on this one. If they ended up going ahead with a plan against Walt, he would burn the whole organization to the ground. Pulling into the mall parking lot, he decided to put all business out of his mind and focus on having fun for a while.

Concord Mills was a massive mall in Concord, North Carolina. It contained everything that a consumer could ever think to buy. The mall had indoor and outdoor entertainment, as well as every kind of eatery to fulfill any craving. He could walk around for days and never catch sight of Alisha or Gabby, so he sent another text to find out exactly where they were. When the reply came in, he told them to stay put and he drove to the closest entrance to their location. He let out a little laugh because, out of the hundreds of stores, if he had to guess, this would have been the first store he would have went looking for two young ladies.

When Manny walked into the huge shoe store that was a woman's dream come true, he nearly turned around and went back out. There were so many women in the store, he thought it would take half the day to find any particular person you happened to be looking for. But it was like his heart sent a message to his brain, which sent a message to his eyes, to look at a certain spot to find the meaning of life.

Gabby was sitting on a couch with what had to be 15 boxes of shoes around her. She sported a beautiful, gleeful smile on her face, and she practically vibrated with joyful energy. She was wearing a pair of lady cross-trainers that matched perfectly with the blue and white skirt set she had on. To see the excitement flowing through her body almost brought tears to his eyes. But that wasn't the sight that nearly stopped his heart.

Alisha was sitting like a Queen on her throne in a chair right next to the couch. She was wearing a sundress that matched the skirt set Gabby had on. Her legs were crossed and the open toe sandals she wore showcased her beautiful, flawlessly pedicured toes to perfection.

She was a goddess. She was his goddess. But even with all the beautiful, dark chocolate skin of her legs, arms, and chest on display, that still wasn't what caused the rest of the world to dissolve into the background.

She was wearing minimal make-up, as her even skin tone didn't need any help to shine bright. Her hair was down around her shoulders, framing the most stunning face he'd ever seen. Her lips had that wet, pink, plumpness that took his mind places they would definitely have to explore in the near future. But even with all that wet dream worthy gorgeousness right there for the world to admire, that wasn't what caused his mouth to go dry.

Alisha had been waiting and watching for him. Saying her eyes are brown doesn't do them justice. Maybe russet or chocolate would better describe the color. With all his formal, and not so formal, education, he couldn't come up with a descriptive word to delineate the hue of her eyes. Right now, he was paralyzed because he was falling deep into the love he saw floating in her gaze. It was accompanied by a look of yearning so intense, Manny associated it with a thirsty man seeing a cold glass of water.

They were both locked in a staring battle that had nothing to do with competition and everything to do with completeness. Neither could move as they shared their most intimate feelings for each other, separated by a crowded store.

"Can I help you with something handsome?" came a flirtatious voice. Manny became aware that the voice had been talking to him for a while. "I hope you need some shoes for your mother or sister and not a girlfriend or wife."

Manny looked over at her and acknowledged that she was a very attractive woman. But her light was a match compared to Alisha's bonfire. He smiled at her and said, "I'm good, thank you. Everything I need is sitting right there on that couch and chair." With that, he walked towards his family like he had blinders on.

Her parting comment as he left was, "Damn. I can't even be mad. Your wife and daughter are beautiful."

About ten feet from them, Gabby caught sight of him. She said, "Daddy! Daddy! Look at my new outfit," as she did a little twirl. "And Mommy told me I could get as many shoes as I wanted. We've already made two trips back to the car to drop off clothes and stuff. This is the best day ever." She ran over and gave him a tight squeeze around the mid-section.

He hugged her back as Alisha started to rise. At 5-foot 8-inches to his six feet, she was the perfect height to fit against his body. He gave her a small peck on the lips because anything more might have been too dangerous for their current location. He was already responding to her feel and her smell. He took a step back so he could gain control of himself. Being her, she noticed what he was doing and why. She let out a small seductive laugh in response.

After they left the shoe store, they had to make a trip to the Explorer. All in all, the family excursion was a huge success. Manny found out that Gabby was perhaps the funniest ten-year-old on the planet as she told jokes and had them laughing the whole time. It was a sight to behold watching her true personality emerge now that she wasn't living in pain or fear. He did notice that anytime she saw a security guard or cop, she would get quiet and grab one of their hands. He would have to do something to extinguish that fear pretty soon. He refused to let her live in fear of anything.

They ate. They walked. They talked. They shopped and had to make several more trips to the Explorer to store their goods. But more than anything, they just enjoyed each other's company. At one point, Gabby was playing a game in the arcade and it left Manny and Alisha alone sitting in a booth watching her.

"Do you feel a sense of completeness now that we have Gabby with us?" Alisha asked.

Manny sensed that she was leading up to something, as her mood had changed after they sat down, so he answered her truthfully. "Yeah, I do. We were happy together with just us, but now I feel.... I don't know. Enhanced."

"Listen," Alisha said with a serious look on her face. "I know this might seem like it's coming from nowhere, but I need to ask you a couple of serious questions. And I need you to be 100% honest with me."

Getting a little nervous, Manny said, "Okay. Ask away."

"I want to have kids and I'd like to know how you feel about that." Alisha was very direct and Manny wanted to laugh and smile and jump for joy, but knew the situation didn't call for that. This was to be a very serious conversation about the future for him and his woman.

"Alisha, I'm being serious when I say this. You give me a number and we'll start on it tonight." He did smile then, but only when he saw the relief flash on her face. "I'm all in with you babe. Anything you want, I will happily give you. And having kids with you isn't exactly a one-way street. The process being what it is, I hope the number is in the teens."

Alisha laughed, but there was still nerves and questions floating behind her eyes. "In that case, I did a little shopping for the two of us also." She looked back at where Gabby had been joined by another little girl, and then turned back to look at Manny with uncertainty in her eyes.

"Our lives are very hectic. Well, more yours than mine now. But we don't really have any certainty in our lives." Manny started to reassure her, but she held up her hand to silence him. "I know what you said about us being taken care of. But Manny, I don't want to be taken care of. I want to be happy."

She reached back and pulled her bag around to her lap. For some reason he couldn't figure out, his heart started to beat a little faster.

Alisha said, "You know how I am. I'm not really the shy, beat-around-the-bush type of girl. I go for what I want and I don't stop until I get it." She reached in her bag and pulled something out, but kept it hidden between her hands.

Beyond Alisha's head was a huge digital clock that read 6:48 pm. Because the arcade was dark all the time, Manny guessed it helped people keep up with the time. He kept his main focus on Alisha, but he also maintained awareness of Gabby and any potential threats to what was his.

Alisha, having finally worked herself up to the point, said, "I love you Manny and I want to spent the rest of my life with you. I want to be the mother of your children and I want to have your last name." As she said the last word, she placed a ring box on the table between them. "Manuel Adams, will you propose to me so I can say yes and we can get married?"

Manny leaned back in his seat and just stared at the amazing, magnificent, woman sitting across from him. He was speechless. Immobile. Alisha didn't give an inch. She just sat there staring right back at him. Finally, able to talk, Manny asked, "Did you buy this today?"

After a few seconds, she nodded her head and said, "Yes. The first store we went to was a jewelry store. I know how you are. You're in the middle of something and you wouldn't even think to ask. I know how you feel, I just wanted to help you move in the right direction."

Manny nodded, picked up the ring box, and opened it. He gave a low whistle as he admired the $200,000 plus ring. "Well, I have excellent taste if I picked this out for you." It was a Le Vian Couture platinum engagement ring with more than 10 carats of chocolate and yellow Ombre diamonds. It had to have been a custom piece that didn't work out too well for someone else. But Manny knew it would shine like the sun against Alisha's dark chocolate skin tone.

If they were alone, he would have dropped down on one knee, but he couldn't draw that much attention to them. Taking out the ring, he looked deep into her eyes, and said, "Alisha Saffiyah Harden, will you do me the honor of being my wife?" He expected her to give him a soft yes and then they would stand up, embrace, and then kiss softly. But that's not what he got.

"On one condition," was what she said. He was astonished. How in the hell could she put a condition on something she came up with? But, because he would do anything to make this woman his wife, he gestured for her to continue.

Then she asked him for the one thing that could bring their world crashing down on their heads. "Manny, I can't change my name to one of your aliases. In order for us to get married, I have to know your real name."

. . . .

In a subterranean office, about a hundred miles away from the mall, a serious discussion was taking place.

"Look," said the young Asian woman. "He's changed a lot over the years and I'm not his biggest fan, but he knows the rules. He's not going to forfeit all their lives just to prove a point!"

The young man that she was arguing with looked at her like she was crazy. "Where the hell have you been the last 13 years? He's proven time and time again that he'll break every rule just to prove a point. I say we kill the whole lot of them and then we can stop wasting man power checking on his ass."

They were sitting in front of a bank of computer screens that, at this moment, showed hundreds of views of Concord Mills mall. The center screen was locked on the couple sitting in a booth in the arcade.

The woman's mouth gaped in shock. "How the hell can you of all people say that? He's your...."

"Fuck him!" the man shouted, cutting the woman off. "How can you still defend him after what he did to you? If it was up to me, he would've been dead a long time ago."

"Well, let's be glad it's not up to you," said a mature voice behind them. Both the young man and woman stood up and remained at attention silently while the small figure made its way into the room. "Mercy is something we all need from time to time. I remember when it was you that everyone wanted to kill. Mercy saved you. I'd have thought you of all people would understand the dilemma he's in."

The man stayed silent, but his jaw worked furiously with the need to defend himself.

When the lights from the monitors revealed the figure, most people would have been surprised. The leader of the WRA was a 5 foot, 60 something year old woman with a head full of gray curls, thick glasses, and the upright posture of the military commander she was.

This woman had started wars and ended them. Dozens of governments only had the control they maintained because of the oppositions fear of her. Those who looked at her and just saw a thin, old lady, did so to their own detriment.

"Well, I already know what his recommendation would be," she said to the young woman. "What do you suggest? And please, take your seats and speak freely."

After taking her seat, the woman said, "We don't have a lot of time to implement it, but I think we should give him something to think about before he makes a huge mistake."

"Tell me what you have in mind," demanded the old woman. After the younger woman laid out her plan, the old woman said, "I like it, but this isn't our normal target. This could go horribly bad, so I'm counting on the two of you to make it work." When the young man continued to sulk in his seat, she said, "Do I make myself clear?"

The young woman quickly said, "Yes Ma'am."

After a few seconds of tense silence, the man said a grudging, "Yes Ma'am."

"Good," she replied back. "Now get back to it and make this thing work."

. . . .

Manny was heartbroken. He would give Alisha and Gabby the world, but what she was asking of him was impossible. He sat back and let out a gush of air.

"I mean, come on. You can't expect me to be Mrs. Manuel Adams when everyone in the world knows that is not your real name. Listen," she said leaning forward. "Sooner or later, something will happen to you on one of your trips. Then I'll be left in the dark without ever knowing my husband's name. Is that what you want for us? Is that what you would want for our children?" she asked as she pleaded with him with her eyes.

"Alisha, I understand where you're coming from. But what you're asking of me is impossible. I have broken almost every rule in the book to fulfill my own personal mission. This is the one rule that, if I break, there is no coming back from. You have to understand, this is for your own protection."

"Manny, I love you. You! I really don't care what your name is. But this is something that I can't budge on. Even if I do take that name, I will not marry a man who doesn't trust me."

Manny's hand flew to his heart for fear that it would jump out of his chest. "You don't think I trust you?" he asked in amazement. "I have given you everything. Access to everything. I keep nothing from you. I love you and you know I trust you. But you have to trust me when I tell you that some information is too dangerous to share."

Alisha looked at him in confusion. "So, you trust me with billions of dollars? You trust me with information that could send you to Death Row? You even trust me enough to plan to have children with me and marry me? I don't understand what I have to do or say to make you trust me fully. It's been over a year. I will never betray you. I love you with all that I am." As she said the last part, a tear tracked down her beautiful face. Angrily she wiped it away.

Manny, looking pained, reached forward and grabbed her hands. He was still holding the engagement ring. He extended her fingers and slid the ring home. He locked eyes with her and said, "I want you to be my wife. I also love you with all that I am. But I told you from the beginning I would never hurt you. If I give you that information, I could be ending your life. I can't take that chance. Let's get married, have our children, and when the time is right, maybe I'll be able to give that to you."

More tears escaped from her eyes as she pulled her hand back and admired the ring she had chosen for herself. Manny saw the decision in her eyes before she committed the act. She pulled the ring from her finger and sat it softly down on the table. She said, "I can't be with you tonight. Please find somewhere else to stay and I'll see you tomorrow." She got up from the booth and started walking towards Gabby.

"Alisha!" Manny said with such force it caused her to turn and look back at him. "Sit down." This was not a request or suggestion. This was a direct order that he knew she would be powerless to obey.

Showing a maturity well beyond her years, she slowly made her way back to the booth and reclaimed her seat.

She was still crying softly with her eyes downcast. "Look at me," Manny demanded. When she looked up and met his eyes, he said, "Alright. I get you. I understand. You don't just want trust, you want me to place my faith in you."

He rubbed a hand down his face and focused on her again. "These people have ruled my life and have ruined my life for too long. I refuse to let them come between us. Put that ring back on your finger!" he demanded.

He watched her as she did what he commanded. His mind made up, he glanced up to check on Gabby as she played the games, and just like that, everything changed. Standing next to Gabby was a familiar face that turned Manny's blood cold. The man locked eyes with him and then made his way to another booth.

"Alisha," said Manny in a tone that conveyed urgency and that the killer was now in control. "Stand up and go get Gabby. Go directly to the Explorer and text me as soon as you are safely inside. Watch for a tail and let me know if anyone follows you. Do you understand me?" At no time did he take his eyes off the man sitting in the other booth.

Alisha, having spent so much time in the gang world, understood that something had just changed the situation. She nodded, got up, pulled Gabby off of the machine, and they made their way out of the mall. Manny didn't move a muscle until the text came through that they were both in the Explorer and on their way.

Then he got up and walked over to the other booth and sat directly across from the man. Forgoing any small talk, Manny said, "If anything happens to them, you will be the fourth to die. I'll make sure it's slow and painful and I won't let you expire until you've seen how I finish off your wife and two kids."

CHAPTER 13

Ghost, A.K.A. Jamar Gorden, was one of the most dangerous men in the world. The WRA agent had more kills on his record than any man in the history of the agency. The nickname came about because of his otherworldly skill to kill so many people and not be detected. To some people, even inside of the Agency, he is just a myth. To Manny, he was just a pain in the ass.

After Manny delivered his threat, Ghost just smiled and tossed his dreads back over his shoulder. At 5-foot 10-inches, 230 pounds, and having almost albino, colorless skin, you would think he would be easy to spot. But, because of his unnatural ability to blend in, and his methodical movements, he became one of the most respected stealth killers in the industry. Even with all of his accolades, they both knew that he wasn't a match for Manny without the element of surprise. As they sat now, locked in a silent battle of wills, they both could conclude that this was a life and death situation for both of them.

When Manny's phone signaled this time, he assumed it was Alisha informing him of a new development. It turned out to be Walt activating the cameras at Jerome Fox's house. When he saw Walt's dumbass without his mask on, he decided to warn the detective so he didn't have to fail his mission.

He excused himself, but only went far enough so the other agent couldn't hear what was said. After he warned the killer in training about his mask, he stalked back over to the booth to finish his confrontation with the legend they called Ghost.

Short and to the point, Manny said, "Tell me what you are doing here or this will be your last day on earth."

Ghost stopped smiling and said in a deep voice, "Half the Agency wants you dead. The other half wants to use you. Sides change all the time depending on what day it is. Or whichever rule you have just broken. For today, no one wants to see you die. So, I was sent here to remind you that some rules you can break, others you can bend. But there are some that no one can come back from once they are broken."

"Is this message from the top or from someone who actually gives a damn about me?"

Ghost sighed and said, "It's from the top and you might be surprised who actually gives a damn about you. Anyway, I've done my duty and now the ball is in your court." He leaned back and said, "For the record, I don't give a rat's ass about you. I don't care if you live or die. But I do understand where you are coming from. As you so delicately put it a minute ago, I have a wife and kids. Some of us are just not meant to be alone, no matter how fucked up we are." Getting up, he left Manny with a small warning. "Just remember, nothing is private. They hear and see everything. So, if you take that last step, be prepared for what comes after."

Manny's phone signaled again. He looked down for maybe half a second, but when he looked up again, the Ghost was gone. He let his instincts roam free and decided that he was safe for the time being. He needed to get home with his family but he had one more crisis to deal with first.

Manny picked his phone back up and watched the video of Walt slowly losing control of the scene. Jerome and Olivia were taking advantage of Walt's lack of experience and things could get ugly really fast if Walt didn't tighten up. Manny sent him another text to that effect then he stood up and made his way out of the mall to the privacy of his car.

Once inside the car, he called Alisha to find out how she and Gabby were holding up.

Alisha answered and got right to the point. "We're on our way home now. No one has followed us but you of all people know that, if they are serious, they wouldn't follow us in a car. I turned on the new black box you gave me just in case they bugged us. So, we should be good on that part."

Manny would always be ten steps ahead of anyone trying to outsmart him. He had given Alisha an upgraded black box that only allowed her phone to talk to his phone when activated. It blocked every signal known to man, including video, audio, radio, and a few that most people knew nothing about. He hadn't even had time to build a device to counter it should someone get a hold to one of his.

The box also sent out a pulse every few seconds that made a drone or satellite surveillance impossible. It just fried the circuits of any video capturing equipment other than the ones that have his own special signature. And no one on this earth could duplicate his signature. He didn't care at all, but as she was driving, Alisha was causing millions of dollars in damage because of that little black box being activated.

After they talked for a while and he was sure that they were safe, and she was sure that he understood that their earlier conversation was not over, they both hung up and Manny was ready to follow his family home.

But for some reason, God, or maybe the devil, had it in for him today. As soon as he went to turn the key to start the car, his phone signaled again, and all Manny could do was laugh and shake his head.

Walt was in a world of shit. The drone that Manny had looking down on Walt had picked up a cop car driving into the vicinity. Manny put his phone on the dashboard holder and watched as the cop car stopped right in front of the Fox residence. As soon as they got out and separated, Manny made the call to warn Walt what was going on.

After the video played for a while, he watched as Walt came out of the house and killed both officers. He pulled back the view of the drone to watch a broader view to see if he would have to use the drone to save Walt's ass. Naturally the drone had a few offensive weapons added to it.

He saw Walt sprint back into the house, so he split the screen to see the bedroom and the area surrounding the house. For the time being everything looked clear on the outside, so he focused on Walt carrying out the task assigned to him.

Manny knew that Walt was a good and honorable man. But the way he shot Olivia and then hacked into Jerome almost brought a tear to Manny's eye. After this exhibition there couldn't be any doubt that Walt was an asset, not a liability. Walt would still have to continue his training but Manny might be able to release the women and remove that chain from around Walt's neck. First things first, Walt had to escape from the hell about to fall all around him when those cops didn't check in.

Walt finished up and ran hard out of the house. Manny switched back to the full drone view and watched Walt running full out down the middle of the street in the dark. He made it to the Honda and was rolling before any back up arrived to the area.

When Manny pulled the drone view back even farther, he gave Walt a 50/50 shot at making it to the highway. There were cop cars heading his way from every direction. Walt was maybe a mile from the highway when the screen on Manny's phone suddenly went black.

He snatched it off of the stand and saw the phone was still active and the drone was still on but the video signal was being blocked. Manny switched to several different frequencies and got the same result; nothing. He closed the app and tried to call up the video of the camera on Walt's shirt. It too showed a connection but the video feed showed only a blank screen.

Manny, still not panicking, dialed Walt's cell phone number. This was a direct-to-direct cell phone. Walt couldn't even dial 411 with it. Now Manny started getting nervous because all he got was a busy signal, which should have been impossible with the program Manny had set up on the phone.

"No fucking way," Manny muttered as he went back to the drone video and hit the rewind button until the video showed Walt closing in on the interstate one more time. He hit the screen jump button until the screen went black and then he jumped it back frame by frame until he had the last visible frame on his screen.

What he saw at the bottom right of the screen, coming up behind Walt, caused a murderous rage to boil up inside of him. He could just see the hood of a black car coming into view and he had no doubt who it was in that car. Maybe not the exact person but he knew who had sent them.

"These mother fuckers just don't learn," he said as he replaced the phone, popped the trunk and exited the vehicle. He went around and opened the trunk and then closed it back after retrieving a little black case. He returned to his seat and unpacked a few small devices and then inserted a small ear piece.

He also pulled out a small screen that, after he typed a few commands, showed a blinking red dot and a blinking green dot on a map. The red dot signified Manny's own position on the screen. The green dot told Manny exactly where Walt was with a constant stream of GPS as well as longitude and latitude coordinates.

Using the map in his head and a constant review of the data on the screen, he knew exactly where Walt was and had a very good idea of where he was going. But he needed to check on something before he went any further.

He called Alisha and she answered with a quick, "We are pulling into the gate now. We are good and as soon as I get up to the house, I'm going to the saferoom and I'm locking both of us in until I hear from you."

A weight lifted off of Manny's chest and he gave a slight laugh. "Alisha. Do you know me as a man who would just have a safe room? That bullshit was there when I bought the house. Put your birthday into the keypad when you go in, and for no reason at all, are you to go back outside. Mines will activate and there will be a two foot, specified path that has to be taken to reach the house. I'm the only person alive who knows the path.

"That code also activates an air defense system that rivals the one protecting the White House. Just stay inside and I'll be home in the morning. I have a few things to handle before I can come home."

Alisha said, "Manny. Please be careful and please come home in one piece." She fumbled the phone around and mumbled something before coming back to say, "I love you and Gabby wants to speak to you." After some more fumbling, Gabby's soft voice came on the line.

"Dad?" she asked timidly.

"Hi sweetheart. Listen, don't be scared. Everything is going to be fine. Just listen to Alisha and I'll see you tomorrow."

"I'm not scared. I just wanted to make sure you're not mad at me for playing all those games and spending all that money. I think I just got carried away because I was having so much fun."

"Gabby, I can never be mad at you. I want you to listen to me and understand what I am saying. Okay?"

"Yes daddy," she said sounding close to tears.

"If you want every day of the rest of your life to be like today, then that's what I will give you. I love you Gabby and I will never stop loving you. I will do anything and give you anything to make sure you are happy. Nothing will ever hurt you again. Do you believe me?"

"Yes," was her soft reply.

"Good, because I am telling you the truth. You are my daughter now and I will protect you with my life. Now cheer up kid and know that you have a real family now." After some heartfelt goodbyes, they hung up and Manny was ready to put in some major work.

There was no way to go back and listen to what had been said before Manny had put the ear piece in, but anything that was said from now on, by Walt or around Walt, Manny would hear it.

During one of their last torture training exercises, Walt had cut his arm pretty bad. Walt, having seen that Manny was a legitimate doctor, let him do his stitches so Walt wouldn't have to go to the hospital. Manny had given him a local to numb the pain, but he had also injected him with a state-of-the-art tracking device that Manny and Manny alone could pick up. No scanner or reader could possibly detect it because it was made out of things already found in the body.

It operated off of the same electricity that constantly ran through the human body. It was situated in Walt's arm but it could pick up sounds from up to ten feet away. It could also pinpoint a person's location down to the foot no matter where they were in the world. Alisha had one in her arm and Gabby would be the next person to get one. He would not lose a single person under his protection. And anyone dumb enough to encroach on what was his, faced the possibility of losing their lives.

He started the car and began the journey to intercept Walt. He wouldn't get there in time to stop the meeting that he was sure was on the agenda. But he would definitely be close enough to make a move if he had to. In the meantime, he would keep the ear piece in and listen to every word spoken by or to Walt. For Walt's sake, he better not try and betray him. If he does, he will die, and a lot of people will join him in death.

Manny was chugging along, heading east, when all of a sudden, he heard his good friend Paul say, "Get out and get in the passenger seat. I have to drive from here on." Depending on what else he heard from him, this very well might be the agent's last day on earth.

The next thing Manny heard was Paul telling Walt to put on what Manny assumed was a mask. When Manny heard, "So I'm authorized to tell you some things..." he plugged his phone into a port on the device so that he could record everything for later reference. Video was always nice, but the next best thing when it came to proof, was someone's own voice on an audio recording.

Now that his family was safely behind the walls of the fortress he had made, Manny dedicated all of his attention to what was being said over the earpiece. He wished that he had The Beast but the modified cop car would have to do. It was no slouch in the speed and power department, and with the official plates connected to it, no cop in their right mind would try to stop him for a speeding ticket.

As Manny drove and listened, he was getting more frustrated by the minute. The agent was telling Walt all the things that, if they came from Manny, would be a declaration of all-out war. It was just another example of the power hungry WRA leadership just wanting control of every situation. And this move on Walt was just another attempt to bring Manny back under their control.

Really, the only thing that surprised Manny was that Agent Stevens was being honest about the things he said. He expected Paul to lie and try to trick Walt into believing that the WRA was the best way to go. The fact that he believed no one could hear him gave a certain honor to the man that Manny didn't know he possessed.

The story about Ann was on a whole different level. Manny knew exactly what Agent Paul was talking about and it cleared up the untouchable tag being placed on her. And Paul was right. When Walt got to the underground compound, he would get the shock of his life. Thinking back, it also explained why Ann was different around him since he had showed her his face. It also left a suspicion in his head that would definitely be cleared up by the end of the night.

When Paul gave Walt the final warning, Manny knew that Paul was genuinely on his side. He pretty much told Walt to say whatever they wanted to hear but to understand that they were lying to him. Manny was using Ann and Denise only as a means of saving all of their lives. The WRA would use them to get to Walt so that they could use Walt to get to Manny. By Paul telling Walt that the WRA didn't know where the women were, he solidified Walt as an ally to Manny.

The truth was, the WRA knew exactly where the women were. They had been trying to hack into the security on the prison since he took Ann there. Manny knew that he was under constant surveillance, but he also knew that he could "ghost" anytime he wanted to. He had been ghosting every time he went to the prison, but he wasn't arrogant enough to think the WRA's I.T. department hadn't picked up some clues from his behavior. Being as he had trained the head of the I.T. department, they should have known about it before he started using it. But with the security parameters he had set up on that prison, anyone trying to go in or out without him knowing would be making a fatal mistake. So even though they had figured out where the women were, the WRA couldn't do a thing about it.

After Agent Stevens finished making his final statement of warning, there was silence for a bit as Manny imagined them walking across the huge open space of the underground headquarters of the WRA. Then he heard the agent speak to what must have been a group of WRA agents. The next voice he heard caused a slow boil to begin in his blood.

He listened to the back and forth between Walt and the speaker before everything went silent except for the sound of footsteps. Manny put half his mind to driving but the other half was prepared to hear all the bullshit that was sure to come from the mouth of this liar. This betrayer. This backstabber. This so called......Brother.

CHAPTER 14

Walt was 49 years old. He'd been working in law enforcement since he was 22 years old. Looking around now, he could not understand how he had never heard of the WRA. This wasn't some rinky-dink, toy soldier operation. This was a fully sanctioned, probably federally funded, Agency that obviously had carte blanche to do whatever it thought needed to be done.

As Walt rode down the elevator that continued to go down, even after he was sure they had reached the Earth's core, he couldn't fathom how big this underground operation had to be. The agents rode down in silence like this was a ride they took multiple times a day, which Walt was sure they did. Paul glanced at him, then at the designated speaker, and shook his head slightly. Walt took it as a warning to be cautious around the other man.

The elevator finally stopped its descent and everyone filed out into what looked like the lobby of a down town office building. No one said a thing, so Walt just kept following behind the group with Paul walking right beside him. As Walt looked around, he noticed no decorations or pictures or anything to make the space look welcoming. Instead, he noticed that everything was clean and only the things that were needed were present. The group didn't look around or hesitate in the least. They headed right for a closed door on the other side of the lobby.

The speaker from upstairs opened the way into a very ordinary conference room that could have been in any law firm in the country. It contained a table with chairs enough to seat 20, and a huge monitor on the wall that showed only a blank screen.

Everyone took seats that had to have been assigned to them because they all sat with no rhyme or reason and it left several open spots at the table. The end of the table closest to the door had two empty spots and Paul started to lead Walt to a seat when a voice stopped them in their tracks.

"What the fuck are you doing Paul? He hasn't earned the right to sit at our table. He stands," said the speaker.

"Don't worry," said Paul with a smile. "I was going to let him sit in my lap."

The speaker lunged up but another man put his hand up and said, "Everyone chill." He looked at Paul and Walt and said, "Sit anywhere except the head of the table."

Paul tauntingly smiled at the other man and took a seat. Walt came and sat down right next to him. Everything was quiet for a few minutes while everyone fiddled with their phones. Then, with an unspoken cue, everyone put their phones away and turned to look at Walt. He had a suspicion they had all been texting one another.

The man who had stopped the violence with just his raised hand said, "We know everything there is to know about you Detective Rogers. You have been a thorn in our sides for a while now. We thought you were working for a rival Agency at one point because it seemed like every one of your investigations had one of our agents in its crosshair. We decided that you had to go."

177

The speech was delivered like he was ordering from a fast-food worker. He said the last part like he was ordering fries instead of admitting to putting out a hit on a senior officer in the North Carolina SBI.

The man continued. "After some deeper research and consideration, we have decided to spare your life and offer you a chance to make a real difference in the world. Before you make your decision, I've called a group of our senior agents to introduce themselves and show you that not all of our agents are homicidal maniacs. I'll start since I've done most of the talking so far. And by the way, these are our real names and titles because we trust that you will make the right decision." With a smile he said, "If you don't, it won't matter. You'll be too dead to tell anyone."

He looked around at the other agents and nodded like a decision had been made. "My name is Reginald Burke and I am head of operations here at WRA. You can call me Reg or Reggie, either is good with me."

Reggie looked to be in his early 40's with his low salt and pepper cut. He wore a black suit that was clearly tailored to show off the rippling muscles on his 6-foot 3-inch, 240-pound frame. He had the dark skin and the ultra-white smile that a lot of women found attractive on a man. But the suave and smooth package didn't fool Walt for a minute. His eyes and his movements marked him as a killer of the highest caliber.

He looked around the table and said, "Don't everyone speak at once." It was said softly, but there was no mistaking the command behind it. Everyone sat up a little straighter and got with the program.

"Hi Det. Rogers. My name is Phung Lei and I am head of surveillance and internal investigations. Pretty much, I just run the I.T. Department."

Phung Lei looked to be in her late 20's and she was probably the most exquisite and dazzling woman in the world. She was extremely pretty with long, raven-black hair, and piercing light brown eyes. With her product launching face and her 5-foot 2-inch, 115-pound body, she could make Hollywood fall at her feet. But, to be the head of the I.T. at this huge Agency, it was clear that her looks were a distant second to her amazing brain.

Walt's head swung when another woman began to talk. "And I'm Kashonda Wilson and I am the head of Intelligence for the WRA. I have two daughters who also work here and would be in this meeting if they were not in the field. Their names are Tonya and Nyaira. You make the right choice and you might get to meet them one day."

The brown skin, hazel eyed beauty looked like she was too young to have kids old enough to be out in the field. She was short, just a tad over five feet, with short, light brown hair and a stunning smile. Walt's head pivoted from Reggie to Kashonda and back again before Kashonda smiled and said, "Yes, he is my little brother. Well, younger brother anyway." Her eyes then swung to the original speaker who seemed to hate Walt on sight.

"I guess I'm next in this little introduction party," he stated snidely. "I'm Delmas Burke and I'm head of mission development. Which means if you don't join the right team, I'll be the one developing the mission to kill your ass."

"And if you can't be a professional instead of a little brat, then you won't be head of anything," said Reggie. He turned to Walt and said, "Our little brother." The tone he used replaced the words with, "Our pain in the ass."

Under closer inspection, Walt could see little tale-tale differences between Manny and Delmas. But they were still close enough to be twins. He even wore Manny's customary outfit of all black. They were both a little over 6 feet. Both weighed about 200 pounds. Both had bald heads with light brown skin. Their voices even sounded the same. Walt knew Manny could change his voice at will, so he had to assume that Delmas could also.

Walt had stayed quiet up until this point because he was soaking in all the new information. "Not to interrupt but that would mean…"

Reggie nodded and said, "Your "Manny" is our youngest brother. We'll get into all of that later on. For now, let's finish the intros."

The next two introductions were short and to the point. Mary Sue Truesdale introduced herself as the property and office manager. Then she gestured towards a younger woman who she said was her daughter, as well as the accountant for the WRA. With pride Mary Sue said that her daughter, Dollis Truesdale, handled all the budgets and payroll for all WRA operations and personnel.

Mary Sue looked to be in her 50's with her long blond hair, green eyes, and her full-figured, mature body. She looked to be mixed with maybe white and black and was about 5-feet 9-inches tall.

Her daughter, Dollis, who still hadn't said a word, was a slimmer, curvier, slightly shorter version of her mother. She couldn't have been over 30 years old. Both women were good looking and obviously smart as well.

Reggie, who Walt figured had to be in charge, pulled out a phone and dialed a number. After a second, he said, "He's ready," and hung up. No one said a word for about five minutes.

All of a sudden, Delmas stood up and said, "Well, this has been nice. Some of us can't just sit behind a desk all day to do our jobs, so I'm going to say bye for now." He turned to Walt and said with a smile, "I might look like him, but don't think for a second that we are anything alike. I'm a real soldier. I follow orders without deviation. So, I'm hoping that you make the wrong choice and you get to see what a real Burke is like when he's your enemy."

Kashonda got as far as saying his name before the door opened and she closed her mouth. Delmas didn't move either as Walt's head swung around to see who had entered that commanded so much respect.

If Walt had been a less trained man, he would have discounted the older woman as the source for the new tension in the room. A closer look forced you to see the power and strength of will flowing through the thin body.

She walked in and made a beeline to the head of the table where she stood and looked at everyone in turn. Before she got to Walt, her eyes lasered to Delmas. "Going somewhere?" She asked him.

"You know that we have work to do," he answered. "You want me to sit here making good with this motherfucker and waste the whole night?"

Fast as a lightning strike, Delmas was face down on the table with a visibly angry Reggie holding him down. "I've had enough of you!" he said. "You disrespect my mother again and I'll knock your teeth down your throat." Just as fast, Delmas got himself free and jumped right in Reggie's face.

He said, "Put your hands on me again, and I'll be the only Burke currently working for the WRA. That's if they don't kill me for killing you."

The older woman turned to Walt, ignoring the two men. "My name is Lucille Drake and I am the head of the World Redemption Agency. Reggie, have a seat," she said, turning her attention back to the brothers. "And Delmas, go do whatever it is you have to do." Like the president had just given a soldier an order, both of them followed her commands without hesitation.

Lucille Drake looked to be in her mid-60's. She was five feet flat with a head full of gray curls and, even though she was thin, she looked healthy and fit. She had light skin that hinted at a mixed heritage and she had the posture and bearing of a 5 star General. As she sat, she adjusted her thick glasses and once again looked at Walt.

"As you can see, even though we are a worldwide Agency, we are still a family run organization." At Walt's confused look at the Truesdale's and Ms. Lei, Mrs. Drake smiled and said, "Mary Sue is my sister and of course that makes Dollis my niece. As for Phung, well dear, you tell him."

Phung turned to Walt and said, "Before, uh, "Manny" took the prison job, we were engaged to be married. Obviously, he never came back, but this is still my family."

The killer? Manny? Engaged to this sweet, beautiful, young woman? It was enough to blow one's mind. There were either levels to Phung that Walt couldn't see or Manny had really changed for the worse. Remembering Paul's comments about how Manny used to be and how he is now, caused a wave of sorrow to pass through Walt. He wondered what all happened to cause the downfall of such an upstanding, talented, young man.

Deciding to throw caution to the wind, Walt said, "Ma'am? Mrs. Drake? If you don't mind me asking, what happened to Manny to turn him into what he is today?"

Paul gave Walt a stern look and firmly shook his head. It was clear he wanted Walt to shut his mouth.

She got a faraway look in her eyes for a few seconds before she came back to attention and said, "Daniel."

"Excuse me?" asked Walt.

"Not Manny," said the head of the WRA. "My son's name is Daniel." Everyone sat still and silent after she made her announcement. "Daniel Burke. He doesn't want to go by that name anymore, but that is the name I gave him. Anyway, that is a discussion for another day. Right now, we need to talk about your future." She gestured for Reggie to take over the talking. She also gave Paul a look that meant his interference would not go over very well.

"Det. Rogers, I really hate to put it like this, but this is a life-or-death situation for you. Your decision to either join us or not will dictate whether you live or die. I understand that this is not an ideal place to be in, but at least you know up front where we all stand." When Reggie stopped talking, Phung raised her hand and looked questioningly at him. When Reggie nodded, she turned to Walt.

"The bottom line is, we need you. As I said in my introduction, I am also heading up the Internal Investigations Department. To be honest, I'm no investigator. So basically, we need a seasoned investigator who can run the department and we can have faith that the work will be thorough and unprejudiced. With your record, and the fact that you are already in our world, you seem to be the obvious choice." She was so pretty, and looked so innocent, it was hard not to just nod and go along with whatever she said.

Walt wasn't fooled. "So, picking me has nothing to do with Manny? Uh, I mean Daniel?"

Mrs. Drake laughed. "We know that you're not stupid Walt. That's the main reason we want you. I know Paul told you from the beginning we wanted Daniel back. And we will use any means, fair or foul, to achieve that goal. We just feel that if we can get him in a position where he needs us, then we can show him how much we really care for him and we want him back in our lives."

Walt looked around and asked, "Does everyone feel that way? Because I just watched someone who should be ultra-protective of a little brother act like he hates him?"

"Delmas doesn't hate Daniel," said Kashonda, joining the conversation. "He, believe it or not, is a strict rule follower. He follows any and every order to its specified end. When Daniel left to do that prison job without consulting anyone, Delmas saw it as a major abandonment of the whole family. He feels like Daniel went AWOL, and as a soldier, you know that that is unforgivable."

Mrs. Drake picked up the tale. "Now, with all the things he's out there doing to people, all of us are disturbed to say the least. He has lost his mind and we feel like the only way to bring him back is if we can get him around his family."

Walt said, "I'm confused. How will me taking this job, or you killing me, bring your family back together? It's obvious that I work with Daniel. Won't this move just push all of you farther apart?"

Reggie responded to the question. "He won't talk to any of us. We have reached out a million times but he never responds to any of our attempts. We really do want you to take this position, but we would also like to force a confrontation that will at least give us a face-to-face meeting with him."

Walt laughed and said, "No disrespect, but I think you have the wrong guy. Manny, uh sorry, Daniel has put me in so many situations that could have resulted in my death. At no time has he came and tried to save me. If you think he will come to rescue me now, you are about to be severely disappointed."

Phung raised her hand again and Mrs. Drake barked, "Girl, if you raise your hand one more time, I'm gonna put you over my knee." It was said as a rebuke, but Phung giggled and said, "Sorry ma'am," before she turned to Walt.

"About 25 years ago, when you were an MP in the Military, you came home on leave and went to a middle school in Philadelphia. I believe it was F.O. Allen Middle School in North Philly. Is that correct?" She asked him.

Walt nodded his head, not sure where this was going, but curious all the same.

Phung continued. "You gave a speech to the students and one of the other speakers was a 12-year-old boy who had just graduated college. Do you remember that?"

Walt nodded again and said "Yeah, I remember. The little boy was from one of the neighborhoods I use to live in and he was said to have the highest I.Q. ever to be tested."

"That boy talked to you afterward and you told him that, if he ever decided to help his country, he needed to join Military Intelligence and figure out ways we can stop American soldiers from dying. Walt, that little boy was Daniel Burke," she said, shocking Walt to his core.

"That's not possible," said Walt. "That kid was from Philadelphia. He was from a poor family in the hood and I think he was actually a foster kid. He developed some kind of game and then moved his family to the suburbs when he sold the program for millions."

"I know it's hard to believe, but Walt, I swear I'm telling you the truth." She paused to read his expression, which still showed disbelief, before she continued. "Everyone thought he would join the CIA when he finished up basic. They were already recruiting him and it's kind of a family tradition. When he joined Military Intelligence instead, the whole family was baffled. To make me understand why he did it, he told me this story. He mentioned you by name. You were still an MP at the time and he said he couldn't wait to see your face when your paths crossed. Then, you left the service and Daniel signed on for the prison job and he never saw you again until he'd changed into 'Manny'."

Lucille Drake cleared her throat to get everyone's attention. "The WRA is a very old Agency that has transformed many times over the years into what it is today. My father, Willie James Burke, was a spy for the government in the 1960's. When he came back from serving his country, he was at a loss as to what to do. Being a man of color meant he could risk his life for the country, but the country wouldn't do a thing for him. He opened up an investigative firm in Washington D.C. and he moved all of us to Philly to live a more peaceful life around other people who look like us.

"He did a couple of spy jobs for some big wigs in D.C. and he just kept growing the company. Pretty soon, word got out to some very powerful people that, if they needed something done, and it had to be confidential, Willie James Burke was your man.

"Me and Mary Sue were the youngest of his kids and the only girls. We had four older brothers, but my father thought it best to train all of us, but in secret. In public we were to continue our lives like normal people while he did all of the dangerous stuff hundreds of miles away.

"My brothers all ended up working and dying for the WRA, along with my father. I followed in their footsteps and I took over the Agency and turned it into the global power it is today. But while I was busy doing all of this, my children had to have cover stories to keep them safe. All of them grew up with different families but in the same neighborhood and they all knew that they were family, but had to keep it quiet. When I established myself and this Agency as a powerful organization, I gathered my children and moved down here because now the Agency itself protects us all."

Walt was awed by the story. This woman was probably the strongest person he had ever met in his life. But more than the story was Daniel's connection to Walt. If the story was true, Daniel had actually followed the advice Walt had given him all those years ago. It's a connection that a boy would always cherish and remember. This explains why Daniel was training Walt and trying to save his life. He'd totally forgotten about the little boy genius. But after 25 years, that boy was putting Walt under his protection so that the people who wanted to kill him would think twice. Now he understood why Mrs. Drake was confident Daniel would come for him.

"Now you see?" asked Phung, reading his mind. "You were a very important part of Daniel's childhood. He has tried to follow your path for him and somehow make you proud. Yes, he has lost his way, but he's not unreachable. With your help, we think we can restore our family and move on from these dark days."

Walt needed time to think. Paul had made these people out to be monsters on par, if not worse, than Daniel. What Walt was hearing was a desperate plea from a family to bring home one of their own. If these people trained with Daniel, then they were excellent agents which would also make them excellent actors. It was time for Walt to throw a curve ball into their carefully choreographed game.

With a side glance at Paul, Walt said, "From what you just said, my death shouldn't even be an option. If you kill me, chances are, he is lost to you forever."

"What you don't get detective," said Reggie, "is you're our last hope. If we can't get him here because of you, and you won't work for us, then you are an enemy combatant that we have no use for. Det. Rogers, don't get it confused. If you don't play ball with us, you will die tonight."

"As you know," said Walt calmly. "Daniel has what I consider two very important people. If I betray him, their lives will be forfeit. If I was willing to do that, I wouldn't have been out there tonight, maiming a guard and his wife. But, if I hear what you're saying, those two women are to be sacrificed either way after tonight."

"We know where Ann and Denise are. They're in an underground prison about an hour from here. We have people working around the clock trying to break the security on that place, but the world doesn't call my son the best for no reason. Regardless, we are not willing to sacrifice either of them. We would like to bring you all on, as all of you are master investigators. As soon as we can free them, they will be given the same opportunity we are giving you."

After the speech by Mrs. Drake, everyone stayed quiet as they gave Walt time to think it through. He decided that he needed to at least try to compromise with them.

"What if I say yes to the job, but I finish all the tasks Daniel gave me so that I can be 100% sure that I get the women back?" Paul gave Walt's leg a tap and mouthed, "Don't try to compromise," then looked back down at the table.

189

Mrs. Drake seemed to think about it but Walt wasn't fooled for a second. Her mind was already made up. She said, "I'm afraid that is no longer an option. Daniel has figured out by now that you are missing, but we can't be 100% certain that he has tracked you to this place. If we let you leave, he will have no reason to come here looking for you. And like we said, we want a face to face with him so we can try and talk some sense into him."

"So again, I say that I am not willing to sacrifice Denise or Ann. And no matter how I go, you are forcing me to end their lives." Walt had had enough. These people were powerful and resourceful, but also ruthless and uncaring. He would sacrifice his life for either of those women and that's exactly what he was going to do.

Walt continued. "So, bottom line is I have no incentive to help you. I've been living on borrowed time anyway since your Agency handed down my death sentence. From what I can tell, there is only one person mixed up in all this who gives a damn about me. Daniel is the only reason I'm alive and I'm loyal to who is loyal to me. So, I'll rely on Daniel, not any of you, to keep my women safe. And you, Mrs. Drake, can do what you will."

Paul looked at Walt like he was crazy and stood up. He said, "Mrs. Drake, if I can talk to him…"

"Sit the fuck down Paul," Walt said, cutting him off. "I've made my decision and I'll live or die with it." Paul glanced around, searching for an ally. When no one spoke up, he shrugged and sat back down.

Mrs. Drake smiled at Walt, then turned to Reggie with a nod. Reggie stood up and removed a very large pistol from a holster under his suit jacket. He said, "Det. Rogers, you have just made a very bad decision. Those two women were going to die one way or the other. Daniel never would have let them live. All you've done is cemented the fact that now, all of you are going to die."

Walt smiled and said, "Mr. Burke, I'm a soldier. If I can't die for what I believe in, it wouldn't be an honorable death anyway."

Reggie nodded. "That is true and I respect you for your fortitude. Now, stand up please." As he said the last, he pointed the gun at Walt's chest.

Mrs. Drake got up and said, "Sorry our business has to conclude this way. You would have made a great agent in our Agency. Unfortunately, my son's search for you doesn't require you to be alive." She walked around the table and opened the door to exit the conference room.

She stood for about five seconds before she took a step back inside the room. She said, "Reggie, go ahead and put the gun away." Walt and the other six agents all looked at her in confusion as she continued to back into the room. All confusion vanished when the figure in the doorway became visible.

A very angry Manny, A.K.A. Daniel Burke, was standing at the door with a gun pointed at his mother's head. He said, "Yeah Reg, put the gun down. And how about the rest of you get with the program of ditching all your weapons too." When Paul stayed seated, Daniel said, "That means you too Paul. I know where your fucking loyalties lie."

When all the agents were disarmed and lined up against the far wall, Daniel sent a long text out on his phone. Then he looked at his family and friends and said, "You all amaze me. After all this time you still think you're smarter than me. You still think it's possible to be ahead of me. Well, you've been wanting a face to face with me. All I can tell you," he said with a laugh, "You should have been more careful with what you wished for." His last statement was accompanied by the sound of his first shot being fired.

CHAPTER 15

Delmas was watching the scene in the conference room play out on his phone when his punk ass little brother stepped into view. That was all he needed to see. Daniel wouldn't hurt anyone in that room, so Delmas cut his phone off as the jet came to a stop on the tarmac.

When he'd left the underground HQ of the WRA, he jumped right on one of the Agency jets and headed toward his targets for tonight. They had just landed in Charlotte about three minutes ago and, now that he knew his targets were alone, he was anxious to get started.

The stewardess opened the back door and Delmas stood and walked down the path to the exit. He was very happy to see that the vehicle he had requested was on stand-by ready to go.

The all black Mercedes-Benz G63 AMG Savage, in his opinion, was the best luxury SUV ever built. He had talked his mother into buying 50 of them. All of them had about $150,000 in additional modifications to bring the total cost for all 50 of them to $25 million. Money well spent if anyone was to ask him.

He jumped in the driver's seat and threw his duty bag in the back before pulling off to finish the last ten minutes of his journey. He was on his way to deliver a comeuppance that was long overdue. Delmas didn't really come out in the field too often. But when he did, it was for these kinds of jobs that required a skill set that most other field agents didn't possess. The ability to mix fear and violence, with a minimum amount of real violence, that resulted in no one getting seriously hurt. Daniel was the best at it, but with his level of training, he should be the best. Delmas though, was a very close second.

Delmas would be lying if he said he wasn't enjoying this. To get one over on the golden child. To do the impossible. To fell what some considered the most talented WRA agent in its long history. But more importantly, to defeat the brother that thought himself so superior to the other siblings.

"We'll see about that," Delmas muttered to himself. He was sick and tired of hearing how great the bastard was. How smart he was. Delmas gave props where props were due, but he was pretty damn good himself. He was also smart. Like he was smart enough not to go to war with an Agency that could squish him like a bug whenever it felt like it. Then again, the WRA would have been ordered Delmas' death if he was out there doing the same shit. Only Daniel could get away with this level of disrespect.

As he pulled into the neighborhood full of compounds, they were way too big to call houses, he switched the vehicle over to its electric mode. The now silent SUV blended into the darkness that only the super-rich and the very poor wished for. The poor, so the darkness could hide their dirty deeds. The super-rich because, well, pretty much the same reason. Neither group could afford for too bright a light to fall on them.

When he arrived at the location, he boldly pulled over at the gate, grabbed his bag, and exited the SUV. This was a stealth mission but his looks were all the stealth he would need this close to his targets.

The Agency had been keeping tabs on this place since Daniel had purchased it. The compound was huge and contained several underground areas. It also boasted some very fine security features that could result in the death of anyone stupid enough to break in. The high walls and the drone blocking technology made it impossible for your average criminal to get a peek inside. For the WRA, it was just a few clicks on a keyboard to send a satellite to observe the comings and goings on the property. But the satellite couldn't tell them everything.

As he approached the gate, he was a little nervous. They needed Phung to be in the room with Daniel, so they had her number two doing all the hacking involved to get him into the house. Even though Jessica was good, she was no Phung. All it would take is one wrong keystroke and his life could end tonight. He took comfort in knowing that his death would start a chain reaction that would also lead to the death of his little brother.

He was wearing all black so, as the gate swung open, thank God Jessica was on point, he merged with the shadows as the gate shut behind him.

There was no going back now. The people in the house would have been alerted that the gate had been opened and closed. It was a good bet Daniel had also been notified. He slipped on his modified shades that allowed him to see in the dark, as well as view the data being sent to him by Jessica.

Everything had the greenish tint that came along with using night vision. But also, little red rectangles in no discernible pattern came up on his lenses. These were the stun mines that had activated when the high alert protocols had been engaged on the security system. The stun mines would knock you unconscious the second you stepped on one. They were dangerous but not designed to kill you. Now, the little purple boxes on the lenses were the real problem.

Phung had developed this program to detect any foreign object planted underground. Jessica was running it and conveying the chemical and physical make up of each item the scan detected. Daniel was ready for a war, and it became evident with what made up the contents of the purple boxes. It was actually two boxes made to hold two different compounds that would detonate near simultaneously to obliterate any enemy. If you stepped on one of them, it was game over for you and everyone around you.

Based on the information being sent to him, Delmas concluded that one box contained C4 and the other box contained a compound that was to act as napalm. The napalm compound would explode first and, within a tenth of a second, the C4 would blow, slinging the compound over the whole area. The compound would eat you alive in seconds and would continue to burn until a counter compound was deployed. It was like the compound Daniel had used on that lieutenant chick from the prison, but this was 100 times stronger. Sweating a little now, Delmas prayed that Phung's program was picking up everything.

When he got the signal that the program was finished with its scan, he stepped away from the wall and followed a pattern that would take him to the front door. He had to backtrack a couple of times but, after 15 minutes of maneuvering, he was at the front door waiting for Jessica to finish the scan on the door and give him the all clear. The technology on the house made all communications impossible once inside. So, after he took this final step, he was on his own until he came back out.

Jessica Signpalm was Phung Lei's protégé as well as her best friend. They had been best friends since Jessica showed up at Phung's High School in the middle of their Junior year fall semester. Phung had been delighted that another Asian girl was at the school, though Jessica was half white and half Filipino. Jessica was smart and loyal and very beautiful, so her and Phung were the perfect match to form a lifelong bond.

Phung was already dating Daniel at the time and they all forged a friendship that only got stronger as time went by. It had been a foregone conclusion that Phung would become a WRA agent, so Daniel trained Phung, and she in turn trained Jessica. The short, dark haired, brown eyed beauty soon proved that she could hold her own in the hacking world. Between Phung and Jessica, they were sometimes able to give Daniel a run for his money. He was hoping that tonight, that was still the case.

The message finally popped up on the display telling him he could enter, but he would have to input the disarm code into the display unit. None of them knew what the inside of the house looked like, but Jessica said the code signature was coming from a unit about 20 feet and to the left of the door.

Delmas took a fortifying breath, removed the soon to be useless shades, made sure all his gear was where it was supposed to be, then he reached out and turned the knob.

The door opened into a wide-open area that contained only art, columns, and chandeliers. He immediately looked for danger and didn't see any, so he walked with purpose over to a column on the left about 20 feet away that was softly emitting a beeping sound.

On the other side he saw the keypad to disable the alarm. He entered the code given to him by Jessica and that's when everything went to shit.

A glass cage suddenly lifted from below the floor and enclosed him in a ten-by-ten area. It glided all the way up to the 20-foot ceiling and a gas slowly started rolling out of hidden vents in the floor. He pulled his gun and was about to shoot at the corner of the enclosure when a voice stopped him cold.

"I wouldn't do that if I were you," said a female voice behind him. He spun around and came face to face with Alisha Saffiyah Harden, one of his targets for tonight.

"The glass is made out of a material that repels momentum instead of absorbing it. So that bullet will bounce around until it hits something that will absorb its power. Unfortunately, that something will have to be you."

The dark chocolate beauty walked closer and stopped about a foot from the glass. She was bare foot with sweat pants and a T-shirt on. Even with the ordinary clothes, no visible make-up, and her hair pulled back into a ponytail, it was easy to see why Daniel was willing to risk war for her. Her calmness over the situation told Delmas that she possessed more than just beauty. She would be an asset to any man in their line of work.

She pushed a button on her phone and the billowing gas abruptly stopped. Fans came on and sucked all the gas back towards the floor. Delmas walked over and stood in front of the woman who now held him captive.

"Normally Manny tells me to do something and I do it. I was sent a text about 30 minutes ago and he told me that you were on your way. It's obvious that you two are related and I want to know what's going on. He instructed me to knock you out with the gas and he would be here in the morning to take care of you." She locked eyes with him and said, "This one time I'm going to disobey him and do this my way. Talk to me," she demanded before sitting on the floor.

Delmas sat down and unloaded all the gear from his body to make himself comfortable on the floor. He then turned to Alisha and asked her, "What do you want to talk about?"

She shrugged and said, "Start with the basics. Who are you and who are you to Manny? Why are you here, and what did you plan to do when you got here?"

Delmas looked at her for a full minute before responding. He chuckled and shook his head saying, "Manny, Manny, Manny. That's actually pretty funny."

He focused on her once more and said, "The day we left Philadelphia to move down here, a turtle was on the sidewalk right outside of our home. We decided that we would take this turtle and he would be part of our new life. Mother didn't want any trace of where we were going to ever come out, so we drove the 500 or so miles to get down here." Delmas looked at her finger pointedly to highlight the ring she was wearing. "Your fiancé, my little brother, named that turtle Manny. So, I guess when he decided to start a new life, he thought about our pet turtle Manny. By the way, the turtle died from old age. Wishful thinking for your fiancé."

Alisha nodded slowly and said, "Okay, so you two are brothers from Philadelphia. It's more than I had, but not enough for me to go against Manny's wishes. You have to give me more than that."

Delmas smiled. "I'm not scared of your gas. I know you can't or won't kill me. He wouldn't allow it. Don't get it twisted, I'm talking because I want to, not because of your threat."

When Alisha just continued to sit and stare at him, he laughed and said, "Your pretty good at this." After a brief hesitation, Delmas said, "My name is Delmas Burke, big brother to your fiancé Daniel Burke, and we are both agents for a deep cover government Agency called the World Redemption Agency, or WRA for short."

He paused and took her silence to mean she wanted more. "The whole leadership of the Agency consist of our family. Our mother is head, followed by our brother Reggie, me, our sister Kashonda, then Phung, then our Aunt and Cousin. You'll find this interesting. Phung was Daniel's fiancé before he took the prison job. He trained her and now all of them are in a meeting that will determine how far all this shit will go."

She absorbed all that information without a flinch, even though he had tried to overwhelm her with the delivery. She said, "So you were sent here to kidnap me and Gabby to make sure Daniel played ball?" She dropped her head back on her shoulders and laughed uproariously. She ended up rolling around on the floor, hysterical, with tears running down her face.

Delmas, getting mad, asked, "What the hell is so damn funny? You think this is a joke?"

She got control of herself and looked at Delmas with a sneer on her beautiful face. "You thought that he would leave us unprotected? You fell into a trap that he probable set up months ago. It's amazing to me that so many people try to outsmart him when they know they can't. You set up a trap for him that was already part of his plan." She reached for the phone that was still sitting next to her.

"Let me show you the text he sent me." She pressed a few buttons, then put the phone up to the glass.

His heart sank the more he read. The text said, "Alisha, I love you. The plan we went through for the intruder will go down within the hour. Set everything up just how I showed you. Deactivate just enough so he has to work, but will be able to make it through. The enclosure is automatic. Once he is inside, deploy the gas. Keep him under until I get home. P.S. He will look like me, but look with your heart. You'll know who he is."

When he looked up, she hit a few buttons and put the phone back down. She said, "We went through the intruder plan about three months ago. He knew you would come before you did." Mimicking Daniel, she said, "When will you people learn? You say he won't kill you? I'm pretty sure this isn't the same Daniel you use to know. You will probably wish for death after you tried to go after his family. His real family."

She stood up and tapped the screen of her phone a few times. The gas started filling the enclosure once again. Delmas jumped up and said urgently, "Alisha, don't do this!

They will kill Daniel for this." He started coughing violently but continued to plead. "Let me go Alisha and I can free Daniel from all of this. I can give you a normal life with your family." He was down on his knees, fighting the gas with everything he had. Right before he fell into unconsciousness, Alisha directed one last comment his way.

"This is normal life for me and mine. You should be more afraid of what the new normal for your family is going to be."

CHAPTER 16

It was a testament to the level of training each person in the room had that no one flinched when Daniel fired his first shot. Or the second. Or the third. Daniel was very proud of Walt because he made no move to stop him or question his decision to shoot random spots around the room.

"Now that no one can see what's going on in this room, we can get down to the business at hand," Daniel said, subtly explaining to Walt that he had shot out all of the hidden cameras. Daniel then swung to face Walt. "Go get all of those guns, and while you're at it, retrieve all the ones hidden in the chairs and table too."

Walt pushed the pile of weapons down to the end of the table closest to Daniel and then went back down the table searching for more hardware. When he was finished with his search, the pile had grown to over 30 weapons. Guns, knives, ice picks, brass knuckles, and even a grenade. That was pretty impressive for seven people.

Daniel asked, "Do any of you have anything you want to say to Walt before he leaves?" No one said anything. "Speak up," he continued. "After this, any more attempts to contact him will result in swift retaliation." Five seconds passed before Mrs. Drake spoke up.

"I would like to say something." She turned and stepped away from the wall with an assurance that said she knew the gun pointing at her would not fire. "Detective, we used you and I am sorry for that. But the offer to work here was a real offer. You are very good at what you do and I think you would prove to be an asset to this Agency."

Daniel turned again to Walt and asked, "So, what's it going to be? My goal was to save your life and protect you from harm. Now that you know what's going on, at least some of it, you can make your own decisions."

Walt glanced back and forth between the two of them a couple of times before he stepped next to Daniel and turned to face Mrs. Drake. He said, "I think I'll stick with the devil I know."

Daniel didn't waste any more time. With his gun still pointed at his family, he said, "Walt, put these on." He handed him a pair of shaded and continued to give him direction. "There is a camera that will transmit everything you see to my phone. Go back the way you came. Ride the elevator back up, get in the car and head back to the lift. The keys are still in the ignition. No one will try to stop you.

"Once you get to the top of the lift, just keep going straight. The door at the front of the hangar will open and just continue down the drive until you hit the street. Take a left and then the first right you come to and then keep going until you see signs for the interstate.

"This is very important Walt, and I need you to follow my instructions. Don't go home. Okay? Make your way to the Charlotte area and I'll give you further instructions when you're close. Do you understand?"

Walt simply said, "Got it." He walked out of the room and Daniel followed his progress on his phone.

When Walt's car exited the property, he told his family to sit down, but keep their hands on top of the table. He took the seat opposite from his mother at the foot of the table. All of the agents now sat bunched together, no longer sitting in their assigned seats. Probably not by accident, Reggie and Paul were closest to Daniel, acting as a unified shield to protect the women.

Daniel tossed all the collected weapons to the corner of the room farthest from his family and laid his own gun on the table, but never took his hand away from it. He wasn't fooled for a second into thinking that there wasn't a hidden weapon that Walt missed in his search.

In his other hand was his phone. He watched Walt's progress as he made his way towards Charlotte. Daniel looked at his mother first.

"The last meeting we had like this didn't end so well. Of course, you didn't have all the family backing that you do now," he said glancing around at the people he once thought of as his family.

"I'm eager to hear what any of you think you can say to bring me back to this corrupt family." He said the word "family" like it was a curse word. Then he sat in silence, almost daring one of them to be the first one to speak.

Reggie was the one to attempt to break the ice. "Daniel...."

"And that's another thing," said Daniel, coolly cutting his brother off. "You just sent a killer at my real family because you feared that I would say my name. Then you go against one of your strict rules by turning around and giving my name away." When he said, "real family" Phung made a sound of distress as if she had been hit with a blow. He was not going into all of that with the rest of his family present. He chose to ignore it.

His mother said, "He is already in our world. You brought him in. I really didn't see a point in trying to hide your identity when he was either going to die or join us."

"I brought him in? I brought him in?" Daniel asked with a raised voice. "No, you brought him in by putting a hit on him. You know what he is to me and once again, in true Burke fashion, you try to kill what you can't control."

"We tried to bring him in through the CIA 20 years ago…"

"And he shot you down," Daniel loudly cut his mother off. "Let it the fuck go. Everyone doesn't have to die because they don't follow your plan for their lives."

Daniel calmed himself visibly after his outburst. He said, "If you have something to say, say it now. I have a lot to do before I can rest with my family."

Reggie said, "So we're not your family? You're big and bad enough now that you don't need us? Fuck you Daniel," he said standing up. "All we wanted to do was talk to your selfish, ungrateful ass. But you come in here with a gun, pointing it at your real family. The ones who protected you when you weren't so big and bad. The ones who trained you and nurtured you when you were just a nerd and didn't understand the world. And this is how you repay us?"

Reggie had been slowly advancing on him during his whole speech. The rest of the family was trying to calm him down and draw him back to his seat. Right before Reggie got close enough to lunge at Daniel, his gun went off which caused everyone to freeze and go silent. When Reggie crumpled to the floor, everyone started to jump to their feet to render aid.

Daniel hopped up and, waving the gun around, said, "Sit the fuck down. Now!"

Everyone could hear Reggie moaning and rolling around in pain. They were too slow to follow his order, so he swung the gun around and shot Paul center mass, causing him to yell out and fall to the floor clutching his chest.

Daniel calmly said, "None of your games can work on me. Now sit the fuck down." The five female agents all sat down with fear showing clearly on their faces.

The two male agents had gone eerily quiet and Daniel didn't even spare them a glance. His mother's face had shed its fear and now settled on rage. She said, "You think you're so smart. You don't want us to be your family? Fine! But now you will feel the full wrath of the WRA. You are only alive today because of my mercy and love. You have rejected me and mine for the last time. When I'm done with you, you'll beg me for that love and mercy that you so callously threw away."

She was spitting and foaming at the mouth while she ranted on, issuing threat after threat. Daniel swung his gun up and pointed it at her head. Her eyes went wide with fright and Kashonda and Phung both screamed and jumped on the table in an effort to protect his mother. After a second, Mary Sue and Dollis joined the other women. They all huddled together, shaking and crying as he lowered the pistol. They were looking at him like he was a deranged killer. In their minds he probably was.

"I will always be 10 steps ahead of you. If you pull this shit again, I won't hesitate to kill you all. You will never get the upper hand. All I want is to be left alone and that extends to my family and the people under my protection." Daniel was back to being calm, but wanted to show them that he was dead serious with his threat.

He pushed a series of buttons on his phone and the screen to his left suddenly turned on. "I want to show you why I reject your love and mercy." On the screen, a live video of Delmas, laid out on the floor inside the glass enclosure, became visible. Daniel gave a sarcastic laugh.

"All of this so you could kidnap a woman and little girl." He shook his head at the five women. "Look what you have loss because of your greed. Because of your quest to rule me. All you had to do was give me my space to find my peace, but I guess that was too much to ask. Now, you'll live with the consequences of your actions."

He backed to the door, but left them with a word of advice. "This was just a warning. It could have been better, but it could have gone a lot worse. Don't try to contact me again, just let me live my life. If I even think that any one of you are thinking of me or my family, I will burn this whole organization to the ground."

At the door, he couldn't help himself. He glanced back one more time and locked eyes with the woman he thought he would love forever and spend the rest of his life with. He let Phung see the hurt and pain from the betrayal he felt. He let her see in his eyes the knowledge that none of this could have happened without her. Not his stay in prison. Their attempt on Walt and his family. None of that could've happened without her setting it up. And even if she wasn't the one doing the set-up, she never tried to stop it.

She couldn't handle what she saw in his eyes, so she closed hers and continued to cry in his mother's arms. He exited the room and ran to one of the secret tunnels he had built while he was a resident here. Since he had upgraded most of the security whenever his mother wanted to expand, most of the time he had free rein to any additions he wanted. He reported some of them, but not all.

He made his way out of the headquarters, never encountering another person, until he came across the guard he had shot on his way in. He was one of the newer guards and Daniel had only seen his face on a computer screen. He walked around the fallen guard and made his way to the spot, about a half mile away, where he had stashed the unmarked cop car.

Daniel wasn't worried about pursuit; they wouldn't risk him retaliating by hurting Delmas. But he knew after the shock had worn off, his mother would mount some kind of rescue mission. The WRA didn't leave agents behind. That's one of the reasons why he still couldn't understand how they could all betray him the way they did.

Anyway, that was in the past. He would just have to make sure he was ready for what they would do in the future. He jumped in the car and backtracked out of the area until he saw the Interstate signs. He got on 85 South and followed the same path Walt had taken not so long ago.

Now that Walt knew his secrets, Daniel decided that it was time for Walt to make a choice. He would never be safe now because the WRA didn't let non-personnel walk around with knowledge of them. And they were so good at killing people, they could make it look like a car accident, or a heart attack, or any other natural cause. Then he would never know if they were responsible for Walt's death, or if it was a real accident.

As much as he hated to say it, the safest thing Walt could do is join the Agency. And when they talked, he would tell him that. But what he hoped Walt decided was to give this partnership with him his all. Jump into the training and let Daniel turn him into a warrior that could hold his own in their world. Walt already had the basics, but Daniel could mold him into something otherworldly. A predator that no one would ever attempt to turn into prey.

Daniel saw on his phone that Walt was nearing his house, so he called him to lead him the rest of the way.

Walt answered with, "I'm right at the city limits. Where do I go from here?"

Daniel gave him detailed directions on how to get to his compound and finished with, "Just wait at the gate. To get you inside without me would take too much explaining and time. I'm about 30 minutes behind you. I'll see you soon." They disconnected and Daniel let his mind wander as he thought about all the possible outcomes to some tough decisions he had to make.

He already knew what he was going to do with Delmas. He had always known this day was coming and he had planned for it. At first, he had thought about turning Delmas over to the police with enough evidence to say he was the Prison Guard Killer. But without the same restrictions in place from his own incarceration, Delmas would be out in a matter of days. And in the process, a lot of people could lose their lives.

Daniel couldn't care less about killing cops, most of them were corrupt anyway. He just didn't want to make it so easy for his family to get Delmas back. Even a large department like CMPD, didn't stand a chance against the WRA. Almost all the agents had reasons for hating the law, and they would have a field day after receiving the green light to get Delmas back at all cost. No, Daniel had settled on a more fitting and secure place for the WRA agent. At least for the time being.

Mostly what was on his mind was what to do about Walt. Daniel played through the many different answers Walt could give to his questions and most of the scenarios were not good. Because of his family, Walt now knew that he possessed a certain amount of power over his situation. He could start making demands that would cause Daniel to cut him off and consider him an enemy. He hated to say it, but a dead Walt was better than an enemy Walt.

Daniel made his mind up on the path he would take as he pulled into his neighborhood. He would have to make some sacrifices, and he would have to trust in people he really didn't trust. But he would have faith in the process he would set in motion. And God help anyone who got in the way of his goal.

He pulled up behind the blue Honda Accord and saw that Walt was still inside the vehicle. Daniel saw the SUV that

Delmas must have been driving and he placed a call to have someone come and get it. They would take the Benz back to the air field where Daniel was sure the WRA jet still sat, and the Agency could retrieve it whenever.

Daniel got out of his car at the same time Walt exited the Honda. He walked over to him and extended his hand. He said, "I'm Daniel Burke. It's nice to see you alive and well Detective."

Walt reached for his hand and shocked him when he pulled him in for a hug. Daniel awkwardly patted him on the back as Walt continued to hold him.

Walt released him and said, "Thank you for saving my life."

"Don't thank me just yet," said Daniel. "You now have a very powerful enemy on your back that you are not equipped to handle." Daniel knew that they were not safe standing in the open like this. There was no telling who Delmas might have brought along as backup. He gestured for Walt to follow him as he made his way towards the gate.

He pulled his phone out and called Alisha. When she answered, he said, "It's me. I have some company, so disable the high alert so we can come in." He hung up after saying that because he didn't want to have a conversation until he could look at her face to face, and make sure she was okay.

With Walt beside him, they stood at the gate while Daniel waited for the all clear on his phone. He was looking at the security schematic and watched as the systems shut down one by one. When the shutdown was complete, he led the way through the gate and towards the massive home.

A commotion at the gate caused Walt to turn around and see what was going on. Daniel already knew it was the crew he'd called to come remove the three cars left outside the gate. Within seconds, all three cars were transported away, all going to different locations to fulfill different purposes.

When they cleared the trees and Walt got his first look at the main house, he gave an audible gasp. Daniel couldn't blame him. The mansion was lit up like a jewel in the night. With all of the glass allowing so much light in and out of the structure, some people would think the house easy pickings. What they would find out under closer inspection was the glass was more secure than the concrete and rocks. The fact was, you really couldn't see inside of the house. The illusion made you see things that were not actually there. Light was the only thing that would pass through the glass.

Walt said, "Let me guess. This is some kind of secret headquarters for some rival government agency? Maybe an underground complex for the CIA or NSA, who are helping you take down the WRA?"

"Nope," Daniel said with a smile. "This is just home. At least for now. I have places like this spread all over the world."

With shining eyes that continued to take in all the beauty, Walt asked, "What does a place like this cost? About $5 million? $10 million?"

Daniel laughed at Walt's question. "Try $150 million. And that was before all the upgrades I gave it. You are now inside of probably the safest place in the world. When all the security features are active, nothing can penetrate this space. I keep my most important treasures here."

213

"What? Like all of your spy gear and secret technology? Gold bars? Vaults full of money? What the hell kind of treasures would you keep in a place like this?" asked Walt.

They were nearing the front of the house when the door was snatched open and Alisha stepped up to the threshold. Daniel turned to Walt and said, "All the things you named, I keep in locations all over the world. But the treasures I'm talking about, I would scorch the earth to keep safe." He nodded towards Alisha. "People who I love and who love me back unconditionally, those are my greatest treasures."

Daniel left Walt at the bottom of the four massive stone steps and bounded towards the love of his life. He scooped Alisha up into his arms and kissed her like it would be the last time he got to do so. Daniel didn't stop even after he heard Walt standing behind him clearing his throat. No. He didn't stop until he felt all the tension and fear melt out of the body of his Queen.

Even after they broke the kiss, they stood staring into each other's eyes, whispering endearments to one another. When Alisha smiled and smacked him upside his head saying, "Don't ever scare me like that again," Daniel knew everything was alright.

He turned to Walt and said, "I'd like to introduce you to…"

"Alisha Harden," Walt said cutting him off. "Yeah, I know. Everyone has been quietly looking for you as a person of interest in the gang massacre. They couldn't find your body, so no one knew if you were running scared or if you had something to do with it. I guess this answers that question," he said while shaking her hand.

Alisha looked at Daniel with uncertainty in her eyes. Silently asking him if bringing Walt here was a good idea. He said, "Let's go inside and I'll explain everything in there."

When they entered the huge receiving room, all three pairs of eyes were immediately drawn to the figure on the floor of the glass enclosure. Walt said, "What the hell? Is that your brother over there on the floor? Is he dead?"

Daniel kept walking but said over his shoulder, "Come on. I'll explain everything in a minute. We don't have a lot of time. Even though the sun is coming up, our night, unfortunately is not over."

He led the group into the kitchen and they both sat around a center island while Alisha went to make coffee and get juice from the refrigerator. Walt let out a small laugh. "Sorry, but isn't the kitchen a little too small for a house this big? I mean, don't get me wrong, it's nice, but my kitchen is bigger than this."

Daniel smiled and said, "First of all, we have more important things going on other than the size of our kitchens. But just to set you mind at ease, this is the family kitchen that I had built because the main one is, well, see for yourself," he said gesturing to a door on the right.

Walt got up and walked over to the door. He pushed the swing door open and then froze in the doorway. Daniel couldn't see what he was seeing, but he had a good idea of what Walt was feeling.

The main kitchen was the size of most people's homes. It was actually about 1,500 square feet and had a mezzanine encompassing the whole second floor just in case someone wanted to watch from above as the food was prepared. Based on all the features on the blueprint, it was a $2 million kitchen.

He walked back over and sat next to Daniel before saying, "I really hate you right now. Here I've been busting my ass trying to catch you for years and you've been living like a king out here in the suburbs."

Daniel laughed and said, "After we finish up with all this bullshit, I'll be sure to give you a full tour."

Alisha joined them, serving the coffee and juice before sitting across from the two men. She remained quiet knowing that was the easiest way to get Daniel to explain himself.

Daniel said, "I know you better than anyone else on this earth besides your mother. How much did you get out of him before you put him under?" He knew his brother would try to talk his way out of trouble. He also knew that Alisha would have been an enthusiastic listener. He had cameras all over the house, but hadn't had time to review their interaction. Eventually, he would, but to speed things up, he was hoping she would tell him.

"Everything," she responded. "I know about the Burke family and the WRA. I know about the turtle in Philly you named Manny. Actually, that was a pretty genius way to tell me everything without you being the one telling me." She glanced at both of them and asked, "What's the plan now?"

"We have to get my brother into a secure location other than here," said Daniel. "Me and Walt will take him because we have some other things to discuss on the way. And I don't think it will be an uneventful trip. Alisha, I'm going to need you to stay in the house for a few days until I can broker a deal with the WRA."

"OK," she said. "I'll just catch up on some of the household things I need to do."

He turned to Walt. "By now, the shock has worn off and the WRA will be out for blood. We have to relocate him and we have to do it fast. There will be traps on the way because they know where I'm taking him. We will talk more later but I need to know that you are with me. No games or bullshit. You know who I am now. I need to know that I can trust you to help me protect the people I love."

It was hard to know exactly what was going through Walt's head, but Daniel knew he wanted to bring up Ann and Denise. Walt cut his eyes towards Alisha and then back to Daniel. He slowly nodded and said, "You can trust me. I just hope I can trust you."

After that, things moved quickly. Daniel went to one of his underground garages and drove out an armor-plated Hummer. It was really a tank disguised as a street legal vehicle. It weighed more than an 18-wheeler and the windows were just smokescreens for the rest of the world, so it appeared normal.

The armor provided 360 degrees of protection with cameras under a bulletproof mesh that projected images on screens where the windows were supposed to be. The Hummer also had an air filtration system that made chemical weapons harmless. The tires were really metal tracks with a rubber outer shell. There was no air in them at all. At $5 million, and with a top speed of 180 mph, the military would kill for a fleet of these. When he made something better, he

217

might provide them with the schematic. Right now, it was the safest and deadliest vehicle he had, so he would be the only one with one.

Daniel and Walt loaded up the unconscious Delmas and secured him in a compartment in the back of the Hummer. Daniel attached a mask to Delmas' face that would continue to keep him unconscious until they had him secured in the next location.

Five minutes later, with the sun shining bright in the eastern sky, they were ready to go. Daniel made sure they were both armed and outfitted in a new body armor that wasn't on the market yet. They would be safe inside the vehicle, but the transfer out of the Hummer could leave them vulnerable without the added protection.

Daniel and Walt exited out of the front door and were just about to enter the vehicle when a voice yelled, "Daddy! You were going to leave without saying bye to me?"

He looked up and saw Gabby standing in the doorway by herself. She looked fresh out of bed. Rubbing her eyes and her hair going every which a way. Bare foot with a long T-shirt covering her body, she waited at the door for Daniel to come back to her.

It had been a blessing from God having this little girl in his life. To see her opening up more and more every day as she started to trust them. She had such a beautiful soul and he couldn't help but smile every time he saw her.

He took off running back up the steps and she screamed and turned to run because she knew what was coming. He grabbed her up and spun her around like she was two instead of ten. She squealed and said, "Boy, you better put me down this instant." She sounded so much like Alisha, who she tried to emulate at every opportunity.

Daniel set her down and asked, "How is my princess doing this morning?"

Now that her eyes were clear, she looked up and noticed Walt for the first time. Her eyes got huge and she said, "I know you! You're that cop who questioned me when my Dad died." She backed up behind Daniel and said, "I'm not going anywhere with you. And if you try to make me, my new Dad is going to kill your ass!"

Daniel watched the shock on Walt's face as it finally registered who it was he was looking at. Alisha chose that moment to step out next to her family. Walt looked at each of them in turn, then focused on Daniel. "Spoils of war?" he asked him. Daniel shook his head as he moved closer to the two young ladies. "Ah! Treasures," Walt said after a few seconds.

Daniel wrapped an arm around his family and simply nodded. Walt nodded back and said, "Well, let's get this done. We have to make sure these treasures stay safe." He got in the Hummer and closed the door.

Alisha took Gabby's hand and pulled her in for a hug. She looked at Daniel and asked, "Are you sure about him?"

Daniel hugged his ladies close and said, "I'll know in a little bit. If I'm not sure by the end of this trip, like Gabby said, Daddy is going to kill his ass."

CHAPTER 17

No alarms were blaring. No armed guards were running to and fro. Her world was crumbling on its foundation, but everything was peaceful and serene inside of the World Redemption Agency's HQ. The five female agents were still in the conference room, but were now sitting silently around the head of the table trying to process what had just happened. They were trying to comprehend how a good plan could go so terribly wrong.

Lucille Drake sat at the head of the table, trying to figure out how she could be numb, angry, and hurting, all at the same time. Her three sons were gone to her now. Reggie, her first born son, lay dead about 15 feet from her. Delmas, her middle son, was being held captive. And Daniel, her youngest child, was responsible for it all.

She tried to work up some feeling for Agent Stevens, whose body lay on the opposite side of the table from her son, but at this moment, she couldn't. He had actually been the first agent she had brought in and he had been a tremendous help to her over the years. But all she could think about right now was the fate of her three sons.

Mrs. Drake looked around at the other four shocked faces and realized that she needed to straighten up and be strong for her remaining family. Her sister and niece wouldn't be a help to her in trying to get Delmas back, so she addressed them first.

"Mary Sue, Dollis, we have a lot of work to do before we are allowed the luxury of falling apart. I need for you two to take care of Reggie and Paul while the rest of us attempt to get Delmas back. Can I count on you two to handle this for me?" Both women nodded but didn't make a move. "Now damnit!" shouted Lucille, which prompted the two women to jump up and start working their phones.

Next, she addressed both Kashonda and Phung. "Okay. So far, we've just been gathering intelligence and information on Daniel to figure out a way to bring him home." She paused as she regarded each one of them in turn. "We will now use that information to get my son back and kill the traitor who took him. From now on, the gloves are off. We will use every resource at our disposal to end this fucker. Do you both understand me?"

Phung said, "Yes ma'am, but are you sure..."

"Look what he did to Reggie!" she yelled, cutting Phung off. "Imagine what he will do to Delmas. I'll tell you what Phung. If you are not up for this, if your feelings are going to get in the way, then you can help the other two women with Reggie and Paul."

"No ma'am," said Phung. "I'm up for it and I'm ready to do what needs to be done. But once you give the termination order, there won't be a take back. Too many of the agents will be out for blood once they find out what he's done."

"Good. Let him experience some of the turmoil he's been spreading around. And what the hell is wrong with you Mary Sue?"

While Phung and Lucille had been talking, Mary Sue and Dollis had called a couple of agents to come down and help with the bodies. Mary Sue said, "Lucille, get over here quick! I don't think he's dead!"

The three remaining women jumped up from the table and rushed over to kneel at Reggie's side. "I couldn't find any blood so I started poking around." All of the Burkes had received some form of medical training to help out in a crisis situation.

"So what? You don't have to be bleeding to be dead," replied Lucille. "Probably some new toy Daniel has cooked up." She grabbed his wrist and put her ear over his mouth. "I don't feel a pulse and I can't feel his breath. Let's take this suit off of him so we can see the damage."

They stripped him from the waist up and everyone just stopped and stared at the odd sight that was revealed. The two male agents had entered while they were stripping Reggie, and they too took in the sight with confusion. The younger one said, "Oh shit! Somebody killed Mr. Burke and Paul."

On Reggie's chest was a grayish ball with spikes attached to it. The ball was maybe a quarter inch in diameter and the spikes extended another eighth of an inch. It had penetrated his clothes, but now sat on his chest like a gray mole.

"Get the med kit," Lucille said to one of the male agents. He ran off and returned with it after about 10 seconds. Phung grabbed it from him and began to lay out the contents.

"Tweezers," demanded the WRA boss. When she got them, she plucked the offending glob off of his chest and everyone waited in anticipation.

No one knew what to expect, but after five minutes of nothing, everyone's hopes began to dwindle. When Reggie gasped and opened his eyes, everyone jumped back in frightened surprise.

Reggie looked around at all of them, noticed that he was on the floor, and asked, "What happened?" A huge cry of relief issued forth and all five women fell on him, hugging him and shedding happy tears.

In a delayed reaction, Reggie sat up quickly and grabbed at his chest. "Did that…? Did Daniel….? That motherfucker shot me!" He looked around in indignation. "I'm going to kill that fucker. He really shot me."

Lucille gasped and said, "Paul! Somebody check Paul." The two men bent down on the other side of the table and called for tweezers after a brief inspection. Another five minutes passed before he too gasped and sat up holding his chest, wondering what had happened.

Phung told the two male agents to go get clean shirts for Reggie and Paul and everyone reconvened at the conference table. One of the agents returned with the two shirts and, now dressed, Reggie and Paul were back to their old selves.

Lucille addressed the agent. "You and your fellow agent helped us in a time of need and I won't forget it. But you and your friend better not breath a word of this to anyone. Am I clear?"

"Yes ma'am," said the agent. "No worries. Neither one of us saw a thing, and I'll make sure of it." He was dismissed and he closed the door behind him on the way out. Lucille knew it would get out eventually, but she wanted to have a plan in motion before it did.

Phung looked at Mrs. Drake who had once again taken her seat at the head of the table. "Does this change anything? He did say as he was leaving that this was only a warning."

Lucille thought about it for a minute as she looked around the table. "I wish it did change what has to be done. No mother wants to be responsible for her own child's death. But Daniel has proven himself to be beyond redemption. With him taking Delmas hostage…"

"Whoa, whoa, whoa. What are you talking about, taking Delmas hostage?" asked Reggie.

Lucille told him about the video Daniel had showed them right before he had fled the scene. She also told him that they really didn't even know if Delmas was alive. "Until we gather more information, we just have to take the video at face value and assume he is only holding Delmas."

Kashonda stood up and said, "Let me go and see what I can find out. I'll get with Jessica and see if it's possible to at least get the vitals on Delmas." She started to exit the room when Lucille waved for her to hold on a minute. She returned to her seat to listen to what was about to be said.

Lucille pulled out her phone and dialed a number. When it was answered, she said, "Stats on Delmas." After a 30 second pause, she asked, "Is it anyway to fake that?" She got her answer and hung up the phone. "At this moment he is alive and well."

She turned to Reggie. "Son, I won't make this decision on my own. I was going to send out a terminate on sight order for Daniel when I thought he had killed you and Paul. But as head of Operations, I'm going to leave it up to you what we do about your two brothers."

Reggie considered for a minute before responding. "Really, the question is how bad do we want Delmas back? We will never get him back with an order of soft retrieval, Daniel is just too good. But if we do a retrieve at all cost, then every agent will be gunning for Daniel under the guise of getting Delmas back. Personally, I say give the agents a shot at taking him down."

Mary Sue grabbed her daughter's hand and looked at Lucille. "What would Daddy say if he could see us now?" She cast her eyes around, shaking her head at the occupant of the room. "This is a member of our family that we are cold bloodedly talking about killing. You seem to forget that I went through most of the same training as all of you. My Dad taught the love of family. He taught us to always be there for one another, to protect each other above all else. That's what the WRA is all about."

She looked around at her family in disgust, daring anyone of them to contradict her. "Now, I sat back and said nothing when ya'll agreed to keep Daniel in prison." She stood up and pulled Dollis along with her. "But I won't sit here and listen to another plot to further destroy this family. And it's funny that you never mentioned anything to me about the plan to kidnap that boy's family," she tossed at Lucille. "Something is really wrong with all of you," she said to the room as she dragged her daughter out of the conference room and slammed the door behind them.

A stunned silence was left in her wake. None of them had ever seen her get upset or heard her raise her voice. The worst part of it all, thought Lucille, was that Mary Sue had a point. They had created the situation that was now coming back to bite them all in the ass. "Alright Reg, what's it going to be? It's up to you and I'll back whatever you decide."

Reggie said, "I think this is a decision we all have to make. Everyone should get their say in the matter. Mom, it's five of us in here, but I know Paul doesn't usually get a vote. Under the circumstances, I think this five should be the ones to decide. Whatever we're going to do, we need to decide fast. We all know where Daniel is going to take Delmas. And once he gets him there, Delmas is lost to us." Reggie looked at Paul and signaled for him to speak.

"I've been with the WRA as an active field agent for longer than anyone currently with the Agency," stated Paul. "Lucille, you brought me in, but you're not a field agent. I'm not exaggerating when I say that this is the deadliest threat we have ever faced. We just had a rogue agent come in here and show us that he could kill everyone in this room if he chose to. Does anyone even know how he got in here?" he asked the room.

In unison all heads shook, responding in the negative. "Which means that he could do it again," Paul continued. "Look, every one of us has emotional attachments to Daniel Burke. Can we honestly say that the man who just came in here is the Daniel we use to know?"

"Okay Paul, we get your point. What do you say we do?" asked Reggie.

"I felt sympathy for him up until this point, but the man is just too dangerous. Too unpredictable." Paul shook his head and said, "I say we terminate."

Reggie turned to his sister. "Kashonda?"

"This isn't a difficult decision. Are we only the WRA or are we a family? Mary Sue has a point. We put him in prison for ten years where we know he suffered unimaginable horrors. This is our brother. Our son. Our nephew. Our friend. This is the youngest of a generation of Burkes. I will do my job as a member of the WRA, but I can't condemn my little brother to death. I vote for a soft extraction to get Delmas back."

Reggie shook his head and said, "We have to stop thinking of him as little Daniel. This isn't a child we're talking about, this is a grown man. He is our family by blood, but not by action. He hates us. For the last three years he has gone out of his way to destroy this organization."

"Give me one example of him trying to hurt the WRA when the Agency didn't strike at him first," demanded Kashonda. "All he wants is to be left alone. He said as much before he left tonight. Nothing he has done, no matter how repulsive the act, has damaged the WRA. Not once has he made an offensive move towards us. Even tonight was because of the threat we made on Walt and Daniel's family."

Reggie wasn't trying to hear any of that. "You're the one with all the connections. You're our Head of Intelligence," Reggie said to his sister. "You of all people should know that there are people who know exactly what he's been out there doing. Important people who can cause a lot of problems for us. And they are wondering why we keep sitting back, letting our brother do these things." Reggie was getting worked up and he did nothing to hide his anger.

"The legacy of the Burke name connects with the reputation of the WRA," Reggie continued. "And every time he does something stupid, it hurts this Agency. He has no respect for the people who suffered or died in the progression of this organization. So, I vote to terminate."

Kashonda started to reply, but Reggie silenced her with a raised hand. He said, "We are running out of time here. Phung, state your case and cast your vote."

Kashonda slammed her hand on the table to bring everyone's attention back to her. "Reggie, I love you and I respect you and your position in this Agency. But don't you dare try to rush people on this decision. We all know time is of the essence, but our brother's life is at stake." She turned to Phung. "Take your time and state your position. Don't be bullied into anything."

Phung held her head high and turned to Lucille as she talked. "I am loyal to this family, no one can refute that. After all the pain and suffering I've been through for Daniel, I've stuck by this Agency and I've done my job to the best of my abilities. But like I said, I am loyal to the family, not the WRA. The WRA is a job, a good job, but a job none the less. I know that all of you have known Daniel longer than me, but I have loved that man since I first laid eyes on him."

Phung paused and looked each of them in the eye. "On his way out the door, Daniel gave me a look that summed up all his feelings towards me. He showed me in those few seconds how I have hurt him and betrayed him over and over with my actions and my silence. I will continue to do my job and follow any orders given to me, but my vote is a soft extraction to get Delmas."

Reggie turned to Lucille and said, "Well, this is fitting. The head of the family as well as the head of the Agency will cast the deciding vote. So, what's it going to be Boss?" he asked in a blatant effort to make her think as the WRA head and not the matriarch of the Burke family.

She examined the faces of everyone at the table. She had known the decision would come down to her. Reggie and Paul as field agents would always see the danger and respond to that. Phung and Kashonda would be more prone to think things through and respond after a careful analysis of the facts. No matter which way she voted, there would be disappointment on the other side.

"Well," she said tapping her fingers on the table. "This is a very difficult decision. My brain and my heart are at war right now. Ultimately, I have a loyalty to both the WRA and to this family. But to me, they are one and the same. So, I am obligated to do what's in the best interest for both. With that being said, it makes the decision a little simpler. As head of the WRA and of the Burke family, I vote to…"

CHAPTER 18

"Oh shit!" exclaimed Daniel. "They didn't waste any time bringing out the big guns."

Walt looked up and down the street as the gate to Daniel's compound closed behind them. "What? I don't see anything." It wasn't even 7:00 am, but the sun was shining bright and the only thing Walt could see was a young black woman jogging towards them on the opposite side of the street. There was no way she could be the threat as she was wearing jogging clothes that left little to the imagination.

"Yeah, this is going to be a fun drive." Daniel looked over and smiled at Walt. "They must have gone ahead with a kill order and they want me to know it." The pretty young woman jogged on by without paying them any attention.

Walt was becoming increasingly confused. "What the hell are you talking about? What is she supposed to be, a distraction?"

Daniel chuckled and said, "Yeah, she's a distraction all right. That's my niece Nyaira. She's one of my sister's daughters and she happens to be one of the top intelligence field agents at the WRA. Her sister Tonya has to be around here somewhere," he said glancing around.

"What's telling is how out in the open she is. With her level of training, we would only see her if she wanted us to." Daniel nodded and said, "They want me to know they are serious. Her revealing herself is a secret warning to me from the part of my family that doesn't want to see me die."

Daniel turned the Hummer to the left and headed for the more populated part of Charlotte. Walt was nervous because he didn't think Daniel was taking this seriously. "Are you sure we have to do this now? I mean, if they are ready for us, wouldn't it be smart to wait?" Walt asked him.

Daniel made a right onto a main street that would take them to the Interstate. "Normally I would say yes," he answered as he surveyed the area. "But then my girls couldn't leave the house. The WRA would engage us in a kind of siege because they would never know when I was taking him out. Basically, it would just prolong the situation and they would be forced to try something stupid."

A car swerved over in front of them and, from under the bottom, some sort of hose fell out lengthwise across the road. Walt yelled, "Watch out!" but Daniel rolled right on over it and nothing happened.

Daniel laughed and said, "Chill man. I told you, as long as we are in this vehicle, there is nothing they can do. Plus, that was just an information cable."

Walt tried to force himself to relax. "Why would you run over it if that's what they wanted?"

Daniel continued driving toward the Interstate like they were out for a Sunday drive. "They've never seen this vehicle, so right now they are trying to get a feel for what they are dealing with. I want them to know how well armored it is so maybe they will conclude they can't stop us. Anyway, they won't make any moves until we are on the Interst...."

Daniel didn't finish the last word of his prediction before he chuckled and said, "Maybe not." A trash truck had crossed the median and was heading right at them for a head on collision. Daniel looked over with joy on his face. "Strap in and hold on tight. We have a long way to go and it's gonna be a bumpy ride."

Daniel slammed on the brakes and turned right, down a side street. The trash truck came barreling right behind them. He hit a button on the steering wheel and, when he pressed down on the gas, the Hummer shot forward like a rocket. "Well Walt, I think we're gonna have to wait to have our talk. But I do need to ask you one thing."

Another trash truck turned onto the street about two blocks up and started accelerating towards them in an attempt to box them in. Walt looked at Daniel and saw that he was still calm, so he said, "Sure, ask away."

"I know back there at the house you said that you were with me. Maybe you're saying that out of gratitude or you think you don't have a choice." Daniel pulled a hard left and a man was standing in the middle of the street with a machine gun. The man started firing as soon as Daniel straightened the wheel. Daniel jerked the wheels left and right as the bullets bounced harmlessly off of the armor wrapped vehicle. Then he floored it and aimed directly at the man.

The move was so fast and unexpected, the man froze for a moment too long and the SUV threw the man twenty feet in the air before he came down in a broken heap. Both trash trucks turned in behind them and continued their pursuit.

Daniel continued with what he was saying as if he hadn't just killed a man. "I guess what I'm asking is if you know what you mean when you say you're with me?"

Walt looked behind them at the trash trucks rumbling after them and said, "I think I have a pretty good idea of what it means."

Daniel shook his head and said, "You really don't and I'm not trying to scare you, but the WRA has you back on its hit list. Without my help, you won't last 24 hours. The thing is, in order to keep you alive, you have to come all the way into my world. You can't be half in and half out."

Walt didn't know if he should drop it, but he needed clarity on that last statement. "So, what are you saying?"

"I'm saying you have to leave your job. You have to leave your home and your cars. I'm saying you can't go visit your family in Philly anymore. You have to leave this world behind and enter a world of darkness and shadows. At least until I can permanently remove the threat."

Daniel hooked another left so he could head for the Interstate. About halfway down the block, another one of the hoses was laid out across the road. Daniel said, "Hold on!" and sped up to go over it. The explosion actually lifted them a foot in the air. But they slammed back down and Daniel expertly regained control over the Hummer.

A woman who looked similar to the jogger from earlier waved at them from the side of the road as they zoomed past. Daniel smiled and waved back, even though she couldn't see him. He turned to Walt and said, "My other niece, Tonya."

Walt wanted to bang his head on the dashboard until he woke up from this nightmare. "If I have to give all that up, I might as well let them kill me. I wouldn't have a life to live."

Daniel took another right and the Interstate signs loomed ahead of them. He got into the right lane and merged onto Interstate 85 North. He said, "I understand what you mean and I would be remiss if I didn't tell you that the WRA would probably still take you if you turned Delmas over to them. And to keep you safe, I'd give him to you and send you both on your way. But to be honest, they will want you to give up the same things. Then we would be on opposite sides of this war."

He paused to let Walt soak all that up. "Make no mistake," he continued. "If I can't barter a truce, the gloves will come off for good. And if you go that route, the next time we see each other, one of us will die."

Walt knew Daniel didn't want that, and he didn't want that either. Daniel had already been at odds with his family, but to save Walt, he had opened himself up for war. There was really no way Walt could leave him and still feel good about himself.

Daniel said, "You got a little time to think about it, but by the time we get to the end of this trip, I'm gonna need your answer. Hell, we might both die today and then it won't matter." Daniel smiled, but Walt didn't think it was funny at all. "Don't worry though, I know they'll come hard for us on the Interstate, but I got a few tricks for them."

They had left the garbage trucks in their dust the second they got on the Interstate. They were passing an 18-wheeler when Daniel said, "Round two so soon? Damn, they want us bad." Walt had no idea what he was talking about until a 15-foot section of the trailer's wall seemed to disappear. Three men were standing there with various weapons. The first guy who went on the attack used a flame thrower.

Daniel laughed and said, "Useless, try again." The man continued the assault as Daniel accelerated to get past the truck. Another 18-wheeler swung over into their lane, making it impossible to get pass. He looked at the screen that showed their rear and saw another tractor trailer coming up behind them. Daniel sucked his teeth and said, "Fucking amateurs."

Walt thought the pursuers were doing pretty good and Daniel had driven them into a perilous situation. If that last truck got behind them, the trucks could then bring their vehicle to a slow stop and the Hummer wouldn't have any means of escape since there was a concrete barrier to their left.

Daniel slammed on the brakes and turned the wheel sharply to the right. With only inches to spare, Daniel got out of the box and the charging 18-wheeler sped by to their left. Daniel said, "The other trucks made their move too fast. The only advantage we have over them on a highway is our ability to maneuver. It would have been a more effective trap if they had waited for the other truck to make sure we couldn't slow down."

Walt didn't have a chance to respond as the two trucks closest to them now picked up the assault. The doors on the back of the truck in front of them rolled up to reveal a man sitting behind a big ass Gatling gun. The barrels were so large, Walt assumed the thing would shoot out missiles.

The other truck had slowed back down and now the panels on its right side disappeared and a man with some kind of hose apparatus took aim at the Hummer. Daniel said, "Oh no you don't," and swerved over to the shoulder as some sort of foam issued out of the hose and landed in the street.

The Gatling gun then swung towards them and started firing at a ferocious rate. Daniel said, "I'm beginning to believe they don't even want Delmas back. Seems to me they're trying to kill everyone in this vehicle."

The bullets were striking the Hummer at such a tremendous rate, it was hard for Walt to hear anything over the noise. "I thought you said we were safe in here!" exclaimed Walt.

"We are," Daniel replied. "I'm doing most of the maneuvering to make them think I'm afraid of their weapons. And this is a $12,000 paint job," he said with a smile. "I don't want those bullshit guns messing it up."

The trucks started swerving erratically, trying to force the Hummer off the road. Daniel said, "OK, it's time to say bye bye to these motherfuckers." He proceeded to drop the hammer on the gas, swerved over into the grass, and literally kicked rocks all over the trucks. 30 seconds later, Walt couldn't even see the trucks out of the back.

"Why didn't you just do that from the get go?" Walt asked him.

"What they are doing now are things they would do to stop a normal armored vehicle. The farther along we get before they realize that we're unstoppable, the less time they'll have to set up some bullshit that will just get a lot of agents killed. The information hose should have convinced them not to even try. But since they want to be hardheaded, maybe we'll just play along for a while."

Daniel's explanation made sense to Walt, but he wondered if he was overestimating himself. He had a lot of reasons to be cocky, but the WRA had out smarted him already the night before. Unless it had been his plan for Walt to get kidnapped.

Walt actually sat up to ask him when he noticed something strange. "Where are all the other cars?" he asked Daniel. On the horizon he could see vehicles entering the Interstate from the right. "And what the hell are those?"

Daniel said, "Shit!" which didn't improve what Walt was feeling. "Those are FRANKS." Daniel didn't seem so amused anymore.

"Man, those are military vehicles!" exclaimed Walt. "I've never seen anything like that. What is a FRANK exactly?"

To Walt, they looked like rockets, sitting on a go-cart frame, sitting on tank tracks. They had to be 20 feet long, and looked formidable enough to blow them off the road.

"The FRANK is an earlier model of the vehicle we're in now," explained Daniel. "It stands for Fast Response Tanks. It looks like they have four of them. While it's not an ideal situation, we'll be just fine." He glanced over at Walt and asked, "Did you play a lot of video games growing up? If you didn't, you might have to drive for a while."

Walt said, "Video games? No, I didn't really play any games except for football."

Daniel said, "Get up. You're gonna have to drive. You might as well get a feel for it before we meet up with the FRANKS."

Walt and Daniel unhooked their harnesses and switched seats. When they were both secured, Walt maneuvered the vehicle around the empty road and realized it handled like a regular SUV. He said as much to Daniel who responded, "For $5 million it should." Walt just shook his head and kept driving.

Daniel said, "Activate LOBI on passenger side." Walt started to ask him how is he supposed to do that when he realized Daniel was talking to the Hummer. A huge screen unfolded from the ceiling that showed what had to be drone footage from directly over the vehicle. At the same time, mechanical ports opened up all over the outside of the vehicle. Walt assumed they were gun ports.

He asked Daniel, "What is Lobby, and what are you about to do?"

"LOBI is an acronym for Lethal On Board Interface," replied Daniel. "Even though lethal is in the name, not all the methods are deadly. I will say, I could take out a whole military base with this thing if I wanted to. Four FRANKS won't be a problem. I just want to be prepared for anything else they throw at us on this drive."

They pulled up to the back of the first FRANK and Daniel said, "Try a PIT maneuver on him. I want to see if they fixed the old problems they were having." Walt slammed into the driver's side rear panel and, instead of the tank spinning to the left, the tracks kept going smoothly straight.

Daniel laughed and said, "Damn, they just made this easy. The whole steering system is computerized." He pressed a few spots on the screen and a red glow highlighted the tank. They were just entering a curve, but the FRANK kept going straight into the trees and crashed.

Walt said, "Let me guess. You activated something like the black box you gave me and you shut down his computer system so he couldn't steer the tank."

"Bingo," said Daniel. "Nowadays, you have to have a strong firewall or anyone can hack your system and shut you down. The WRA's IT department is top notch, but you can't defend against something that you've never encountered." After seeing all this, which Walt was sure Daniel had done mostly on his own, he was really starting to believe Daniel was the best.

As they caught up to the other three FRANKS, Daniel would wait until they came to a curve and activate the jammer. They never had to fire a shot to put all the tanks out of commission.

The next two hours was more of the same. The motorcycles came and Walt just patiently bumped them off the road. Then came the helicopter. They actually had people rappel down onto the top of the Hummer with massive saws in their hands. Daniel pressed another button that caused an electrical pulse to travel through the vehicle, which caused all the saw wielders to fall off after losing consciousness.

Then came the drones, which fell victim to the drone that Daniel had protecting them from the sky. He treated it like it was a video game as he sent up cheers every time, he downed one of the enemy drones.

239

Daniel switched back to driving as they finally exited the Interstate. Walt was tired as hell, but Daniel told him to stay on point because they were getting close and this would be when the WRA tried something desperate.

On a long country back road, they ran over a few more exploding hoses and were peppered by sniper fire. But nothing stopped, or even slowed down, the progress of the Hummer.

Daniel pulled into a field that had a rundown shack set a ways back from the road. Walt remembered the description from what the girls had told him and he figured this was the above ground entrance to the prison they were being held in. He was excited to get the chance to see them, but he was apprehensive of what the WRA could do once they exited the modified Hummer. He had on the body armor, but that could only stop so much.

They pulled up next to the shack and what materialized was something out of a science fiction movie. From out of nowhere, like they appeared from another dimension, what had to be 100 gear laden soldiers surrounded them. Walt didn't know what to expect but Daniel calmly pulled out his phone, dialed a number, and put it on speaker.

Lucille Drake answered with, "I had to go through all this to get you to call your mother?"

Daniel was all business now. "This might be a joke to you as you sit in your headquarters safe and sound. I don't think it will be a joke to these guys about to die."

"Well, if you want, you can give me my son back and we can all live to fight another day?" she responded, still sounding amused about the whole thing.

Daniel flipped a switch on the dash and said, "Mrs. Drake, leader of the WRA, Mom, I am begging you. I can send a pulse attack that will kill all these men. Or you can call them off and we can all live to fight another day," he said throwing her own words back at her.

"Live. Die. I don't give a fuck about those soldiers. As far as I'm concerned, they were born to be cannon fodder!" screamed Mrs. Drake. "You kill them and a hundred more idiots will be waiting when you come out. And I'll keep sending them until one of them gets lucky and kills you."

"I have an enclosure that will guarantee none of your guys can get to us while we do the transfer," said Daniel. "I am giving you this option to show that I am merciful. If one person shoots when I get out, all of them will die. Call them off. Remember, you had your warning last night. There won't be another." Daniel hung up.

He continued to talk. "You see how your leader feels about you." It was only then Walt figured out that he had broadcasted the conversation for all to hear. "I'm not bluffing. I don't care what you were ordered to do, if any of you shoot, then you all die."

Daniel hit a series of buttons and a clear enclosure emerged from under the ground to protect their access to the shack. He maneuvered the Hummer so that the driver's side doors would open into the protection of the glass. He told Walt to put his helmet on and, after they were both geared up, Daniel deactivated LOBI and opened his door. Walt prayed that no one would shoot.

He stepped out and faced the soldiers with a key fob in his hand. When he talked, his voice came from the hidden

241

speakers he had used to communicate with them before. "You can't hurt us and you can't stop us. In five minutes, I will press this button. When I do, everyone within 200 yards will die. Everyone within half a mile will be knocked unconscious. Leave now and this doesn't have to end in a mass killing."

Walt knew Daniel wasn't bluffing, but he also knew the men wouldn't leave. Daniel reached in and cut the speakers off. He said, "I'm sorry Walt, but I can't let them call my bluff. Chances are high that these men are going to die."

Walt nodded that he understood and said, "Let's get him in fast and they might leave while we're inside." At Daniel's silence, Walt said, "Man it's worth a shot."

Daniel didn't say anything, just walked over and removed the lock from the shack's door. Walt went ahead and opened the back door to the Hummer, but waited for Daniel to help him move Delmas. Walt turned to see what was keeping Daniel and what he saw made his stomach drop.

One of the soldiers was walking towards the enclosure with what appeared to be a grenade in his hand. Daniel just stood watching, but Walt raced to that side of the enclosure and screamed, "No! Don't do it man. Just stay back!" By the way his words were thrown back at him, he could tell they were not being heard outside of the glass.

Walt raced over to the Hummer and flipped the switch he had seen Daniel use to communicate with the soldiers. He repeated his message while waving the man off, hoping to prevent a massacre.

To Walt's surprise, the man stopped and removed his helmet. He was a light skinned guy with short dreads and his brown eyes were locked on Daniel's armor covered form.

Daniel walked closer to the SUV and said, "What the hell are you doing here? Did you get demoted or something?"

The man shook his head. "No man. This is an all-hands-on-deck situation. Look, I don't have a lot of time, but I wanted to let you know something."

Daniel said, "Corey, whatever it is will have to wait. You need to get out of here now. If you don't, you'll die with the rest of these guys."

"That's what I wanted to tell you," Corey said, shaking the dreads out of his face. "We ran a scan on the glass and the building, so we know none of our weapons can touch you. But we have orders. If we don't try to get Delmas back with everything we have, she'll send agents after all of us. You know, the real scary agents. The ones who will kill us and our families. But we heard your conversation with Aunt Lucille. I know you Daniel, and I don't know all the details on what happened, but killing all these innocent people is not what the cousin I know would do. We really don't have a choice."

Daniel seemed to think about it for a minute. He said, "You always could talk me into anything cousin. You guys do what you have to do. I'll give you five minutes to shoot so you can say you tried. But Corey, in five minutes I'm pressing this button. Oh, and I'll be calling to return this favor one day." Daniel cut off the speaker.

Corey nodded, put his helmet back on, then hurled the grenade at the glass. He turned and ran, but inside the

243

enclosure, when the grenade went off, Walt barely heard a sound. He had no time to marvel over the makeup of the partition because as soon as Corey was out of harm's way, the small army fired everything they had.

Daniel told Walt to come on. They hefted Delmas' unconscious body inside the structure, and now Walt could see that the rundown shack image was only skin deep. The walls of the structure were probably two feet thick with layered metal and concrete. The guy Corey was right, nothing would reach them short of a nuclear bomb.

Daniel did something on his phone and the elevator door opened up. They settled Delmas against the wall, then he went back out and secured the outside door. He took his helmet off and told Walt to do the same. He said, "This is the point where I need your answer. I've never let anyone in here that didn't end up in a cell. So, I need to make sure you are 100% in or you will have to wait in the Hummer."

Walt didn't have to think about it. He had been all in since Daniel had put a gun to his mother's head to free him. He said, "I'm in, but if we are partners, we need to be…"

Daniel held up his hand to cut Walt off. "We'll get to all that in the near future." He stepped back into the elevator and pulled his phone back out. He pressed some buttons and said, "Ladies? I'm sorry, but I need you to lock down for a little bit." Walt watched on the phone's screen as Ann and Denise made their way back to their cells. Daniel locked them in and then turned to Walt. "Welcome aboard. Now how about we deposit this son of a bitch into his new vault?"

As the elevator doors closed, a new set of doors was opening in Walt's life. It would be all new to him and he would be out of his element for most of it. But for some strange reason, he trusted the killer. Manny. Daniel. More than anything, Walt just wanted to live. He just hoped he didn't live to regret placing his trust in the other man. But one question was burning in his mind that he had to voice. "Where the hell were the cops during all that?"

CHAPTER 19

Ann needed some fresh air. She knew her time in the prison could be measured in weeks, but it felt like years since she had been outside. Having worked in law enforcement for almost 15 years, she never sympathized with the inmates she locked up. Thinking the way they ran prisons now a days was more like summer camp than any type of punishment. She never understood the concept of just being locked up was a torture in and of itself. She definitely understood now.

The one benefit to the situation was that she was in the best shape of her life. Her second week there, Manny had come in one day and showed her and Denise the gym. And gym really wasn't the right word to describe the open space. It was more like an underground sports complex and had everything from a full court basketball setup, to free weights and machines, to a track and field with artificial turf. There was a Pickleball court and even mirrored rooms with big screen T.V.'s to do yoga and calisthenics.

Even with her own sports complex, and her heavenly bed, and her luxurious bathroom, and all the decadent food she could eat, it was still just a prison with a lot of fluff added to it.

And on top of missing the sun and the wind and even the rain, she was pretty much down here on her own. After the altercation with Denise, the only person she could talk to was the killer.

Denise almost never left her room, and when she did, she acted as if Ann didn't exist. Not one word had come out of

Denise's mouth since her declaration after the smack heard around the world. Ann had apologized a million times, but Denise would keep doing whatever she was doing and act like she didn't hear it.

Detective Ann Grace had her pride and she was not going to beg anyone to talk to her. So, she left Denise alone, and concentrated on preparing herself to make her move.

She was under do delusions that she could beat Manny in a fair fight. The man was four inches taller and 70 pounds heavier. But it gave her something to focus on. She was not going to sit around reading romance novels or watching bullshit movies all day. No! She was going to do something to better herself and possibly help her escape. She would need the element of surprise and a hell of a lot of luck, but in her mind, it was doable.

The one thing she did indulge in was the news. She hardly ever missed the morning, noon, or nightly broadcast. Even though it was all bad news, it still kept her up to date on what was going on out there. A lot of it involved the Prison Guard Killer.

One thing they updated every day was the status in the search for Channel 5's own, Denise McCarthy. They had the F.B.I., S.B.I., Sheriff's Office, and local Raleigh P.D. all out continuously searching for the beautiful rising star of the journalism world. As the weeks rolled pass, less and less was said about the kidnapping. But obviously, the reporters felt it was their duty to keep one of their own in the forefront of the viewers minds. Even after all this time, they flash her picture at least three times a day.

When it came to Ann, it was the complete opposite. No story. No reports. No pictures. Nothing. No one out searching for her. As far as she knew, only a few people knew she was missing. She didn't have any family left, at least none that would search for her. Her mother was none existent in her life, and her father had died while she was in the academy.

The only friends she had worked for the S.B.I. and had no doubt been told to keep their mouths shut. And that was if Will and Walt didn't decide to tell everyone she was undercover somewhere. It was a glimpse into her future that she didn't like one bit. She could disappear forever and no one would care. No one would question. No one would mourn.

She tried to shake off her mood as she headed to the kitchen to get Officer Green's food and water. She had cornered Manny the third day the officer was down here and asked him why the man was being treated this way. The darkness that entered his eyes had made her take a step back. He told her to follow his wishes because the man deserved everything he was getting. So, she fed him his dog food and water and tried to ignore the horrible stench that permeated that end of the hall.

Denise was in the kitchen when she got there, wearing a form fitting pair of blue jeans and a yellow tank top that seemed to make her skin glow. She padded back and forth in her white tennis shoes, making a meal for one. Ann watched her for a minute before her anger got the best of her.

"Good morning, Denise," Ann said snidely. "What are you dressed up for? All you're gonna do is eat and watch

T.V. all day. I don't think Walt would still want you if you lost that fabulous body." Ann knew she was being a bitch, but she was sick and tired of Denise.

The previous morning Ann had gotten up early to go work out. She had never been a morning person, but found time ran differently when you were locked up. The more you sleep, the more sleep you need. The less activity you do, your body seems more lethargic instead of being energized.

Anyway, she had gotten up and fixed a big breakfast for both of them. After her workout she made her way back to the kitchen and found Denise sitting there eating a bowl of cereal right in front of the plate Ann had left her. She'd wanted to knock the woman senseless, but just shook her head and went to take a shower.

Now, Ann just wanted Denise to respond to her in some way, even if it was negative. "You know Denise, you're not the only one down here. You're not the only one going through this. I mean, not once have you taken that poor man his food or water," she said gesturing down the hallway. "You can act like your tough shit all you want but, the longer we stay down here, the harder it's going to get. And I might have been the one who slapped you, but you dealt the first blow with your comments."

Denise ignored her and kept making her meal. "What the hell is wrong with you!" demanded Ann. "What do you want from me? I've apologized. I've gone out of my way to try to be nice to you. Why are you being such a fucking bitch to me?"

And finally, a reaction. Denise slammed the pot into the sink and looked up at Ann. She remained silent, but anger

249

raced across her features. Then the mask of indifference settled back in place and she went back to cooking.

Ann said, "This is your last chance, Denise. I promise you, if you don't say something now, this will be how it stays between us forever." Ann walked over to Denise, but stopped a few feet away. "When we get out of here, how much do you think this will affect Walt? I can tell how much he likes you Denise, but Walt is my family. Do you want to make his life hell by always having to pick one or the other?" Denise remained steadfastly silent.

"I've been Walt's partner for over six years now. I've known him over eight. I know him, and I know what he will and won't do. You've made your decision, but I want you to ask yourself this. Are you so selfish that you would make his life hard just to feel like you got the better of me? And at the end of the day, do you think he will choose you over his job? More importantly, will you make him make that choice?" Denise silently sat down and began to eat her food.

Ann shook her head and grabbed the food and water for Officer Green. She steeled herself to ignore the smell, and made her way to the punishment cells. Both the food and water were in bags that could be slid under the door. She slid both in as she watched the disgraced officer lunge for them like the starving man he was.

Over the past almost three weeks, the officer's appearance had drastically changed. He had loss so much weight and was so filthy, it was hard to imagine he was the same proud cop from the news.

The night after the officer was brought here, Ann had watched the report on his abduction. They said a man had impersonated an FBI agent and requested a meeting with the officer at a Wendy's. The video showed Officer Green following a black car from the restaurant, but his car or his person had not been seen again. The man and vehicle had disappeared without a trace.

The Dunn Police Department had only good things to say about the man and said at every turn how good of an officer he was. Mr. Green looked nothing like the photos they still showed from time to time. Ann wondered what the man had done to get on Manny's radar.

One thing she knew for certain was that the officer wasn't going to tell her anything. In fact, he wouldn't say anything at all. Ann had tried to engage the man on several occasions and the man would shake his head and cower away. Whatever threat Manny had used on the man sure worked. She bet it had something to do with the man's family who had been on T.V. begging for the officer's safe return.

All of a sudden, Manny's voice filled the air telling them to return to their cells. As she made her way back to her end of the hall, she couldn't stop the waves of apprehension from crashing over her. Manny was just so dangerous and unpredictable. He tried to treat them with respect and dignity, but there was always the threat of death whenever he came around. After that one time he had locked them in their cells and released some type of gas, she felt death could come at any time. It frightened her that the man could kill them and never give them a chance to fight back.

As soon as she entered the cell, the glass door slid into place. She watched Denise walk by and knew she was being locked in also. Sometimes he would black their windows so they couldn't see him and he couldn't see them. Sometimes he would talk to them one on one, and sometimes together. She hated talking to him one on one because she knew Denise was imagining some conspiracy at best, and an illicit liaison at worst. Without those one on ones, Ann felt Denise would have thawed towards her by now.

From her cell, Ann couldn't see the doors to the elevator open, but she could see anyone who stepped out of them. The first person she saw was Walt and it made her heart skip a beat. To her cop mind, Walt would only be down here for two reasons. Either Manny was no longer a threat to him or, more likely, he was about to become a resident of the underground prison.

She wondered what that would mean for her. If Manny was a friendly now, would she be able to go free? And if Walt was a prisoner, did that mean he had failed one of his missions and now Ann would die as a result? She tried to regain control of her racing heart and wait to see what happened instead of imagining the worst.

Ann watched Walt as he looked around in wonder. Suddenly he turned back around and entered the elevator. After a few seconds, he emerged with Manny and a third guy who they were carrying between them. For some reason, a wave of recognition hit her but she didn't understand it because the man had a mask over his face. Then all she could see was the back of him as they led him towards the punishment cells.

She tried to watch them through the glass command center but they were too far away to make out any details.

252

She did see them remove the mask and toss the man into the cell next door to Officer Green. Ann figured it had to be another enemy by the way they handled the man's body.

After the new prisoner's door closed, she watched as Walt and Manny talked and then Walt's head turned towards her. Manny waved him away and Walt took off back towards Ann's end of the hallway as Manny stayed in front of the new guys cell. Walt was halfway there when her door opened and she rushed out to greet him.

She felt a wave of embarrassment as she remembered she was in her yoga pants and sports bra and didn't have on a bit of make-up. What she looked like should have been the last thing on her mind but hell, so what if she was a little vain. She might die today and she didn't want his last image of her to be of a hot mess.

Then Denise ran pass and damn near pushed her into the wall to get to Walt. Ann decided to stayed back a little, and she watched as the model perfect woman jumped in the air and Walt caught her and spun around as they kissed, and kissed.

They were so enthralled by one another, Ann took the free time to study Walt. He was dressed in some kind of black body armor that highlighted the definition of all his muscles. He looked so happy as he held Denise and they murmured endearments back and forth. Ann admitted she felt a little left out, but she was also happy to see him happy. It made her heart and soul warm to see him smile and hear his laughter. She really did love the man and she had to face reality that it wasn't just a sisterly love. But she would play her role and try not to impede his happiness.

Ann was so focused on the loving couple, she didn't hear or feel Manny come up behind her. "It's beautiful, isn't it?" he asked, making her jump.

She scowled at him. "What's beautiful?"

He frowned. "Come on Ann. I know you're jealous but even you can see that new love is beautiful."

Ann spun on him. "Jealous? What the hell do I have to be jealous about? He's just my partner."

Manny put his hands up in the classic surrender pose and said, "Easy Det. Grace. I'm just messing with you." He sobered up quickly and said, "Let's give them a minute. I have something I'd like to show you."

Ann followed Manny around the loop where he stopped her outside of the new prisoner's cell. He gave no indication that the horrid smell of the officer bothered him, so she ignored it too. He said, "I wasn't sure I should do this, but I didn't like seeing the fake happiness on your face." Ann glared at him even though she knew he was teasing her.

He glanced towards the cell, pulled her back a few steps and whispered, "I don't want you to get upset. It's just something I had to do to keep everyone safe. He's going to be fine. I won't hurt him and you better not tell him I said that."

Ann had no idea what he was talking about but she walked over to the door when Manny motioned her to go ahead.

She looked into the cell and at first her mind didn't comprehend what she was seeing. She actually laughed and shook her head because she thought it was a hallucination.

The man started to move and then rolled up on his elbows facing the door. His eyes blinked open and he also shook his head like he couldn't believe what he was seeing.

Ann placed her palm on the glass, no longer aware of what Manny was doing. The man stood up and walked to the door of the tiny cell. "Ann?" the man questioned.

"Delmas?" was her question back. She never heard the answer. Too many thoughts were swirling in her mind. She couldn't breathe. Her heart was pumping. She was on overload. Then the darkness swam up to offer her blessed relief. She embraced it with gratitude, never hearing the men calling her name.

CHAPTER 20

"Ann? Ann? Can you hear me, Ann? Wake up." Daniel was cradling Ann's head in his lap, trying to get her to come around. He had caught her before her head could hit the ground, so whatever was making her not respond was in her mind.

"Get your fucking hands off of her Daniel! I swear I'll kill you for this!" Delmas was slamming his fist and feet into the glass door over and over again. He only stopped to spew more hatred towards Daniel.

"Shut the fuck up Delmas! I'm trying to help her. Remember, I'm the doctor here. And seeing your face is what caused her to drop like this." Daniel kept his fingers on her pulse and watched as her chest continued to rise and fall with her breathing. As long as neither one of those things changed, then he felt Ann would be okay.

"Open the door!" screamed Delmas. "Open the door now!" Daniel ignored him with his back to the cell because Delmas knew there was no way in hell he would open his door.

All of a sudden, Daniel heard the sound of the door opening. He heard Delmas running at him from behind, but his reaction time was a little too slow. Delmas executed a perfect flip kick to his chest that caused him to stumble backwards and slide all the way into the cell.

Delmas screamed, "Close the door! Close the door!" and the cell door slammed close with Daniel trapped inside.

Delmas said, "Yes!" while raising both hands high. "I finally got your ass. Who's the smart one now Doctor?"

Daniel watched as Walt and Denise walked up and started to assess the scene. Walt was quick, but Delmas was ready and much faster. Walt pulled his side arm, and even got off a shot, but Delmas was already too close to him. In a glorious combination that was as startling as it was efficient, Walt was laid on the ground, and Delmas stood over him pointing his own gun at his head.

Delmas looked at Denise and asked, "Do you want to try something? I'll kill him and leave you down here to be Daniel's play thing." Denise's eyes went huge and she threw her hands in the air, shaking her head. "Good," was all Delmas said.

He told Walt to stand up and slowly remove all of his weapons. Walt stood and glanced at Daniel locked behind the glass. Daniel said, "Do whatever he says Walt. No reason for anyone to get hurt."

Delmas squeezed off a round that nipped Walt on his shoulder. Walt was a trained soldier, so he didn't react to what he knew hadn't hurt him. "You look to him still?" asked Delmas. "It's over for him. You want to save the life of your little girlfriend, you better get with the new program."

Walt still hesitated, but then started removing weapons and dropping them on the floor. He was also ordered to take off the body armor. Once that was done, Delmas told him to step back and place his back against the control booth.

All of the gear was moved down the hall so it was out of everyone's reach. Delmas returned and knelt beside Ann.

His whole demeanor changed once he was staring down into her face. "My beautiful Ann. I'm so sorry I let them take you away from me. I promise you, we will be together from now on. But I need you to wake up. Come back to me." As if by his own will alone, Ann's eyes fluttered open and they both froze, gazes locked in wonder.

"I thought I was dreaming," said Ann. "But it's really you." Ann brushed her fingertips over Delmas' face and chest. He stood and carefully pulled her to her feet. His hands migrated to her waist and her arms circled his shoulders like they were about to slow dance. Their eyes remained locked firmly on each other. Finally, they embraced and Ann started crying as Delmas assured her everything would be all right.

"If you believe anything he says to you Ann, you're a fool," said Daniel, cutting in on their moment. Ann looked over in confusion as she noticed he was in the cell. "He is nothing but a do boy for his mother who has a hit out on you, Walt, and Denise."

Delmas' gaze burned into Daniel, but it softened when he turned back to Ann. "I won't let anything happen to you. I will die before I let them hurt you, I swear it."

"Where was he when those agents came and threatened you all those years ago? I'll tell you," said Daniel. "His coward ass was sitting in front of a bank of computer screens, hundreds of miles away, watching drone footage of them approaching the cabin he had told you to meet him at."

"Shut the fuck up Daniel," snarled Delmas.

"The thing is Ann, he was begging for your life like a little bitch because he swore he never told you who he really was. Which now everyone knows was a lie," continued

Daniel. "They had been sent to kill you and he never once tried to fight, all he did was cry and beg. At the last minute, his mother decided to show you mercy, but all she really wanted was a hold card to play if Delmas ever got out of line."

Ann was listening raptly to Daniel talk, but Delmas turned her face back to his. "He is lying Ann. They never told me they would kill you. My mother simply said they couldn't allow me to see you again and she sent some agents to make sure you wouldn't talk about us. My brother is just sore because I got the best of him."

"I have proof Ann. You know I watch and record everything. I did back then too," confessed Daniel. "My phone isn't working right in regards to security, but I can access my cloud videos just fine. I'll show you what a cowardly, backstabbing, little momma's boy he really is."

"Enough!" roared Delmas. "Ann, you know I love you. I always have and I always will. I tried to get the WRA to bring you over as an agent, but I was shot down. This time I won't give them a choice."

"But what if I don't want to be a WRA agent?" asked Ann softly. "What happens if all I want is a nice, normal life working at the SBI? Can you give me that? Will you fight for me to have what I really want?"

Delmas dropped his head so it was Daniel who answered. "He doesn't have a say in any of that and he's too chicken shit to go against the family. Tell her the truth Delmas. Tell her that Mommy dearest put a hit out on her and I locked her down here to save her life. Tell her that you're going to take her to WRA headquarters where you know for a fact, they will kill her and Walt and Denise."

Up until this point, Denise and Walt had stayed silent. Now Denise gasped and said, "OK, that's the second time you've mentioned my death. Why kill me? I don't know anything about this mess."

Daniel said, "The WRA does whatever they think is good for them. When you did your first exclusive report on me, they tagged you. When you aired the videos, they assumed we were working together, so they started watching you. As soon as you began consorting with the super stud, Walt, they added you to the list. Ann and Walt were already on the list because of some other investigations, but I held the WRA off as best I could. They didn't see any more value in Ann, so I put her here where they couldn't get to her. Only after I hid her did they have a change of heart and say not to hurt her. I can only guess Delmas did some more of his begging."

Denise laughed and turned to Walt. "You don't believe any of that do you?" She went on before Walt could answer. "Manny, or I guess Daniel now, is a monster. He is a fucking serial killer. In my book, anyone who wants to lock him up is a friend of mine. We need to be helping this man Walt, not trying to fight him."

"There is a lot you don't know about Denise. I don't even know what I can tell you, but Daniel is right. He just saved my life hours ago." He pointed at Delmas. "That man's family told me that none of us would be allowed to live. Not you, me, or Ann. Now, I don't know how much pull this guy really has, but from what I saw, his mother's word is law. She said we would die, so Denise, that is what I believe."

Ann backed away from Delmas and glanced at Walt. "Delmas, Walt is my family. If you're going to kill him, then you have to kill me too."

Delmas laughed. "I watched you over the years Ann. Throwing yourself at this old, soft ass motherfucker," he said with disgust. "Mooning over him, embarrassing yourself over and over as he ignored your childish advances. Now you're ready to die for him?" He shook his head. "I'm tired of this whole thing. I'm taking all of you to the WRA headquarters and I'll let my Mom figure it out."

A small voice from the end cell said, "What about me? Can you let me out of here?"

Delmas sighed and said, "Open the last cell." About five seconds later, the cell door whisked open. The officer stepped out and Delmas shot him four times center mass. All of them stayed silent, listening to the man struggling to draw one more breath. Then all went quiet.

He pointed the gun at Walt's head and said, "All of you, walk to the elevator." He then turned to Daniel. "I guess someone will be down to get you later. You can't even use your pulse weapon now without fear of killing your team. Mother still wants you dead, but she'll insist on doing it the right way." He walked off, following his three captives, leaving Daniel and the dead man without a backwards glance.

If he would have looked back, he probably would have wondered what his trapped, defeated, little brother had to smile about.

CHAPTER 21

"What in the hell happened?" demanded Reggie. "How did they make it to the prison? That bullshit armored SUV shouldn't have made it out of Charlotte."

Reggie had just come back from the hospital wing after being checked out to make sure he had no lasting effects from the fake bullet. Paul and the other guard who had been shot were still down there being tested. It seemed that the only real bullets used where the ones Daniel had shot out the cameras with. It was unreal how well Daniel planned everything.

Now, the whole management team was sitting in the all-glass suite overlooking the command center in the heart of the WRA headquarters. Below them, agents were running around from station to station transferring information and probably trying to figure out how they had let Daniel and Walt make it to the prison with Reggie's younger brother. He had only been gone a few hours, but the instructions he'd left should have ended the pursuit before it started.

He glanced up at the screen everyone was so intent on and saw something that made no sense to him at all. The big screen down in the command center showed a drone view of the area around the prison's entrance. Reggie could see the Hummer parked next to the shack. All of the soldiers were packing up and leaving the scene which is the reason Reggie had rushed to the suite for answers.

But the smaller screen in front of him showed Daniel and Walt dragging a masked Delmas down a hallway and stopping at a cell. They dumped him in and the glass door closed. "What am I looking at here? How are we getting this footage?"

At no time had they ever had a view inside the prison. From the angle of the video, Reggie could tell it was a camera installed inside the prison, not one they had somehow snuck in. Phung pressed keys on her keyboard and more views from different cameras popped up on the screen. They watched Walt run off one way and Daniel slow walking in the other direction. Ann and Denise came out of other cells and Walt and Denise embraced as Ann looked on.

When nothing else happened, Reggie said, "Will someone please tell me what's going on. How are we seeing this?"

Finally, Lucille looked up from Phung's computer screen and said, "Relax and have a seat, Reggie. We have this operation under control."

"What operation do you have under control? Delmas is sitting in a prison cell that we can't get to." Reggie walked over and stood next to his mother so he could look at the computer screen with them.

Phung was typing furiously and talking on a headset. "All right Jessica, we have to attack this last firewall from both directions. You continue the inside hack and I'll initiate the new one."

Lucille looked at Reggie with a please smile. "We're gonna have to give Phung, Delmas, and Jessica bonuses after this. Their plan is working to perfection. Pure genius!"

"Plan? What plan?" demanded Reggie. "The plan was to stop the SUV and get Delmas back." Reggie got a sick feeling in the pit of his stomach. "Please don't tell me ya'll came up with another plan without consulting me."

"No Reggie," his mother said. "This was the plan all along. It's an I.T. plan so there was no need to include you in it. And please don't talk to me like us women couldn't come up with a plan without a big ole strong man to lead us."

All of a sudden, red lights flashed and a buzzer noise issued from below. Phung said, "That was it Jessica, we did it. We are now in total control of the prison."

Lucille Drake reached down and hugged Phung to her chest. "I knew you could do it. I had complete faith in you and Jessica. When Delmas gets back here we're going to celebrate your success." Phung beamed as she started testing how complete the hack was by moving the cameras and opening cell doors where no one could see.

"Am I the only one who heard the buzzer and saw the flashing lights? Doesn't that mean we just got hacked?" asked Reggie.

Phung smiled and said, "No Reg, that was the last firewall being brought down on the prison security. It was just a signal to tell us our system is now connected to his."

Reggie did not look reassured. "Okay Phung, tell me what your original plan was."

She took the headset off after telling Jessica good job and then turned to Reggie. "The security on the prison was top notch. Is top notch. It's exactly what you would expect from the greatest computer mind in the world. But part of the security, really the greatest part of it, was proximity. From outside of the prison, the only door into the prison, technology wise, is Daniel's phone. And trust me, he is the only person who can use that phone.

Reggie nodded his head. "Yeah, I know about the phone. Something about a biometric and DNA scan that is impossible to fake. You remember, we got his phone when he went on the prison job and it's still being worked on to this day."

Phung, ever in a good mood, smiled and said, "Oh yeah, I remember. I'm the one still trying to crack it. Anyway," she said to get back on topic. "Based on trial and error, and after trying different kinds of attacks, we concluded that the only way to defeat the security was to launch a coordinated attack from the inside and the outside.

"So, with that in mind, I hid a microchip in Delmas' foot to act as a relay from the inside, then Jessica and I hit his firewalls with everything we have. We were in within minutes."

Reggie didn't like it. Something still felt off. "Wouldn't Daniel scan everyone for things like that before he ushered them into the prison?"

Phung gave him the megawatt smile. "You can thank LaCora for that. She developed a type of microchip made out of human nerves. That way, if anyone scans for any kind of device, it won't come up as a foreign object. It's a prototype, but she guaranteed it would work and would be undetectable."

LaCora Clay was the WRA tech inventor. She was also a cousin to the Burke siblings. If she said something would work, then you could take it to the bank.

"If you have control over the prison, why is Delmas still in the cell?" asked Reggie. "You could open his door now and he could make it to the elevator before Daniel even knew he was free."

"Well," said Phung, flashing a worried look at Lucille. "Momma Drake wants to bring Ann, Denise, and Walt back here. So, Daniel has to be locked in a cell and Delmas has to figure out a way to do it."

Just as she was saying that, they noticed some activity was going on in front of the cell Delmas was being held in. All of them knew that Ann and Delmas had history, so it wasn't a surprise to see her being led to his cell door.

"Phung, where's the sound?" asked Reggie. "I want to hear what's being said."

She started typing again and, out of hidden speakers, Daniel's voice could be heard giving Ann a warning to prepare her for what she was about to see. They also clearly heard him say that he wouldn't hurt Delmas. They couldn't see Ann's face, but she was hesitant as she walked towards the cell.

Everything was quiet for a minute and then Ann placed her hand on the glass and whispered, "Delmas?"

This caused Reggie to slam his fist down on the table and scream, "I knew it! That lying little bastard. All these years Ann's been walking around knowing exactly who we were."

Reggie was in a rage and didn't care one bit when Ann passed out and Daniel caught her. "I told you we should have killed her," he said to his mother. "Who knows how much information she's leaked over the years." He listened as Delmas and Daniel bickered back and forth while Daniel helped Ann.

Delmas screamed, "Open the door! Open the door now!" Phung frantically entered the code to open his door and they watched Delmas explode out of the room and deliver a kick to Daniel's chest that sent him careening into the cell Delmas had just vacated. Everyone was screaming, "Close the door," right along with Delmas.

When the door slammed shut, they all watched as Daniel pulled out his phone, hit a few buttons and put the phone away. Everyone started cheering and celebrating except for Reggie. Something was not right about this whole thing. Reggie had trained with his brother, and Daniel was acting like he was right where he planned to be.

On the screen, Delmas easily defeated Walt and made him disarm himself. Reggie wasn't buying it. "Run diagnostics on our system right now," he said to Phung.

His mother said, "Chill out Reggie, we got this. Everything is under control."

Reggie shook with the urge to break something. "Phung. I'm not going to ask you again. Don't forget who you really work for. Run the diagnostic now!"

The party atmosphere suddenly died and Phung, looking dejected, sat back down at her computer to do what she was told. Mrs. Drake looked at her son with disapproval and said, "That was uncalled for. As a field agent with so much experience, I'd expect you to have better control of yourself."

"As the only field agent in this room, I would think that anything I say should be taken more seriously." He turned to his quiet, analytical cousin Dollis and asked her, "Based on everything we know about Daniel, and everything that's happened in the last 24 hours, what is the probability that this plan of theirs works?"

She cocked her head in thought and slowly shook her head. She looked at Reggie and said, "Not good. I would place our odds of coming out on top of this situation at about ten percent."

"Ten fucking percent," he said to his mother. None of them had really been paying attention to the exchange on the screen. When Reggie tuned back in, Walt was explaining to Denise why he was on team Daniel. Reggie didn't care about that, they had more important issues.

"You can't just throw a plan together when you're up against an adversary like Daniel," Reggie explained to the group. "Do you see how calm he is? Do you think if his security was really taken over, he would have checked his phone once and put it away? Something isn't right here."

They all turned back to the screen when Delmas said loudly, "Open the last cell." Phung leaned over to another computer and opened the last cell door for Officer Green to come out.

They had watched as Daniel forced the man inside the prison. At the time, the WRA was still playing nice, trying to get Daniel to talk to them. So, everyone had sat back and done nothing. Officer Green meant nothing to them anyway.

With no warning, and for no apparent reason Reggie could see, Delmas shot the cop and left him dying half in and half out of his cell. Reggie shook his head and said, "What a fucking mess." He turned to Phung. "How is the diagnostic coming along? Anything looks out of whack?"

Phung said, "No, not really. We're using slightly more power than I anticipated, but that might just be what's needed to keep the firewalls of the prison from closing on us. Everything else looks good."

They all focused back on the screen as Delmas led the three captives back to the elevator. Reggie's blood turned cold. He ran to the monitor and pointed at Daniel. "Why is he smiling? I thought everything…."

He didn't finish the statement. His breath froze in his lungs because the whole command center suddenly lost power and they were all plunged into darkness.

CHAPTER 22

Daniel always felt euphoric after one of his plans ended exactly as he foresaw it. Walt, Ann, and Denise were now behind the glass doors leading to the cell area, while Delmas and Daniel were in the prison's receiving area. He was the only one conscious at the moment, but the others would come around soon.

When Delmas had walked away from him 15 minutes ago, he had pulled out his phone once again and got to work. He had activated the sleeping gas release valve in the elevator area. Within seconds, all four occupants were on the floor sleeping soundly.

Daniel opened his cell door and turned on the exhaust to get rid of the excess gas. When everything was clear, he'd entered the receiving area and moved Walt, Ann, and Denise to the cell area. He had stripped all the weapons off of Delmas and himself and secured them in the central control booth. Then he'd locked the doors to give him and Delmas a little time to work out their differences, without anyone interfering.

All he was doing now was waiting for the gas to wear off so they could get this show on the road. Walt, being the biggest one, would show the first signs of waking up. Denise, being the smallest, might be out for an additional five minutes.

As soon as Walt's hands and feet started moving, Daniel walked over to Delmas and injected him with the paralysis drug. That way, Delmas would wake up but Daniel could talk to him before things turned deadly.

Walt sat up and Daniel walked over to the door with a smile on his face. "I'm proud of you Walt. You passed your test. I hate to say it like this but, if at any time you would have wavered in your decision to join me, I would have had to kill you."

Walt stood all the way up and looked from Ann, to Denise, and then to Delmas before smiling and looking at Daniel. "You just might be the best after all. But there's no way in the world you can tell me this was part of your plan."

Daniel laughed and said, "The best plans have a beginning, an outcome, and a lot of flexibility in the middle. As long as you stay fluid, you don't panic if anything goes wrong. Like, I didn't think they would kidnap you until next week, but it didn't matter because we ended up in the same place."

Ann started moving so Daniel figured Delmas had to be awake. He turned around and noted with satisfaction the fury in Delmas' eyes. He turned back to Walt and said, "Hopefully this won't take long. Listen and you might learn something. Either way, be ready for a good show."

Daniel walked over, leaned down, cocked his arm back and smacked the shit out of Delmas. He laughed because all Delmas could do was increase his breathing. Daniel stood up straight and said, "That was for going after my family. Anyway, this stuff should wear off after another 15 minutes. In the meantime, I'm gonna fill you in on some stuff."

He glanced over and saw Walt helping Denise to her feet. Now that everyone was up, he started his speech. "I'll go ahead and tell you the worst of it now big brother. I have control over the whole WRA mainframe now because of your dumbass, half-baked plot. That means all of the money, all the assets, all the information belongs to me now. And it's all thanks to you, Phung, and probably Jessica."

Daniel walked around his brother's prone body as he filled him in on just how fucked the WRA was. "The thing is, even I couldn't hack my way into the command center from outside the room. I designed that system so that it updated itself and learned as it was being attacked. With ten levels of protection, no one, not even me, could force their way in. And once it locked you out, you had to come up with all new attacks because none of the old ones would work. I trusted all of you so much, I didn't even build in a back door.

"So, I went back to my military intelligence days," Daniel continued. He noted that Walt and the two women were listening intently to what he was saying. "I locked myself in a room for two days until I came up with the perfect plan. No food. No water. Just me and my thoughts." He turned to face Walt. "So that you understand how I play the long game, that two days in the room was over three years ago."

Daniel watched the interaction between Walt and Ann and knew that they were plugging that information into their time line. "Yes," he said to them. "Some of the killings were personal, but most of them were geared towards bringing this day about. Ann, I had no idea you had a previous role in any of this until after my mother warned me not to hurt you. Which was ironic because I never would have taken you if the WRA wouldn't have placed a hit on you. Anyway, that's when I went back and viewed the recording of your situation.

"Denise, you just had the misfortune of being good at your job and answering your phone. I had called ten reporters before I reached out to you. If you don't answer, then it's another reporter here and you'd still be at channel 3 getting peoples coffee," he said snidely, reminding her she was a nobody before he turned her into a star.

"Walt, you were always meant to be right here. As soon as I found out you had taken over the homicide unit for the SBI, I knew what I had to do to get you standing behind this door when the time came."

He turned back to Delmas. "Now, my dearest big brother. I had no idea if it would be you or Reggie laying here, but I'm kind of glad it's you. First off, Reggie probably wouldn't have fallen for the trap. But secondly, out of everyone, your betrayal hurt me the most. We were practically twins growing up, and just like that," Daniel said, snapping his fingers. "You turned your back on me and left me locked up for ten years. If the shoe had been on the other foot, I would have burned the whole state down to get you out."

Daniel saw his hand twitch and knew it was almost showtime. He took his phone out and leaned it on the wall near the elevator.

"Only one of us will be leaving this prison," Daniel continued. "Right now, the whole WRA management is trapped inside the command center without power. Everything is frozen. I haven't moved any money or assets and you'll have the chance to keep it that way. If you beat me in a straight up, one on one, man to man, fight, then you can put me back in my cell, take my phone, and you'll have control over the prison and the WRA mainframe. But if I win, you go back in the cell and I drain the WRA down to the bone."

As Delmas was gaining more and more movement, Daniel stripped off his body armor and threw it behind him. This would be a tricky fight for him. He didn't really train to win fights, he trained to kill his opponent. He did not want to kill his brother, but if he had to in order to survive he would.

The funny thing was, Daniel had never won a fight against either of his brothers. Reggie was always too big and strong, and Delmas was always more ruthless. Where Daniel would pull back on a debilitating blow, his brothers showed him no mercy. Delmas would be overconfident, never guessing the beast that lurked inside Daniel now. He knew this wouldn't be easy, but he also knew failure wasn't an option. He was fighting for more than just himself, as pictures of Alisha and Gabby flooded his mind.

Delmas sat up with a look of pure hatred on his face. This prompted Daniel to have a sudden thought. He walked over to his phone and organized a little watch party back at WRA headquarters. He tapped into his mother's phone so that they would be able to see and hear what happened between the two brothers.

He set his phone back down and waved at the camera as Delmas was getting to his feet. "For those of you just joining us, we are about to fight to see who will take control of the WRA mainframe and this prison. If Delmas wins, I will stay down here and he will take my unlocked phone, which will give him access to everything here and at the WRA. But if I win, then Delmas will remain my guest down here and I will drain all assets of the WRA. Last I checked, it was somewhere around $600 Billion, so I have no doubt who you will be cheering for."

Delmas laughed and said, "I only heard one mistake in your little speech."

Daniel cocked his head and asked, "And what might that be Brother?"

"You said you would be going back into a cell, but that won't happen," Delmas said with a nasty smile. "Your next stop will be a shallow grave or the ocean floor. And for taking me through all this, I'm gonna pay another visit to your little family. But don't worry, we look alike. I'll have both of them calling me daddy real soon, but obviously for two different reasons."

Daniel's whole persona changed. "Delmas, you really shouldn't have said that. You just made this a lot easier."

Delmas ran at him, shouting as he threw a high knee aimed at his head. Daniel dodged to the right avoiding the knee, but ended up taking an elbow to his forehead. Daniel didn't even have time to register the pain as Delmas kept his offensive momentum with a combination of kicks aimed to end the fight fast. These powerful kicks had to be dodged because any body part used to block would more than likely break on impact.

The elder Burke didn't seem to tire as he kept his younger brother on defense. There was no way he would be able to keep up this ferocious pace, thought Daniel. They had been fighting for almost two minutes and he hadn't seen an opening yet.

Walt yelled, "Come on Daniel. Stop toying with him. Don't forget who's waiting on you."

Delmas backed off and sneered. They circled each other as he said loudly, "So you think he's toying with me? I guess he never told you what his record is against me. Just don't get your hopes up that his first win will come today."

Daniel knew Walt didn't like hearing he had never beaten his brother. He probably thought of Daniel as Superman and couldn't fathom him losing in a fair fight.

Delmas, not even breathing hard, ran at Daniel to begin his second attack. This time Daniel had a few surprises for him. As each one of Delmas' kicks went flying by, Daniel would push the leg to alter the attacks momentum. This caused Delmas to either spin with the kick or use his other leg to slow his motion. On the fifth kick, Delmas decided to spin and Daniel stepped in and delivered a vicious kick to the planted leg just below the knee.

No one could take a kick like that and stay up. Delmas proved that he was not the exception to the rule. His back smacked the ground and Daniel punched him twice in the face before Delmas could roll out of range and get back to his feet.

Delmas touched his nose and mouth and his eyes narrowed as he looked at the blood on his fingers. "Still pulling your punches I see. Let me get you in that position and it's game over for you."

They battled. With Delmas being the aggressor, they traded blows, each giving and receiving damage. This was no show fight, but it was methodical, each fighter knowing that one mistake would be life altering.

After 15 minutes neither man appeared to be winded at all. Daniel hated to do it but he was going to have to seriously hurt his brother or he would be forced to kill him. He took up a different fighting stance that he knew his brother had never seen. This style of fighting was only to be used to end a life. He prayed his brother was strong enough to at least survive what was to come.

Delmas laughed. "All right Bruce Leroy. Let's finish this."

Daniel faked a high kick and, when Delmas' arms came up to block, Daniel stopped on a dime and threw a punch that signified the beginning of the end of this contest. The quad punch connected and Delmas screamed in agony. Daniel rose into a hip toss position and slammed his brother to the ground. The straight finger jab to his solar plexus caused Delmas to go eerily still. It wouldn't last long, so Daniel had to strike hard and he had to strike fast.

He rolled on top of Delmas and delivered a savage knee to the thigh of Delmas' right leg. He then repeated the process on the left leg. Both of his legs were now broken. Delmas was making a low moaning sound in his throat that Daniel knew was the only outlet to pain at his disposal.

Daniel did a 180-degree spin and sat up with Delmas' head between his knees. He proceeded to hammer down on both of his brother's shoulders until he heard his collar bone snap. He joined both his fist together so he could deliver the final blow to his brother's head, but stopped when he registered someone screaming.

Ann was pounding on the glass and screaming, "Don't kill him! Please don't kill him!" over and over again. Tears were raining down her face as she pleaded with him to spare her former lover's life.

Denise was nowhere in sight, but Walt was looking at him with a mixture of awe and fear. It was a look you give a man when you understand that he could kill you at any time. The look also said that he believed in Daniel and would follow him to the end.

The phone rang and Daniel glanced at it but ignored it because he knew who it would be. He looked down at his brother who was watching him with fear in his wide eyes. "I'm supposed to kill you," Daniel told him. "You have threatened my family and told me numerous times that, given the chance, you would kill me. The hate and fear I see in your eyes tells me you will never stop. But I want you to think over the last 24 hours and see how many times I spared your life."

Daniel stood up and looked at the camera his family was watching him through. "Do we have to keep going through this?" he asked them. "Why can't you just leave me and mine alone? Will I have to kill every one of you for my family to be safe?"

He pointed back at his fallen brother and said, "This is the last chance I will give you. I'm going to take him up to the surface and leave him for someone to come pick him up. I'm going to restore all WRA control back to you. I won't touch your money or assets. But I won't stop going after the people on my list. And if any of you make another play at me or anyone under my protection, I promise that I won't pull any more punches."

He walked over and picked up the phone, not surprised to see the missed call from his mother. He terminated their connection to the prison's camera, restored power to the WRA command center, but left them locked out of their system for the time being. He opened the cell area doors and Walt and Ann walked over and looked down at the incapacitated WRA agent.

"Is he going to be all right?" asked Ann, having got control of herself, but still looking concerned.

"He won't be threatening any more women or girls for a while, but he'll be all right."

With a serious look, Daniel told them, "We need to talk," before leading them into the kitchen area. Once there, he said, "I've already talked to Walt about this but Ann, you can't go back to your regular life. The WRA will find a way to kill you. They'll make it look like an accident or in the line of duty or some other way that won't trace back to them. But once they put out a hit on a non-agent, there is no taking it back."

"So, what do you want me to do? Stay down her for the rest of my life? I'm no coward Daniel. They don't scare me."

"Well, you're a moron if they don't scare you," said Walt. "Before last night, I had no idea who or what these people were. Now that I had a glimpse, I know it would be suicide to try and act like they don't exist."

"OK, fine. They're dangerous and they'll kill me," said Ann. "Where does that leave me? Because I'm not staying down here hiding from the Boogie Man."

Daniel said, "That's why I wanted to talk to both of you. See, you can't go back to your normal lives now, but that doesn't mean you can never go back."

Walt, looking confused, said, "I'm not following you. If we go back, we die right?"

"If you go back as you are now, yes, you will die," said Daniel. "But, if you let me train you on how to survive in my world, then you'll both be able to live a somewhat normal life in the not-so-distant future."

"How long exactly is the not-so-distant future?" asked Ann.

Daniel considered for a moment. "If you really put the work in and dedicate yourself to the training, I'm thinking one year, 18 months max. The training wouldn't stop there, but you would know enough to return to your lives with a good chance to survive."

Ann looked at Walt with questions in her eyes. Walt said, "This is your decision to make Ann. I've already told him I'm in. After seeing what these people can do, and what they are willing to do, this is really the safest action to take."

Daniel was not going to try and convince her in any way. If she wanted to live, she would sacrifice a little time so she could live a full life. If she wanted to die, he would drop her off at her house and she probably wouldn't make it to the end of the week. He did not want her to die, but he wasn't going to force her if she wanted out.

Ann said, "If I have to stay down here, it's a deal breaker. I'm getting too pale. I need the sun."

Walt wrapped his arms around her and smiled. He said, "Our new benefactor has more money than he knows what to do with. I'm sure we can figure something out."

"Wait," said Ann. "What about my house and all my stuff? Some of it is irreplaceable."

"I'll have someone go through and get all the personal things from both of your houses. So, if you have some secret stash, you might want to tell me so I can pass the information on."

They started poking fun at each other, talking about porn stashed and sex toys, when Walt looked up with alarm in his eyes. He shouted, "No Denise!" which caused Daniel and Ann to spin around in that direction. Denise was standing in the doorway holding one of the guns Delmas had stripped off of Walt.

She pointed the gun right at Daniels head and said, "This is the part when you give me a good reason why I shouldn't blow your fucking head off. From what I just heard, you and your two friends here are about to run off and play super soldiers. And where does that leave me? On the streets where your crazy ass family can come and kill me? Or stay locked up down here? No way. You're gonna give me some answers or we all die down here."

Walt and Ann looked desperate, but they both kept still and silent with their hands reflexively raised in the air. Denise looked like an unhinged beauty queen with her dead serious expression, bare feet, and big ass gun. There was no doubt this was a life-or-death situation. That's why they all looked at him crazy when Daniel burst out laughing.

CHAPTER 23

Lucille Drake was terrified. One second, she was feeling on top of the world. The next, total devastation. All she could do was assume the worst, that Daniel had turned the tables on them once again. "Phung, what happened? What's going on?"

It was pitch black as whatever was being done prevented the two backup generators from coming on. Phung said, "I'm not sure. Could be we were using too much power and fried all the circuits."

"If you believe that, it's no wonder it was so easy for Daniel to trick you," said Reggie. "We're under attack and you opened the door wide enough for the whole army to march in." Lucille knew she had messed up, but now wasn't the time for I told you so's.

"Reggie, if you're not going to help, then do me a favor. Shut the hell up!" shouted Lucille. "You were right. Is that what you want to hear? Now help us fix this instead of making it worse."

Someone rattled the door and Reggie was smart enough, and still had enough sense to turn on his phone's flashlight. He illuminated Agent Paul Stevens standing on the platform trying to get in. The room was totally sound proof, so Reggie called the agent's cell phone.

Reggie said, "Yeah, we've been hacked. Since the power is off, these doors won't open for security reasons." He listened for a few seconds and said, "Stand back, I'll give it a try."

Lucille watched as Reggie propped his phone on the end of the desk, pulled out his gun, and aimed at the corner of the glass door. They all knew the door was bulletproof, but you shoot something enough times in the same spot, it's liable to break. He fired six shots, hitting the same spot each time, before the whole door spider webbed. He picked up an unused computer monitor and heaved it at the center of the door, causing the glass to shatter and cascade to the floor.

By now, everyone in the control center had their phones out with the flashlight activated. Paul stepped in and said, "I saw the big screen before the power went out. How in the hell did they make it to the prison? Did something go wrong?"

Reggie didn't give her a chance to answer. "That's no longer relevant. We need to figure out how to get power back, because right now we're not getting any air pumped down here."

"Bad news Reg," said Phung. "I've tried to access parts of our network on my phone and it's a total lock out. Whatever Daniel did, he controls everything now. He controls the whole WRA mainframe. From the lights all the way up to our top-secret data. And with the new firewall he's dropped into place, there's nothing we can do about it."

"How is that even possible?" asked Lucille. "A lot of our data is stored off site."

"I'm not exactly sure," confessed Phung. "To be honest, I've never seen a hack on this level. I didn't think Daniel knew how to do something on this scale. All our backdoors have closed. To put it in perspective, just to keep us locked out would take a thousand computers running a thousand programs simultaneously."

Lucille felt a lump form in the pit of her stomach. "So, what are you saying Phung? Is he receiving help? Possibly from the inside?"

Phung glanced around the room before shaking her head. "I don't know. It's possibly coming from the inside, but it's more likely he's struck a deal with another agency that wants our assets and intel. Then again, this is Daniel we're talking about. He could be doing this with some supercomputer hidden under his compound."

"So, bottom line," said Reggie. "We have a hostile in a secure location with a hostage. A hostage we are not willing to sacrifice. And he has control over the whole WRA mainframe as well as our lives because without power we can't get back to the surface or pump air in here. In other words, we're fucked and we just have to hope Daniel shows us mercy."

Everyone remained quiet so Reggie turned to Paul. "You have any suggestion? Daniel used tunnels to get around down here. Can any of them get us out of here?"

"In my opinion, if Daniel had a tunnel that led into here, he wouldn't have waited so long to hack us. Anyway, if there is a tunnel, we would never find it, or be able to use it. The one tunnel I saw him use back in the day was activated with his phone." They all knew that meant the tunnels weren't an option.

Reggie looked at Lucille and asked, "So what do we do? Maybe we should call him and ask him to at least activate the air pumps. If Kashonda, Dollis, and Aunt Mary were outside of the headquarters, he would probably let the rest of us die. Maybe one of you should call," he suggested.

Lucille damn near had a heart attack when her phone started vibrating in her hand. She looked at the screen and gasped. "Everyone come quick. I'm getting video from inside the prison."

Everyone gathered around her trying to get a good view of her screen. Phung pulled out her own phone again and started poking furiously at the screen. Finally, she said, "Everyone should have this feed on your own phones now." They all locked in on their phones to see what was going on inside the prison.

They listened as Daniel explained that he and Delmas were going to fight and exactly what was at stake. Daniel seemed calm enough, but Lucille could see the fury on Delmas' face. If he could channel his emotions, Lucille was sure this would be over quickly.

After some basic male posturing and trash talk, they began to fight. Delmas stayed on the attack and everyone was indeed cheering for him. The only troubling part to her was that Delmas couldn't seem to hit his brother as Daniel danced around him still looking calm.

On top of that, Reggie was getting on her last nerve, shouting advice at his phone like Delmas could hear him. When the first break in the fight occurred, Reggie looked at her and asked, "Why isn't Daniel fighting back? I saw ten different times he could have tried an attack."

She didn't answer because round two started and everyone's focus went back to their screen. Delmas went right back on the offense and, for no reason she could see, Reggie said, "No! No Delmas. Stop! He's setting you up." Fast as lightning, Daniel stepped in after a missed kick and delivered one of his own that dropped Delmas onto his back. Daniel sent two more punches at Delmas before he seemingly let him get back to his feet.

Lucille had been taught to fight but, other than the occasional spar, she never indulged in hand-to-hand combat. Even she knew Daniel was pulling his punches. Which didn't make sense to her unless he was still running some kind of game. When she looked at Reggie, she could tell he was thinking the same thing.

The fighting started again. Even though they both took hits, none of the damage appeared serious. After about 15 minutes of back and forth, Daniel stepped back and did something that ripped the air out of her lungs. She heard Paul gasp and they locked eyes across the room.

Reggie looked up at them and asked, "What? What's going on?"

All she could do was shake her head. Paul said, "No fucking way! It has to be a coincidence. He's been dead for…"

Lucille jumped up pointing at him. "Shut the hell up Paul! Not another word." She heard gasps coming from the other occupants of the room and quickly focused on her phone.

Phung said, "Oh God, he's going to kill him." Lucille frantically tried to get her mind to work as she dialed Daniel's phone number. She was watching Phung's screen and gave an audible cry when Daniel raised both his fist to finish Delmas off. She sagged in relief when he froze and looked at Ann as she begged him not to kill Delmas.

Lucille finally got control and hit the call button on her screen. Daniel glanced at his phone, but ignored it as he gave his brother a message before standing up to deliver his message to them. Afterwards, the video feed stopped, but the power came back on in the command center. Reggie told Phung to run another diagnostic, but she responded by saying they were still locked out of the system.

Reggie cut his eyes from her to Paul. "One of you tell me why you freaked out when Daniel took up that stance. I've never seen it before but it must mean something to you two."

Paul threw his hands up and said, "Talk to your mother. I don't have anything to say on the subject." Reggie stared him down but it was clear to everyone that Paul wasn't saying a word.

Lucille ignored him and focused on Paul. "I need you to go get Jessica and LaCora and bring them to me immediately." She turned to Mary Sue. "And please call someone to fix this door."

Paul hurried off and Mary Sue got on her phone to get maintenance up there. Lucille looked at her family and said, "Let's go. We need privacy to discuss some things." She sent a quick text to Paul on where to bring the women when he rounded them up.

They followed her as she exited the vault-like command center door, walked about 30 yards, and entered a conference room identical to the one they used last night. Everyone took their normal seats and remained silent even though she could see the questions on everyone's faces.

After five minutes the door opened and Paul entered with Jessica and LaCora trailing behind him. When everyone was seated Lucille stood up and pulled a gun from behind her back.

Everyone jerked in surprise but no one got up or said a word. Lucille walked around the table as she talked. "Someone in this room is a spy. A traitor!" As everyone started to object, she shouted, "Shut up!" She didn't point the gun at anyone, but they all knew the threat was real.

"Phung," she said, startling her adopted daughter. "Go stand on the wall." Lucille could see the fear on her face but she bravely went to the spot indicated. "Reggie, pat her down and make sure she's unarmed." At the end of the day, Reggie was a soldier and her son. With uncertainty in his eyes, he did what his mother told him and removed a gun and knife form Phung's body.

"Jessica, go stand next to her," demanded Lucille. "Reg, same thing with her." Reggie took the gun from her ankle holster and she leaned on the wall next to Phung. WRA agents were required to be armed at all times. Didn't matter if you worked in I.T. or the field, you went armed.

"LaCora, you're next." She started to protest and Lucille pointed the gun at her head. "Just humor me. I'm not saying you're guilty, just do what I say." LaCora frowned, but walked over to Reggie and let him disarm her before she joined the other women at the wall.

Lucille said, "Like I said, someone in this room is the traitor. I have a very good idea who it is, but it really could be anyone." She took her seat but kept the gun pointed in their direction. "I'm gonna tell a story that will explain the situation you're currently in. I'll give you one warning and it's not a threat, it's a promise. Whoever betrayed this organization, your life will change today. And if I can't determine which one of you did it, then I'll kill who I think did it."

That announcement sent a shock wave through the room, but everyone stayed quiet. Lucille let it sink in before she went on. "Most of the people in this room already know this story. In fact, you are the only three who don't. 30 years ago, when the WRA was still fighting for government contracts, we kept having setback after setback. It didn't matter what we did, the contracts just kept slipping through our fingers. My husband and father to my children, Alan Lee Drake, was running the Agency with me and Mary Sue because our last brother, Glendo, had just been killed.

"I was a mess, as Glendo had always been my closest sibling, and I let Alan pretty much have control over everything. Then one day Mary Sue came to me and said we had a spy in our midst. Kashonda, even at such a young age, was amazing at gathering intelligence and she came across a startling development."

Reggie said softly, "You don't have to do this. We have interrogators for this. Lie detectors. Truth serums. Let them handle it."

She smiled at Reggie but shook her head before continuing on with the tale. "It seemed that another up-and-coming Agency kept getting all our contract. When Kashonda dug a little deeper, she found that the Agency was paying out a percentage of every contract to an unnamed consultant. This wasn't unusual for that time, but it was unusual that the payouts only went out on contracts they won over us.

"Kashonda brought this to Mary Sue's attention and they started digging together. Eventually they tracked all the money to an account in Switzerland that was owned by a series of shell companies. After months of untangling a web of aliases and false leads, they were able to connect the account to none other than Alan Lee Drake."

She paused to gauge the reactions of the three women. All of them were nervous but they had their most innocent faces on. "I approached him and gave him an option. He could either leave the country and never return, or I'd shoot him in the head. But he could only get the first option if he confessed his betrayal.

"He swore he was being framed but we actually had video of him setting up the account in Switzerland. I tried everything, even begging, to get him to confess so I wouldn't have to kill my children's father. In the end, he maintained his innocence so I shot him in his head." Phung and Jessica had tears rolling down their faces. LaCora, a true Burke, looked at her watch and rolled her eyes in annoyance.

"So, I'm giving you the same option. Come clean and you can live out your days in another country. Or don't, and I kill you right now." Everyone remained silent so Mrs. Drake huffed out a breath and stood up.

Phung said, "Please Mama Drake, you know none of us would betray you. Just because Daniel is better than us doesn't make us traitors."

"You are absolutely right Phung. And if this was the only evidence I had, I'd chalk it up to Daniel's brilliance," said

Lucille. "But we've been having leaks here and there for a few years when it pertained to Daniel. To tell you the truth, I've known about this traitor for a while now. But this person is so good at playing their role, and since nothing major happened until today, I let it go. A little intel here, a little lie there. Pretty soon a pattern started to emerge. Anyway, I have proof who the traitor is and this is your last chance to get out of this with your life."

Everything was silent for two minutes while Lucille stood in front of the room with the three women. "Well, I guess that's it. I did give you a chance but you remained the coward I knew you to be."

She brought the gun up and fired one shot right between the eyes of the traitor. Reggie said, "Oh my God! What have you done?" The survivors were visibly shaken as everyone watched the death throes of the judged and executed traitor.

Lucille walked over and looked down at the body. There was blood and brain matter leaking from the wound, soaking into the carpet. With a smirk, she said, "At least this is the last leak we'll have to deal with from this fucker."

She looked at her son. "Reg, we need to set up transportation to retrieve Delmas. And people," she said addressing the room. "This day is not over. Let's see if we can work up one surprise for the always prepared Daniel Burke."

CHAPTER 24

Daniel couldn't stop laughing. Every time he thought he had himself under control, one glance at Denise pointing the huge gun at him had him in hysterics once again.

"You think this is a game?" Denise asked him. "You think I won't shoot you?"

Walt was grinding his teeth and clenching his jaw in an effort to stay quiet. Daniel thought if he looked in his direction it would help him control himself. But when he saw how terrified Walt and Ann were, he lost it once again.

The sound of a shot being fired caused Walt to jump, Ann to shriek out loud, and Daniel to glance back at Denise with a smile on his handsome face.

"That was just a warning," she said. "You better take me seriously or the next one goes in your head."

With a couple of last chuckles, Daniel turned all the way around and gave her his full attention. "Okay killer," he said to her. "What do you want to know?"

"I want to know why you pulled these two for a private meeting and then never mentioned me at all?"

"Because I knew you were going to get the gun so you could make a fool of yourself," he answered her.

She adjusted her grip on the gun. "Can't you be serious and give me a straight answer? Just tell me what you plan to do with me."

"You're the one with the gun. Tell me what you want?"

She hesitated like she hadn't thought this far into her plan. "I want to get training too so I can live a normal life."

Daniel was already shaking his head before she finished. "Denise you're weak. You have no training at all that I can build on. Just to get you up to their level would take years. You don't have the instinct or reflexes needed to become what you would have to become. Bottom line, you would whine and complain and become an obstacle, not an asset."

Her eyes stayed locked on his. She didn't like his frank appraisal of her, but deep inside, she knew it was true. "So where do we go from here?"

Daniel pondered her question. "Nowhere. You either stay down here or you go back to the world and wait for the WRA to kill you."

Her grip faltered for a second, but then she firmed back up. "No! You're gonna take me with you and you're gonna train me too."

Daniel smiled and said, "No, I'm not."

"Yes, you are," she snapped back at him.

He stood up and Denise tensed her whole body. "You ever shoot anyone Denise?" All laughter was gone from him. If she wanted to get serious, he would give her the real deal. "You ever point a gun at a person and purposefully take that person's life away? Because I have. Many, many times. So, I'll make a deal with you." He looked back at Walt and Ann.

"I'm only gonna train two people," he told her. "If you want to live a normal life, you can either live it down here, or you can shoot one of them and take their place in the world."

"What the fuck man!" shouted Walt. "Don't tell her that!"

"Relax Walt. She's chicken shit. She's not gonna shoot anybody. She thought she could come in here with a big gun, look and act a little crazy, and we'd fall at her feet in fear."

Denise was sweating now. Her hands were starting to shake and a frantic look was rising in her eyes. "I'm not chicken shit," she said between clenched teeth.

"Prove it then. Prove to me you're not just a scared little girl with a big gun." Denise stared at Daniel for a few more beats, then swung her gaze to Walt and Ann.

Walt pulled Ann behind him and said, "No Denise!" He turned to Daniel with disappointment on his face. "Why would you do this? We need to be coming together, not pushing each other away. I don't know if this is another one of your tests, but this is wrong Daniel."

He nodded at Walt and then turned to Denise. "You have ten seconds to make up your mind. Do you come with me or stay in this prison forever? Do you live a normal life or go back to the world on borrowed time? The choice is yours." With that he started counting down.

Walt continued to talk to Denise. Promising that she could stay in the prison and they would protect her when the time came for them to return to the world. Begging her to not shoot and put the gun down.

Daniel was about ten feet from her when he reached three on his countdown. Denise screamed, turned the gun so it was pointing at his chest, and pulled the trigger.

The shot was deafening and Walt reached as if he could catch the bullet and screamed, "No!" Daniel stood looking at her with a smile on his face.

Denise thought she had missed so she squeezed off five more shots, all aimed at his chest. When she stopped, he still stood there with the same smile.

Daniel turned to Walt. "Understand something. I want and need for you, Ann, and Denise to be as close as possible. I need all of you to be a team. For the last few weeks, Denise has shown nothing but hate for Ann. There was no way I could let that same attitude infiltrate our training. I needed to see if Denise was selfish enough to sacrifice one of you to save her own life."

He turned back to Denise. "While all of you were unconscious, I switched the live ammo for blanks. I knew you wouldn't forget that Delmas had stashed those guns down there. You're smart, resourceful, and very observant. Those are the traits you need to stay alive. And with my training, you'll learn how to spot irregularities that signify danger, and then the skill to neutralize the threat."

He continued, now including them all. "Not everyone in my world is a killer, but everyone in it has to be a survivor. If you're not smart enough to identify what kind of threat you face, then all the skills mean nothing. You have to know when to run, where to go, and at what pace is the best for a given situation. As one of my mentors use to say: 'If common sense was common, it would just be called sense.' You'd be surprised how many agents escape fire fights without a scratch only to get hit by a car running away because they didn't look both ways."

He paused and studied each of their attentive faces. "You'll have plenty of time to hear me preach when we get to the compound, but I need to make one thing clear. I'll be taking you into a place that is sacred to me. Once you enter, you'll be in a position to hurt me tremendously. I will offer you this one warning: If you attempt to take advantage of that position, I will kill you where you stand. No hesitation and with no remorse, I will end your life. Make no mistake, the surroundings are nicer than this, but you won't leave until I'm satisfied you can survive on your own. If this is not agreeable, speak now." He studied each of them, looking for any doubt hidden within their eyes. When he was satisfied, he said, "Good. Let's get this show on the road."

Before they left the room, he said, "One more thing. Denise, after you killed me, what was your plan to get out of here?" Her look broadcasted clearly that she had no idea. Daniel said, "It's okay. Sometimes your objective is not to win yourself, but to make sure the other guy doesn't win. Anyway, let's go."

He issued assignments for each of them as they prepared to leave the prison. Denise and Ann had gotten deliveries of their own clothing, so Daniel instructed them to pack up anything they wanted to take with them.

Daniel went into one of the cells and called his mother. The call went straight to voicemail, so he left a message. "Delmas and the dead officer will be placed in front of the shack. Since he killed him, he is now your problem. Walt, Ann, and Denise are coming with me back to my compound. We make it back without a problem, I'll unlock your mainframe and unfreeze your assets." He paused before adding, "Give me time and I'm sure we can work something out where we can coexist." Knowing his plea would fall on deaf ears, he hung up and helped everyone prepare for the journey.

It had been a long and stressful day and Daniel hoped his mother wouldn't do anything else until him and Walt could get some sleep. Daniel was use to going days without sleep while out on dangerous missions, but he knew Walt was affected by the adrenaline highs and lows. And no matter what he threatened his family with, he would have to be on point for the drive back to his place.

After they loaded Delmas and Officer Green on the elevator, Daniel told the women to stay put as they took the bodies outside for the WRA to pick up. Just in case his mother was still in attack mode, Daniel made sure they were both encased in body armor for the trip.

They got Delmas laid out nice and comfortable as he cursed them both for the pain jostling his body caused him. Officer Green didn't complain as they heaved him a few feet from Delmas. Daniel stood there looking through the glass enclosure wondering how night had crept up on him so fast.

Darkness would make the drive more dangerous, so he pulled out his phone and called up a drone view of the area surrounding the prison. He saw nothing that alarmed him, but he would still be ready for anything. He closed the drone app and sent a quick text.

He put his phone away and walked over to the Hummer. He crawled in and pulled a phone out of the center console. Handing the phone to Walt, who had been standing quietly by the shack, he said, "This is an exact replica of your phone." He glanced at Delmas and tilted his head to direct Walt back into the elevator area.

Once inside, he closed the door and continued talking. "I need you to talk to someone at the SBI and let them know the three of you are safe, but will be gone for a while. That way, when you all return, it won't catch everyone off guard. Let them know as much or as little as you want, but you have to trust this person explicitly. They have to be in a position where they can explain the absence without too many questions. You stay up here and handle that while I go down and get the ladies."

Daniel got on the elevator knowing Walt was going to call Cpt. William Graham. Walt knew and was friendly with people higher up, but Will was probably the most powerful person in the SBI. No one would question anything he said.

While he rode down, he sent a text to both Alisha and Gabby letting them know he was okay and he loved them. Within seconds they both responded, letting him know they had been waiting for contact. Mentally kicking himself, he knew he would have to make it up to them for the worry he had put them through recently.

Ann and Denise were standing by the elevator doors, bags all packed and ready to go. They were smiling at each other with tears in their eyes, so he assumed they had used the alone time to settle their differences. He hoped it was genuine on both sides and reminded himself to have a talk with Walt about his relationships. He couldn't allow Walt to drive jealousy and resentment between these two women. Their training would be dangerous and they would have to like and trust each other to get through it.

Even though he hoped to never come back to the prison, Daniel sent out another quick text to bring in the cleaning crew. He never let them come when guests were there, but now that it was empty, he would get the place spotless again. Never could tell when a high-level prisoner would need to be housed.

Daniel sent Walt a quick notice that they were coming up and Walt told him to come on, everything had been taken care of. Daniel hoped he was right because Walt's disappearance could spark investigations into places that would make his return impossible. Daniel had done his best to protect him as he went about his task, but you never knew when that small piece of evidence could bite you in the ass.

They met back up in the shack and, after a quick check outside, Daniel told the women to go ahead and stow their bags in the back of the Hummer. He watched them for a moment as they worked together to load everything into the cargo area from the back seat. Delmas was still cursing them all except for Ann, who he was trying to sweet talk. Luckily, she ignored him and settled into the back with Denise before closing the door.

Daniel turned to Walt and said, "I know it's not fair to ask you this knowing what I have at home, but I'm gonna need you to kill the romance until you leave the compound."

Walt looked crestfallen. "Why? What's it hurting?"

"You're too smart to ask me that question." Daniel sighed when he saw genuine confusion on Walt's face. "Both those women are in love with you and it's driving a wedge between them."

He laughed. "You're delusional. Ann is like a sister to me."

Daniel shook his head at Walt's naivety. "She settled for that role because it was the only one you offered her. You have no idea the relationship they had down there. They're happy now because they're leaving, but any signs of affection for one or the other will bring that resentment right back to the surface. I need you to trust me on this. You'll all need to work as a cohesive unit for this training to work. If either one of them is holding a grudge, it could get all of you killed."

Walt clenched his jaw, not liking it one bit, but he nodded and said, "You're right. I'll have a talk with both of them when we get there."

Daniel smiled at the older man and they both stepped out of the shack. Just in time to see an armor-plated vehicle ram the back of the Hummer, pushing it up about five feet and exposing them to the gunfire that suddenly erupted.

Epilogue

Ghost woke up with a major headache and something all over his mouth. He was disoriented and all he could hear was ringing in his ears. Images were slowly creeping into his mind, but they were disjointed and didn't make sense to him.

With difficulty, he opened his eyes and found himself face down in the grass. Although his memory was fucked up, he did remember that it had been dark outside at the beginning of his mission. Now, the sun was bright and strong, high overhead, informing him that he had been unconscious for a while.

The WRA super-agent spit the grass out of his mouth and labored to his knees to better see his surroundings. The sight of the shack in the middle of the field brought his memory back with startling clarity.

He climbed to his feet looking around wildly. What he saw and what he expected to see were at opposite ends of the spectrum. He expected to see mayhem. Bodies littering the ground. Carcasses of burnt vehicles scattered across the field.

What he saw was a meadow that looked peaceful and serene. Completely undisturbed by the battle that he knew had taken place. He staggered around, holding his aching head, wondering why the ringing would leave only to return moments later.

"Oh God," he murmured when he figured out it was his phone. He fished it out of his pocket, only now realizing he didn't have any weapons, and looked at his screen. "Shit," he cursed when he saw the name on the display.

They probably had a satellite or drone looking down on him, so he answered the call. "Hello," he said to Lucille Drake.

"Damnit, why haven't you been answering your phone? What the hell is going on out there?" She was spitting mad, but he didn't have the answers she was looking for.

"I don't know what's going on. Can you tell me what you're seeing from above?" he asked her.

"The bastard still has us locked out, so I can't see anything. I can't reach any of our soldiers. Please tell me everyone's gear was fried but they are alright."

He wanted to make a crack about why she was acting concerned for them all of a sudden. In the mood she was in, he'd have every available agent on his ass in minutes.

She sounded desperate but also resigned to hearing bad news. "All I can tell you is what I know. We used the soldiers to keep Walt and Daniel penned down as we retrieved Delmas, but then everyone fell sick. We assumed that Daniel had activated his pulse device but on a low setting. After that, him and Walt came out and started picking us off at will.

"Walt carried Delmas back to the Hummer as Daniel walked through executing every soldier he could find. Some of us recovered enough to mount another attack and I took Daniel down with a long-range shot. He was wearing body armor, but I hit him center mass. I watched him go down and he stayed down.

"I moved in to finish him off but, as soon as I reached him, someone came up behind me and stuck a needle in my neck. You know no one sneaks up on me. I don't know who this guy was, but he moved like a shadow. I stayed conscious for a few seconds and I heard Daniel ask the guy what took him so long. He replied that he moved pretty fast for a dead man. I have no idea what happened after that because I just woke up five minutes ago. But I can tell you the scene is spotless."

"Spotless?" she asked, confused. "What do you mean by that exactly?"

"Here, I'll show you." He used his phone to make a quick video of the scene. He sent it to her and waited for her response.

"Damn! Against all evidence, I was hoping it wasn't true, but I have to face reality. He's still alive."

"Who's still alive?" he asked her.

She was quiet for so long, he checked to make sure the call hadn't dropped. Finally, she said, "Come into headquarters Jamar. There was nothing you could do. But they left you alive for a reason. I just pray we can make them regret that decision."

She hung up and left him with more questions than answers. With no vehicles in sight, he started to walk. He wondered how much more infighting the WRA could take before the whole Agency crumbled to the ground. He'd keep his head down and do what he did best, blend in. Because one thing Ghost was sure of, change was coming. He just prayed the changes wouldn't result in him becoming his namesake.

BEYOND REDEMPTION

About The Author

Leon A. Burch was born in Philadelphia, PA; and now
resides in North Carolina. He attended Temple University.
To contact him with questions or comments,
you can reach him at
authorlaburch@gmail.com

Coming Soon

Reparations

Book Three Of The
Masterminds Series

By L.A. BURCH

Made in the USA
Columbia, SC
19 March 2025

55379741R00190